IP

Pisgah Press was established in 2011 to publish and promote works of quality offering original ideas and insight into the human condition, the realm of knowledge, and the world around us.

Printed in the United States of America

Published by Pisgah Press, LLC
PO Box 1427, Candler, NC 28715
www.pisgahpress.com

Book & cover design: A. D. Reed, MyOwnEditor.com

Library of Congress Cataloging-in-Publication Data
Wilson, Robert F.
Deadly Dancing/Wilson

Library of Congress Control Number: 2016933514

ISBN: 978-1942016151
ISBN-10: 1-942016-15-8
Mystery/Fiction

First Edition
May 2016

This is a work of fiction. Any resemblance to actual events or persons living or dead is coincidental.

THANKS TO:
- Beth for her continued support, encouragement, and love
- Western North Carolina Mysterians, for their early reading
- Jossie for her close reading
- The rest of my family for treating me as a working writer
- A.D. Reed for getting this book to see the light of day

Deadly Dancing

by RF Wilson

For Jerry

Deadly Dancing

1

I blamed my weakened state of mind on too much alcohol the night before, but the probable cause of the seizure was seeing the dead body in the parking lot. They loaded me in an ambulance and brought me to the hospital for observation.

When I regained consciousness, a nurse told me a couple of police officers were waiting outside to talk to me. I told her to send them in. A guy in a khaki suit with a shaved head accompanied by a sepia-skinned woman in police blues ambled into the room. I managed to push myself into a semi-upright position, then fell back against a couple of pillows. I thought I caught the woman looking furtively at the place just below my shoulder where most people have a left arm.

"Mr. Ryder," the suited figure said, holding a badge out toward me. "I'm Detective Henderson, Asheville Police. We met earlier this morning. This is Sergeant Simpson. How are you feeling?"

I vaguely remembered him.

"All things considered, like shit, Detective. But thanks for asking. You can call me Rick."

"Sure, Rick. I'm sorry you're not feeling well. But we do need to ask you a few things."

"Do I need my lawyer?"

"You're entitled to one, of course. But this isn't an interrogation."

I closed my eyes. The picture came into focus, where part of her head had been shot away.

"We don't know her name, Rick. Her clothes weren't found, there's nothing to I.D. her with. From your reaction we thought you might have known her."

"Her name was Debbie. That's all I know."

"How did you know her?"

"From The Doll House."

"The strip club?"

I nodded.

"How well did you know her?"

"I'd seen her dance there."

"That all?" he asked.

I nodded. Anticipating his next question, I said I'd seen her twice. "She danced as 'Tiffani'."

"Then how do you know her name was Debbie?"

"She told me."

"Couldn't she have made that up, too, like she did Tiffani?"

"I don't know, Detective. She told me her name was Debbie. That's all I can tell you."

His demeanor didn't change in the face of my annoyance.

"Ever see her outside the club?"

"Once, at Bill's Sporting Goods store, before I saw her at The Doll House."

"Never anywhere after you'd seen her dance?"

I shook my head.

"Know anything else about her, where she lived, who she hung out with?"

I shook my head again. He said they'd talk to The Doll House people and thanked me for my time. Sergeant Simpson was already out of the room when Henderson turned back to me.

"Oh, yeah, Rick. I meant to ask you. Can you tell me where you were late Saturday night, early Sunday morning?"

"Home."

"Anyone with you?"

"Nope."

Henderson nodded that cop nod, the one that lets you know he thinks you're probably lying. I wasn't lying, so far as I knew. I knew I had awakened at three-thirteen this morning in my bed, a two-thirds empty bottle of scotch on the night stand. I knew I'd come across a dead girl, a girl I had met a few days ago. What I didn't know was what had happened between eleven o'clock the previous morning when I'd ordered my second beer and waking up sixteen hours later with an unholy hangover.

I thought back over the events of the past few days.

2

Three days earlier, Jay McIntyre was maneuvering our old Jeep down the mountain road while I dozed in the shotgun seat. A roar, the sound a flash flood makes, woke me up. I looked back over my shoulder to see a truck stacked high with logs bearing down on us. I put a death grip on the door handle with my right hand, wishing I had a left to brace against the dash. I was thrown up against the door when Jay jerked the steering wheel. The Jeep came to rest straddling a small creek. The truck sounded like thunder as it went by.

"Guess he had the right of way," Jay said as he backed and turned and headed up the embankment, as if this was no more challenging than parallel parking downtown. "Everybody's pants dry?"

My heart was still racing five minutes later when he said, "I think we're being followed."

I saw a car in the side mirror about thirty yards back.

"Been there since the truck went by, about a mile. Stays the same distance back if I speed up or slow down."

Thirty minutes later, when we turned into our parking lot, the car went the other way, going on up toward town. It was a large sedan, dark green. I recognized the grill ornament.

"I think I've seen that car somewhere," Jay said.

"Not like it's the only green Buick in town."

"Actually, there aren't that many of them. I've seen one like it recently. I can't remember where, though. You know that's gonna bug me now."

We climbed out of the Jeep and entered the renovated warehouse on the river. I strode into Zella Jefferson's office, making a display of excavating a miniature tape cassette from my pocket-sized recorder and tossing it on her desk.

"A statement by a Mountain Timber and Mining employee confirming that they are responsible for cutting and removing standing growth from National Forest Service land," I announced.

She stepped toward me and gave me a hug.

"Good work."

I glowed. A smile from my boss always hit me like a mild dose of cocaine.

We told her about the logging truck and the car tailing us.

"Couldn't it be coincidence? The log truck going too fast and some other guy tailgating?"

"I could have written off the truck," I said. "You get one of those mothers moving, you don't want to slow down if you don't have to. But the Buick was obviously tailing us and didn't care if we knew it."

"You suppose the guy you got on tape told someone you'd been out there?" she asked.

"Out there" was a tract in the National Forest where it had been alleged the lumber company had been cutting trees illegally. Jay and I were tromping around trying to pinpoint the area in question when we were accosted by a guy who told us we were on Mountain Timber and Mining property. Big guy, six-six, two-seventy-five or so, dressed in jeans and flannel shirt, a camouflage hat displaying the NASCAR logo perched on his head. He said we were trespassing.

"We just passed a red stripe on a tree," I said. "Means we're on National Forest property."

"Yeah. But Mountain Timber leases the land."

I swept my arm in an arc, indicating an array of newly minted stumps.

"Mountain Timber responsible for all those?"

"Yeah, that's what they lease the land for," he said, exasperation thick in his voice, like maybe we were playing one card short of a full deck.

I shrugged and looked over at Jay. "I guess we wandered off the trail." We turned to head back the way we came. I felt the man's glare like a laser aimed at the back of my neck.

"Got 'em," I said when we were out of the big guy's view.

"Got who?" Jay asked.

"MTM. Or at least their lackey. Admitting on tape to what they're doing."

Zella was probably right. The guy in the woods must have let somebody know we'd been up there and they didn't like it.

I left work a little after five, still high from having got the tape. The Buick still nagged at me a little, but I had about convinced myself I was feeling paranoid because of the logging truck. Basking in the warmth of Zella's approval, I didn't even notice the red pickup truck coming at me until it almost ran me off the road and over the embankment.

3

My breathing was back to normal by the time I stopped at Bill's Sporting Goods where a new racket was being strung for me. Waiting for the clerk to retrieve it from the back, I was experiencing buyer's remorse, ogling the ones I hadn't bought. I didn't notice the young woman come up next to me until she spoke.

"There're an awful lot to choose from, aren't there?" she said.

I turned and took in the khaki short-shorts and hot pink T-shirt with CHARLESTON SOUTH CAROLINA emblazoned across her chest. I guessed her to be in her late teens, early twenties, five-four or -five, short blond hair framing a pretty face.

"Yeah, like toothpaste and potato chips," I said. "Way more options than we really need. You just starting to play?"

"I used to play a lot as a kid, but it's been years since I've been on a court. What would be good to get started again?"

The clerk called my name.

"Be right there," I called back. I knew I was flirting and thought she might be reciprocating. Although in my mid-forties, I'm in reasonably good health, stay trim playing tennis, hike when the weather's good, work out in my basement gym. Brown hair with a little gray at the temples that my wife says is distinguished. Having only one arm was off-putting to some, but this young woman didn't seem to pay any attention to the pinned-up shirt sleeve.

"Any of these would probably be okay," I said, pointing to the mid-priced models. I was in mid-sentence, talking about the kind

I used, when the clerk came up and handed me my racket. I could feel blood rush to my face when the girl smiled and thanked me for my help. I wandered around for a few minutes, then came up behind her in a check-out line even though the next one over was shorter. She had a racket and a can of balls.

"You made a pick," I said.

She turned. "Yeah. I kind of just closed my eyes and pointed where you suggested."

She paid for her things and went out the door. I hoped to catch another glance of her in the parking lot, but the clerk seemed to be in a "How-Long-Can-You-Take-To-Check-Out-One-Item" contest. When I finally got outside, I scanned the lot for her; my sigh may have been audible across the acre of parked cars. I wondered if she lived in the area, if I might bump into her again.

About two miles out Riceville Road, I noticed the green Buick behind me. It stayed on my tail when I turned onto Cove Road, past the sign that read, "Paved road ends 4.5 miles ahead." The pavement gave way to gravel just past our driveway. After parking my car, I walked back down to the road. Thirty yards away, the sedan stopped and made a K-turn. It was just far enough away in the waning afternoon light that I couldn't make out the license plate number, although I was pretty sure the state was Georgia.

Kathy's call came at ten-thirty. I'd complained the night before about how much she'd been on the road lately. She said it didn't seem to make much difference since I'd been so distant when she'd been home. I got defensive. We'd exchanged cheek pecks when she'd gotten in the car.

"We got some guy on tape admitting that Mountain Timber has been cutting live trees in the National Forest," I said on the phone.

She didn't say anything.

"It's a pretty big deal."

"Congratulations." It could have been sarcasm or just my state of mind.

"I'll be home around six on Sunday," she said. That meant she'd have to leave Lexington around noon. I wondered why she wasn't leaving earlier but didn't say anything. I didn't bother mentioning the logging truck or the green car. Or the girl at the sporting goods store. Neither of us offered the rote, "I miss you."

I knew I tended to remoteness, something related to my upbringing by a controlling mother and my need to escape. Or so it was suggested and re-affirmed by a succession of therapists who had tried to help me with my drinking. I knew I had some habits Kathy didn't find endearing. I also knew it took two people to keep a relationship out of balance.

I didn't want a drink, but I had that old edginess that comes when an alcoholic is dry but not sober. When I woke up Thursday morning, the last image I could remember before falling asleep was that of a young woman in a pink T-shirt.

4

Lying in bed with my eyes closed as the sun sent its early warning that another morning had arrived, I saw the girl again. I scolded myself. I actually did miss my wife. Maybe that was why I was seeing images of young women. Very young women. Way too young for me. I got up to end the discussion.

The Bluetooth car phone rang as I was backing out of the garage.

"This is Rick."

"You on your way in?" Zella asked.

"Just leaving."

"We had visitors last night. The place is trashed. The police are here and I want you to tell them what you were doing yesterday."

Carole, the office manager, was crying when I walked in. It was as if a sea of paper had broken through the walls, flooding the office, leaving small piles of flotsam at random on the floor. Nothing but paper seemed to have been touched. No capsized or smashed furniture; no torn upholstery; no broken equipment.

Zella introduced me to Detective Hammer.

"Rick is our lead investigator as well as being an attorney," she said. "He seems to like tromping around in the woods more than the more mundane work of lawyering."

10

"Ms. Jefferson thinks this is more than simple vandalism, said what you were doing yesterday—your tromping around, as she calls it—might be relevant."

"I think she's right," I said and told him about the guy in the forest and the logging truck and the green Buick.

"And you think this car was following you? Didn't just happen to be behind you?"

"I even came to a stop so he could pass us," Jay said, "and he just lay back, thirty, fifty yards or so."

"And," I interjected, "he followed me home last night." All eyes in the room turned to me. "With all the commotion this morning, I almost forgot about it."

"Someone followed you home last night," Hammer said, looking at me with a deadpan expression.

"Yeah. I'd stopped at Bill's Sporting Goods to pick up a restrung racket. I was on Riceville Road when I noticed it."

"How do you know it was the same car?"

"Okay. To be technical, it was a car like the one that followed the Jeep. That Buick medallion on the front is noticeable and it was a dark sedan. Pretty coincidental if it wasn't the same car. Then, when I stopped and got out to look at it, the driver did a quick turn-around in the road and took off back the way it had come."

Hammer shrugged, giving that cop look, like he might buy it … or might not.

"What'd the driver look like?"

"Couldn't see him—or her."

"You think you pissed them off by being out there in the forest and they retaliated by doing this?" he said, his gaze sweeping the room.

"That'd be my guess," I said.

We stood in an arc around the detective.

"This happened because we are investigating a major force in the destruction of the environment," Jay started in. "They are a greedy, soulless corporation who will destroy anything that interferes with their ability to make a profit."

Hammer looked at Jay, then at me. I shrugged. The detective said, "You mean there's nobody else out there who might have reason to come looking for stuff. I mean, you're lawyers, right? You go after people, bring lawsuits. I'd think there'd be a lot of people with an axe to grind. Who was the first person here this morning?"

"I was here at eight-fifteen," Jay said.

"Your usual time to get to work?"

"More or less. Maybe a few minutes earlier."

I looked over at Zella. Jay didn't usually come in until nine. She gave a little shrug.

"Why'd you come in early?" Hammer asked.

"Why does it matter why he came in early?" I asked.

"I'll conduct the investigation, if you don't mind, Mr. Ryder," the detective said, giving me a weary look, like he had to do this all the time.

For the next hour, that's what he and his uniform did. They found no footprints outside, no tire tracks, no random incriminating evidence. In fact, not much at all except a bunch of fingerprints, all of which I assumed would be ours.

When they had gone, Zella called me into her office, opened her briefcase, and pulled out the little cassette.

"I don't know why," she said, "but a small voice said to me before I left last night, 'You ought to take this home and listen to it again.'"

"You think they came looking for it? That guy up there didn't know I'd been taping him, the recorder was in my pocket."

"I don't know what to think."

I thought about Jay's early arrival and I didn't like what I thought next. By the expression on her face, I could tell Zella was having similar thoughts.

"It couldn't be, could it?" I said.

"I don't want to believe it."

"I think they're just trying to intimidate us, you know, leaving their calling card, letting us know we'd better be careful what we do. They know we were out there. The tape is irrelevant. So is the time Jay got here."

The nod she gave in reply was unconvincing.

Detective Hammer was right about people getting mad at us. We were an environmental defense firm, and we called businesses on their bad behavior. Although a small shop, we'd had some major victories in the decade we'd been around.

❧❧

By the end of the day, we had managed to get most of the mess straightened up, and nothing had surfaced to dissuade me from the belief that MTM was behind the mayhem.

As we were leaving the office, I asked Jay if he wanted to join me for dinner.

"Thanks. But I'm meeting Zoey."

"Working on your project?"

He nodded. I thought I detected his eyes shift.

Zoey was his girlfriend. I'd met her once, at a Christmas gathering at our house. Cute, small, slim, sexy, funny. I could see how they'd get along. He'd been secretive about this "project" since he first let it out a couple of months ago that he and his girlfriend were working on a movie. He'd immediately changed subjects, as if he'd said too much. When asked, he wouldn't say anything else about it, said we'd be among the first to know when it was completed; when I'd pressed him, he got impatient, repeating that he'd tell us when it was done. I let it go.

But there was something in the way he averted his eyes when I mentioned it this time that let me know he really did not want to talk about it, that the mere mention of it spooked him.

I fixed a quick meal at home before going to the AA meeting at St. Luke's, getting there early enough to help set up and have a cup of bad coffee. I had had every intention of heading home after the meeting, but fifteen minutes later I was in the parking lot of The Doll House, "A Gentlemens' Club" according to the sign.

5

A guy deep in conversation with a young woman wearing tight blue jeans and a dramatically full yellow tank-top stood at the door. He stuck out a hand with the radius of a pie plate to swallow my five-dollar bill. Pictures of dancers, all with names like Teri and Barbi and Cindi, adorned the walls of the short entrance way. I took a stool at the bar. A disembodied voice asked the audience to "give it up for Angi." The barmaid, a pretty, thirty-something-ish redhead named Donna, turned my way.

"Hey, hon. What'll it be? Oh. You're the Coke drinker, aren't you?"

"Doesn't take long to get a reputation around here," I said, smiling. The Coke cost as much as a mixed drink, and I slapped a ten on the bar to cover that and a tip. Semi-naked women wandered through the crowd trolling for lap dances or private performances in one of the booths along the far side of the room. A young man sat down next to me.

Turning toward me, he said, "I'm Jimmy."

I said I was Rick.

"I seen you here before, ain't I?" he asked around a thick tongue. The beer in his hand was not his first of the night.

"Possibly," I said. "I think I've seen you."

"Yeah, I work here, ya' know. Clean up after hours, do a littl'a this and that for Tom and Sally—they're the ones own this place."

A smattering of indifferent applause met the next girl who pranced onto the stage, a rap song droning around her. A fuzzy white angora-like top with matching hot pants, white cowboy boots and hat, all worked to give her a slutty Dallas Cowboys cheerleader look. She seemed very young and very self-conscious thrusting body parts at us.

A few minutes later, a voice came over the air to introduce Tiffani. Men were shouting, calling her by name as she came out onto a dark stage. Jimmy popped his elbow against my side.

"This chick is amazing. You're gonna like this."

The lights came up slowly to reveal a woman I guessed to be a couple of years older than the previous dancer. About five-four, long black hair, a pretty face that was vaguely familiar from thirty feet away. I didn't sit nearer the stage because from close range you can see the toll that crack and booze and the rest have taken. Tiffani was young enough to appear innocent, as innocent as someone could be while disrobing in public.

She wore black: gaucho hat, cape, skin-tight body suit, high heels, all black. The music was Latin-flavored. The crowd knew her act, shouting, "Olé," when she threw her cape across the stage. Like a toreador working a bull, she had them cheering each time she tossed off another piece of her outfit. About half the house was standing and cheering when she finished her set. I had finished my two Cokes, it was close to ten o'clock, and I thought, now is the time to leave. Nothing was likely to get any better.

"Wha'd I tell ya, man! Pretty hot, huh? I seen her dance in Atlanta. Can't imagine what the hell she's doin' up here. I mean the place I saw her, that's a class place. Bet she made two, three times what she makes here."

Donna came by again. Jimmy said he'd have another. I passed.

"Driving, huh?" our girl said with a wink.

Jimmy said he'd buy me one of whatever I was drinking. I declined. He wanted to argue. I assured him it was nothing personal, that I never had more than two when I came here. Holding my hand out to him to say goodbye, maybe soothe his ego, I heard a voice behind me.

"How about a Sprite, Donna."

Tiffani noticed me turn and smiled. She was in street clothes—jeans, sweatshirt, tennis shoes. It was only then, without the black wig, that I recognized her. My hands got sweaty, like they did in high school when I was around any attractive girl who would talk to me. In place of something witty, all I could think to say was, "That was you at the store last night, wasn't it?"

Before she could answer, Jimmy said, "I seen you dance in Atlanta."

She looked over my shoulder at him. "I don't think so."

"Sure. At that Club Elegant."

"Never been there," she said.

"Oh, yeah, it was you. Different color hair. But it was you."

"Let it alone, Jimmy," I said. "She says she's never been there. Drop it."

"Who the hell are you tellin' me to drop it?"

His voice was loud enough to attract Donna. She told him to cool it.

"Man, the girl's lying."

"Tough shit," Donna said. "You can't start yelling or I'll have to call Dewey over."

"Fuck you all," he said, and walked away. I didn't watch where he went.

"An admirer," I said to the dancer.

"Not anymore."

Remembering my manners, I said, "I'm Rick."

She held her hand out toward me. "Deb ... shit ... Tiffani." Her eyes rolled upward.

"Deb Shit Tiffani. Interesting name."

She looked straight at me and said, "Tiffani." End of discussion. Then she said, "So, Rick, what's a nice guy like you ..."

"Doing in a place like this?"

She smiled.

"One could, of course, ask the same of you," I said.

"It's a living," she said. The smile disappeared. She turned fully toward the bar. "I'm going, Donna. See you tomorrow."

"I was just getting ready to leave myself. Mind if I walk with you?" I said.

She shrugged, and I followed her past the gift shop replete with porn and related accessories and appliances, past the office and out the back door. Standing next to her as she unlocked her car, I felt like I was saying good-bye to a date.

When she was seated behind the wheel, I leaned forward conspiratorially.

"You want to play tennis some time?"

She looked at me like I'd spoken in a foreign language.

"Yeah. It's a little crazy, I know. Here," I said, and handed her a business card. "If you do want to, call me on the cell number."

She looked at the card and back at me with eyes narrowed. She started her car and looked at me one more time with the same question on her face before driving off. I shook worse than when the truck had almost run me off the road earlier in the day and had to steady myself against a nearby car to keep from falling over.

As I walked toward the Honda, I saw Jimmy and some other guy pass a glass pipe between them.

"You got some kind of a problem, man," he said, glazed eyes beaming in my direction.

I ignored him, knowing the likely outcome of anything I

might say to this cracked-out redneck would be for him to come over and get physical. In my distraction, I almost didn't notice the green Buick at the edge of the lot, aimed outward like a weapon.

Headlights followed me all the way to Riceville Road, then disappeared when I turned onto Cove Road.

The red light flashed on the answering machine as I walked into the kitchen.

"Hi, Hon," Kathy's voice greeted me when I pushed the button. She went on about how good the conference was and how she thought she'd picked up some new clients. The message ended with her saying, "I miss you. Sorry I've been bitchy lately. Call me when you get in." I tasted scotch and was glad there was no liquor in the house.

The next message was from her father, Ted. He described in detail a disorder of his kidneys, his latest physical complaint. The man was a lonely hypochondriac.

Working hard to keep those ugly twins, shame and guilt, under wraps, I called Kathy. We exchanged pleasantries, each acknowledging we were out of kilter. I attributed my state to her absence, as well as to the vandalism and being tailed around town.

"Why would someone be following you?" she asked.

"We've gotten the attention of Mountain Timber and Mining, the company owned by Senator Simmons. Well, technically, it's owned by his family so it's not considered a conflict of interest that he sits on the committee that has oversight of logging in the national forests. Damn, don't let me get started on that. I think they're trying to intimidate us, get us to back off the case."

"Think you ought to have the gun with you?"

She meant the one we kept in the bedside stand. I'd gotten licensed as a private investigator several years ago when I was working in the state environment resources bureaucracy and needed a hobby. I'd never carried the pistol, but it seemed like a good thing to have when we moved west to the mountains and to this semi-isolated house in the woods.

"I don't really feel threatened, just kind of unnerved."

"Is anybody else being followed?"

"No one's said anything."

"Why single you out? Why not Zella? She's the director."

"Good question. Oh, I almost forgot. Your dad called. Thinks we're screening calls so you won't have to talk to him."

"Oh, for crying out loud. That man. If I don't talk to him three times a week he thinks I'm hiding from him."

"Aren't you?"

"Only because I can't get away from him. Please don't start giving me grief about him."

"Just messing with you. I know he's difficult."

"Difficult? Try suffocating." She took a breath. "Sorry, he just aggravates me. If you talk to him, tell him I'll call him when I get home Sunday."

There was none of the tension of the night before. I brewed a cup of decaf and sat on the deck, listening to the advance stirrings of summer. Lightning struck off in the distance, and a rumble echoed through the mountains. When I closed my eyes, all I could see was Deb-Shit-Tiffani in a G-string.

6

It wasn't an alcohol hangover, but I sure felt lousy. It was insanity, going to a strip joint, inviting one of the dancers to meet me outside the club. No possible good could come of it. Just the opposite was likely. The part of my brain where rational decisions are made understood this. Unfortunately, decisions about this kind of behavior, what is obvious to others as self-destructive, are made in another part of the brain, a primitive part where reason has no influence.

I went to the office early to do a little detecting of my own. Jay's and Carole's cars were there when I arrived at eight-thirty, a half-hour earlier than I usually showed up. They both appeared to be putting away files when I walked in.

"You guys are at it early."

The look I thought passed between them may have been nothing more than a projection of the suspicion I walked in with.

"Thought we'd get a jump on it," Jay said. "We've about got everything back in its place. Now we need to do an inventory, see what's missing."

"We aren't going to find anything," I said. "If they wanted something, they'd take pictures, or make copies, download files—"

Carole cut me off. "I checked yesterday and nobody'd used

the computer after we left the night before."

"My point is, they wouldn't leave a track that would direct us to anything in particular. If anything is missing, it'll be a red herring. I'm still convinced it's related to the MTM case, in spite of Detective Hammer's suggestion that it could be someone else with an axe to grind."

Zella arrived a little after nine attired as usual in a colorful dress, hose, and heels. She believed there was African and Arabian royalty in her blood lines and carried herself accordingly.

"What's the verdict?" she asked.

I repeated what I'd said to the others.

"So let's get back to work. They know we've got the goods on them and they're desperate. Let's keep the pressure on."

The fun part of the investigation into the activities of MTM was over. Now it was all paperwork, the most exciting aspect of which would be driving into town and filing motions in the courthouse, the kind of work an intern is good for.

After work, I took a walk, following the creek up the hill behind the house, admiring the great white blooms of rhododendron, the delicate bluets along the trail, the occasional flame azalea. By eight o'clock, I had eaten dinner and was back in the car. I had been to The Doll House five or six times over the past couple of years, never more than once every few months, and never two nights in a row. I was crossing a line and seemed powerless to do anything else.

I was parked before I realized the pickup truck next to me was the one I'd had to dodge the previous day. Jimmy was leaning against the driver's door, smoking something that did not look manufactured. Whatever drug it was, it might explain why he drove erratically.

"So that was you about ran me off the road yesterday," he said, smiling, like we were pals.

"I think it was the other way around."

He smiled and sucked on the joint. I kept walking.

"You know that bitch is lying, don't you?" he called behind me. "I seen her in Atlanta."

The familiar tattooed arm greeted me at the door and took my five dollars. I took my place at the bar, said "Hi, Donna," and got my Coke. The first two dancers looked like they were on autopilot, what was meant to be erotic merely tawdry. I was about to leave when the music changed. It was familiar, of a kind I associated with a different sort of establishment. I swiveled to look at the dark stage. Thirty seconds into the music, a spotlight burst on the dancer, setting her in a pool of light. She was dressed all in black, like a German cabaret dancer—high heels, garter belt, hot pants, bustier, a bowler on her head. And a cane. A smattering of boos greeted her as she began to strut around the stage. The mood changed when her bra came off. She leaned over the cane, shaking her breasts toward the front row. She seemed to be enjoying herself. Whether or not she had danced in Atlanta, she was unlike anything they were used to seeing here. At the end of the song, the crowd didn't need to be coaxed to "give it up for Tiffani."

As soon as she was off stage, I felt a black cloud descend. I was focusing on my Coke, a voice inside me saying it was time to leave, when I heard, "Hi, Rick."

She had on a satiny white robe over her black G-string, still wearing the garter belt and stockings. My pulse quickened. She remembered my name.

"Why the long face, cowboy?"

I nodded toward the empty stool next to me.

"If I sit, you're going to have to buy me a drink."

I waved Donna over. She took a five-dollar bill from my pile and returned with a glass of ice and clear liquid and a dollar change. I figured I'd just paid four dollars for ice water.

"I think this is the last time I'll be in this place," I said.

She scanned the room. "Oh, why ever so?" she asked, a Cheshire-cat grin drawn across her pretty face.

"Of course, I'll miss the stimulating companionship, and all. But I don't think my spirit is well served here."

The robe gaped open when she leaned toward the bar for her drink. I closed my eyes.

"Nobody's spirit is well served here, Rick." She sipped from the glass. "I hope to get out of here soon myself."

I wanted to ask where she would go, what she would do, why she was leaving, but Donna came over and gave her a discreet nod.

"Gotta go. My public calls," Tiffani said.

"That's the first time I've ever heard Leonard Cohen in a strip club," I said as she was turning away.

"He was my mother's favorite," she said, leaning back toward me. I didn't close my eyes. She gave me a peck on the cheek and whispered, "My real name is Debbie." I was glad she hadn't mentioned my suggestion for tennis, but I did have a fleeting thought about moving to a table and spending twenty dollars to have her dance for me. Instead, I pushed the dollar bills remaining in front of me toward Donna, waving at the barmaid as I got up. She smiled and waved back.

I didn't see the Buick in the parking lot.

I punched the numbers into the alarm pad as I came into the house. It beeped when I walked away. I looked back at it and saw the red light was on, meaning I had failed to disarm it—punched the numbers in wrong, maybe, or forgot to set it when I left earlier in the evening. I went through the procedure again and the green light came on. I was relieved there was no light on the answering machine and was almost asleep when the phone rang.

"Sorry it's so late," she said. "A bunch of us went out to dinner and got yakking."

"I think I'm a little weirded out from all that's been going on the last couple of days."

"Well, don't go off and do anything, you know ..."

"Stupid?"

"Yeah, that."

I wanted to get indignant, to justify going to a strip joint, just the kind of behavior she was referring to.

"I miss you," I said.

"I miss you. Doing anything fun tomorrow?"

"No plans," I said. "Go to a meeting. I hope to get outside some if the weather's nice."

"Just try to keep it between the lines, okay, sweetie?"

I smiled. She'd started saying this to me when we were dating, after she'd found out that I'd lost my arm in car accident. It was affectionate, like a light tickle on the ribs. I knew that I had been out of bounds and hoped I could get back before someone called foul.

7

Charley Eagleston called at seven-thirty Saturday morning to ask if I would play doubles at the Racquet Club at four o'clock.

"I'll be there," I said.

"You been watching the French Open?"

"Don't have cable, Charley, remember?"

"Well, the women's semis come on about nine this morning, and they ought to be terrific. I know some guys don't care about the girls game, but for me good tennis is good tennis."

"Kind of like Miles Davis about music."

"How's that?"

"Only two kinds of music. Good music and bad music."

"Yeah, that's it. Anyway, you're welcome to come down here. I'll be watching it."

"Down here" was at the far south end of the county, almost into the next one. I thanked him for the offer.

I made the nine o'clock meeting at St. Luke's. There was a voice message when I turned my cell phone on after leaving the church.

"I could play a couple of sets today," the recording said.

My hands shook. If I took her up on it, I wouldn't tell Kathy about and it would become a secret that would inhabit the space between us. My fingers felt like sausages as I tried to punch buttons. When her phone rang once, I hung up. Stopped at the red light by Jackson's Sports Bar, I thought I might go in, have a couple of Cokes, see if they had the tennis on, maybe figure out what to say to Debbie. When the light changed, I turned left into the saloon's parking lot. I was staring at a gargantuan TV screen when the barman came over, asking what I wanted. I ordered a Heineken. A few minutes later, I ordered another.

❦

The numbers 3:13 glared red on the face of the clock radio. I wasn't sure if it was AM or PM. I saw a mostly empty scotch bottle on the bedside stand. Despair fell around me like a shroud. Suicide rose in my consciousness. I forced myself to get up and look outside. It was dark, early morning. I wondered where I'd been, what I'd been doing since the second beer.

I stood in a steaming shower for fifteen minutes, dressed, drank Alka-Seltzer and a quart of water, took a hike up behind the house, drank a shake of frozen banana, ground almond, apple and orange juice, drank more water, took another shower and dressed again. Wanting to occupy my brain in some way other than ruminating on the possibilities of what might have occurred during the sixteen hours for which I could make no accounting, I decided I'd go into the office. I grabbed my wallet and keys off the dresser. It wasn't until I put the key in the ignition that I realized I was using my spare set. I wondered where the other ones had gotten to.

The weather was misty, gray and foggy, like an old Sherlock Holmes movie. It reflected my mood. As I crested the hill and headed down toward the river, rain refracted strobing blue and white and red lights into psychedelic streaks. I thought I might pass out. Yellow tape stretched across the entrance to the parking lot. A handful of black-and-whites, an ambulance and several civilian cars swarmed over the area from the river to the street. I parked along the road among the half-dozen cars of sight-seers and walked under the barrier. A uniformed policeman came up to me.

"Can I help you, sir?"

"I work here," I said. "What's happened?"

"I'll let you talk to the Lieutenant, sir. Please follow me."

I followed the cop to the far end of the parking lot where small groups of uniforms and plainclothes were milling around. He led me to a man with a shaved head wearing a khaki suit and told him that I worked in the building.

"Ted Henderson," the cop said, extending a hand.

"Rick Ryder," I said, reciprocating.

"Got a call about a half-hour ago, said there was a body down here. The Medical Examiner is checking her out. This your office?"

I nodded, thinking how surreal it was, like walking onto a movie set. A dead body in our parking lot. On a Sunday morning.

"Maybe you should take a look, sir, see if it's anybody you know, anyone you've seen around here."

The policeman guided me through the clots of law enforcement people. I saw a white sheet laid over something on the ground, a man in civvies kneeling close to it.

"Doc," the Lieutenant began, "This is Mr. Ryder. He works in the building."

As the officer continued to speak, the doctor turned the body so I could see the victim's face. A wave of nausea overtook me as the pavement moved rapidly upward toward my head.

When I awoke, something was stuck to my arm. Opening my eyes, I saw the needle connecting me to a bag of liquid hanging from a pole. Wires grew out of my chest. I heard the regular beep of what I took to be a monitor of some kind. My head pounded. I felt like I'd just run a marathon. My forehead hurt. When I touched it, I felt a gauze bandage. I shut my eyes, falling into a non-sleeping, non-waking fugue until the nurse came to tell me I had visitors, and Lieutenant Henderson and Sergeant Simpson came into the room.

8

I fell asleep soon after the cops left. The room lights were down when I opened my eyes again, the tube still sprouting from my arm. The door to the corridor was closed, and blue was draining from the patch of sky I could see through the window. A meal tray perched on the bedside stand. Hushed noises came from the corridor, the sounds of second-shift people, most of the work day behind them. I punched up my pillow and propped it behind me, lifted an edge of the meal tray cover, and quickly closed it. Apparently I was on a soft diet. I sipped some water. My head still hurt. An ache haunted the ghost of my left arm. Debbie's face, then only half of it, appeared in my mind. I was able to grab the bed pan before I vomited.

A nurse came into the room dressed in pastel lime pants and a matching print shirt. Her name badge read "June Christie, R.N."

"You okay?"

A burst of laughter seemed to frighten her.

"I'm sorry," I said, "it just seemed absurd. I don't really know how I got here, I assume by ambulance, after I saw the dead body of a young woman I know with half her face blown away, and I passed out. I was in a blackout for hours before that. The police have questioned me. My body is suffering the effects of an overdose of alcohol. Other than that, yeah, I guess I'm okay."

She stuck a thermometer in my ear, held my wrist, then wrapped my arm in a blood-pressure cuff. She let the air escape and undid the apparatus.

"So, according to the instruments, how'm I doing?"

"Temp is fine. Blood pressure's a little high."

"How curious."

She was about to leave, and I felt panicky at the idea of being left alone.

"Any idea how long I'll be here?"

"As long as you don't have another seizure, you'll probably be out of here tomorrow. Do you take meds for those?"

"Uh huh."

"Maybe you need to up them."

"Or stop seeing corpses early on Sunday morning," I said.

She smiled. "That, too. Can I get you anything?"

I shook my head.

"There's the call button," she said, pointing to the cord hanging off my right shoulder.

Before she got out of the room, I called, "Nurse?" She turned. "Are there any police outside my room?"

"Nope," she said, giving no indication she thought it a strange question.

I wondered where everybody was. Kathy'd said she'd be home by six or so. Judging by the sky, it must have been well after seven. Of course, things happen, had happened. I wouldn't know if she'd called because I didn't have my cell phone, which was in the console of the Honda, which was...? Certainly, the police would have contacted Zella, who would have gotten in touch with, or tried to get in touch with, Kathy. Charlie Eagleston probably wondered why I hadn't shown up for our match, probably gave me a call, incensed at my irresponsibility, leaving three other people in the lurch. There was a phone on my bedside stand. I could call any of these people, but I was going to have to get my story straight first. Not everyone needed to know that I'd been an acquaintance of the deceased or had drunk myself into oblivion the night before. I couldn't account for myself for better than half a day. Maybe it was just as well I didn't have to talk to people—in addition to the police—who would be interested in explanations.

There must have been a sedative in the I.V. to keep me from having another seizure because I drifted off again, coming around when I sensed a presence in the room. A woman was seated, apparently asleep, in the chair in the corner of the room. Even in the faint light, I knew it who it was.

She raised her head and saw me looking at her.

"I got here as quickly as I could."

Love, fear, gratitude, panic came all at once.

"How'd you hear?"

"Zella called. How do you feel?"

"Worn out."

I lay still with my eyes closed.

"Are you tired or just avoiding me?"

"Probably both."

"Did you know the girl?"

It was like when I was a kid and had been entangled in some mischief my parents heard about but didn't know for sure if I was involved. When asked about it, I would weigh the likelihood they would find out against the chance they wouldn't.

"Yes," I said, after a pause. I couldn't make eye contact with her. "I talked to her a couple of times."

"Where she worked?"

I nodded.

"Rick, you may not get this. And at times, I'm not sure why.

But I love you. I just hope you haven't screwed it up for good this time."

She stood and walked out of the room. I didn't know when or if I'd see her again, except maybe from the other side of a divorce attorney's table.

I hit the call button, hoping to see June Christie. An older, grandmotherly woman appeared. She looked at her watch when I asked what time it was and said it was nine o'clock. She asked if there was anything I needed. Nothing came to mind other than recovering the missing hours of my life.

9

Sunlight slipped into the room. The tube coming from my arm reminded me where I was. My headache had disappeared but my body ached, reminiscent of mornings after high school cross-country runs. The self-pity I'd been wallowing in the previous day had lifted, replaced by outrage. What, I wanted to know, was going on? A young woman, yes, a stripper, with whom I had had two conversations and the poor judgment to suggest we might play tennis, was murdered and her body dumped where it would draw attention to me. Why?

A woman in white pants and flowered tunic, holding a blood pressure cuff, with a badge proclaiming her to be Cynthia McFadden, LPN, came into the room. She was young and pretty, and my thoughts started to drift toward where young and pretty women always lead them.

"Are you okay, Mr. Ryder?"

I was inclined to say, If I was okay, this is not the place I'd be. I chose to be polite.

"Yes, Cynthia, I'm just fine for the shape I'm in."

She took my vitals.

"How'm I doing?"

"I believe you'll live."

"Any chance I'm gonna get out of here today?"

"Don't know. Your doctor ought to be in soon."

"I think we all know what 'soon' means when we're talking about doctors, Cynthia. Sometime before Friday, maybe. What day is it, anyway?"

"Monday."

"Good. That's what I thought."

A man in whites came in bearing a tray, excusing himself as he put it on the bedside stand. I lifted the lid, peeked and closed it back. Cynthia winked when she said she'd be back soon. Another orderly, I.D.'d as Gregory Benson, appeared and wheeled me into the bowels of the building where they took pictures of the workings of my brain. It was a mildly disconcerting procedure but distracted me from the drama of my life. Gregory wheeled me back to the room, where I saw a great black bear seated next to the bed. A bear with an unlit short cigar sticking out of his mouth. I felt safe.

I smiled. "Hi, Nate."

"Yo, bro."

Next to Kathy, Nate Chatham was my best friend, though given my current standing with my wife, he may have moved to the top of that list. An old civil rights lawyer turned cynic, now in his mid-sixties, he still carried vestiges of the offensive tackle he had played at Notre Dame. I met him two years after I'd gotten sober, when he walked into a room and said, "Hi. My name is Nate and I'm an alcoholic." He didn't go to meetings much anymore, but we had a regular Monday coffee date. He could have retired into a very comfortable life but instead kept a small practice, defending people of modest means he believed were getting screwed. He was very likely the smartest man I knew. And he still had great connections downtown.

"I was wondering if this had anything to do with why you

missed coffee this morning," he said as he held up a copy of the local daily newspaper so I could read the headline. He handed me the paper.

Dancer Found Dead in Office Parking Lot

The nude body of a young woman was found by police at 8:30 Sunday morning in the parking lot of the offices of the Mountain Center for the Defense of the Environment on Riverside Drive. The Asheville Police Department received a phone call at 8:15 from the manager of a nearby restaurant who saw the body as he was going to work. The identity of the woman was not immediately known, as no clothes or identification were found nearby. The police believe she was in her late teens or early twenties and may have worked as an exotic dancer at a local club.

An employee of the Mountain Center, Rick Ryder, appeared on the scene soon after police arrived. Mr. Ryder was hospitalized for an unrelated occurrence, according to police. A spokesperson for the Center said she had no information about the slaying or the investigation.

Nate was watching me as I set the paper down. "So, Counselor," he said, rolling the stogie between his lips. "It seems you've been having an extracurricular life you've not been sharing with your old friend."

"What can I say, Counselor?" The first time I'd called him "Counselor" eight years ago, he'd reciprocated. We'd been doing it ever since.

"Kathy know?"

"I told her when she stopped in last night. Didn't seem real happy about it when she left."

"Imagine that."

"I've been trying not to."

"Well, you'd better, because whatever you were doing with this girl is gonna come out, and it's gonna come out in the press."

"Woman, Nate. She was a young woman."

"I'll bet the distinction was comforting to Kathy. Anyway, I've been to the courthouse and police station. Want to know what the talk is?"

"Shoot."

"Poor choice of language, perhaps. You know a Jimmy Crawford?"

"I met a guy at the club, called himself that. What's he got to do with this?"

"Seems he was arrested last night at The Doll House. Got drunk, was asked to leave, wouldn't, started fighting with the bouncer— never a good idea in my experience—then fought with the cops when they came—a worse idea. Got him for drunk and disorderly, resisting, two charges of assault on an officer. The latter are felonies. He's a two-time loser. If he's convicted of another felony, he'll be facing ten years, minimum. Jimmy's a certifiable lowlife, but he's not cut out for prison life. So he offers a deal. Reduce everything to misdemeanors in exchange for information about the stripper murder. This is only, what, sixteen hours after she'd been found, hadn't even hit the papers yet. Here's the good part."

I picked up the paper cup from the bedside stand, poured some water, waiting to hear what could possibly be the good in this narrative.

"He tells them you were out at the club the night before, talking to him about how much of a bother this dancer had become, making some kind of demands, and you said you were going to have to do something about her."

We exchanged deadpan looks.

"That's it?" I could feel the blood in my face. "Some drunk felon wants to keep his ass out of the penitentiary and he serves them this? And they believe him?"

"The other thing I hear," he continued in the matter-of-fact-way of lawyers, "is that there is pressure to get this thing resolved quickly. You may be a handy patsy. You knew the girl. You had a motive."

"According to them."

"Yes, according to them. That's all it needs to be according to. They will be the ones to arrest and prosecute you. They are your adversary right now."

I thought Kafka would understand how I felt.

"This is crazy, Nate."

"Your trouble is you've been brought up to believe things will turn out like they're supposed to. The good guy—in this case, you—will win. The bad guy—whoever really killed the girl—will lose. I'm operating on the assumption, of course, that you didn't kill her."

"Thanks."

"Where I come from, nobody expects things to be fair. We are prepared when someone tells us our world is not what we believed it to be. Welcome to my world, Counselor. The world where truth and justice and fairness are irrelevant."

"Okay, Nate. You're not running for anything. I get it. The wheels of justice don't always ensure justice is done."

"Just a reality check. Don't know if they've got enough to convince a judge you might be guilty of anything other than incredibly bad judgment, possible felony stupidity. But you better hope they find something—somebody—else soon, 'cause right now you're the default perp."

"And why is it I would I leave the body in the parking lot?" I asked, hoping my fear wasn't obvious, because it was at that moment, in the asking of the question, that the full range of possibilities of what might have occurred between the time I ordered that second Heineken and awoke at three-thirteen a.m. sank in, like something thrown into a pit of quicksand.

"Try this on. You take the girl back to the office for a little hanky-panky, can't take her home, after all, and don't want to be seen at her place. Things go bad, she won't back off. Next thing you know, you have a body to dispose of. So, you think of the old 'I'll make this look so obvious they'll assume I'm not the one who did it' ploy."

I shook my head. It sounded like a scene from a TV cop show.

"The question is," he said, "who knew these two things: one, where you work; two, that you knew the girl?"

"Will you quit calling her a girl?"

His eyes rolled upward.

"Twenty-one year old females are still girls in my book," he said. "But whatever you want to call her, she was way too young for you to be taking an interest."

"It wasn't like that, Nate."

"Of course not. The question is, as I was saying, who knew those two facts?"

"And," I continued doggedly, "who's responsible for the Buick that's been following me around? I thought it was the MTM people, but then it showed up out at the club the other night. Leading me to believe that MTM is somehow involved in all of this."

"MTM?"

"Mountain Timber and Mining. Company owned by Senator Simmons's family. The Mountain Center is working with a consortium of environmental groups to get them to stop clear-cutting. I think we may have pissed them off."

"And you've been followed?"

"Yep. Jay, you know the intern who works with me, he and I were out documenting what they've been doing on National

Forest land when this car appears behind us. Follows us down the mountain. I've seen it behind me a couple of times since then."

"Does add a twist to things. Means there's some interesting detective work to be done here. Unfortunately, it doesn't seem that the local gendarmes are interested in doing it."

A wrist shot out from the white shirt under the black suit jacket, exposing a gold Rolex as his hand sought mine.

"Oops. Gotta run. Love to stay and chat, homey, but I do have a practice of sorts. If I don't see you here before they let you go, check in with me."

I called after him. "So, who's going to do the investigating?"

"Isn't that what you do for a living?" he said.

"Environmental predators, Nate. Not murderers."

"What's the dif'? Anyway, you know my man Dominic. He might be able to help."

A candy-striper appeared at the door with her cart of books and magazines and snacks. I guessed her to be about sixteen and the cutest thing yet to come into my room. Nate paused in his move to the door, gave her a quick glance, and was gone. I wanted to call after him and say, "THIS is a girl. I KNOW the difference."

10

I was a murder suspect. I couldn't imagine what could be on the candy-striper's cart that could provide a distraction from that fact, but I scanned the neatly arrayed rows of glossy romances, thrillers, and westerns. Stuck in the middle was an older paperback whose faded spine appeared out of place and caught my attention. She handed it to me. It was a Perry Mason novel, The Case of the One-Eyed Woman. I doubted that she knew what kind of small treasure had been buried in plain sight. She was sweet and shy and I tried not to flirt.

I hoped the mystery would occupy my mind as I waited for a couple of shoes to drop. One from the "what's going to happen to me and Kathy?" pair. The other from the "where do I stand with the police?" pair.

I had gotten to the part in the book where the famous lawyer, having just sat down for dinner, gets a phone call from a woman frantic for his services, when the phone in my room rang. It was too spooky. I looked at the handset for a second before picking it up.

"When are you getting out?" she asked. A wide grin blossomed on my face. "I've got to leave again tomorrow and I was hoping we'd have a little time together."

One pair was complete. I could feel my entire body soften. I couldn't speak. I didn't want to cry but couldn't help it. She was patient. My voice returned.

"I haven't seen a doctor but can't imagine why they'd keep me much longer. They took pictures of my brain this morning"—I almost heard her stifle a snarky comment—"and I'm still tired, but I can rest at home much cheaper than the hundreds, heck, thousands of dollars a day it's costing here."

"I was hoping there might be time for something requiring a little activity on your part."

I was just getting into the fantasy of what that homecoming activity might be when there was another knock on the door. A man in a white lab coat stuck his head and torso in the room. I waved him the rest of the way in.

"Dr. Bright's here," I told Kathy. "I'll let you know what I find out."

When I first met the neurologist almost a decade before, I wondered if it was his real name, or one of those ironic monikers one gives people, like Shorty for a guy six-foot-seven. He looked like a basset hound on downers, perhaps from too much time looking at how people's brains aren't working right. We exchanged pleasantries, and he told me that a cursory glance at the MRI images didn't show anything to contradict his assumption that my seizure was stress-related, possibly brought on by seeing a corpse as had been reported in the newspaper.

"A radiologist will review the pictures, but you seem to be all right in the head, physiologically speaking. Another major stressor would be alcohol withdrawal. The toxicology report showed a low level of alcohol. Not a big deal in itself. Except it was about nine o'clock Sunday morning when it was drawn. So, either you'd been drinking before you went into your office, or you'd been drinking the previous night—a lot, for you to still have a measurable level. I mention this for two reasons: one, you know about the relationship between drinking and seizures; and two, the last time we talked, you told me you'd been abstinent for several years. I'm not asking for an explanation, you understand, just pointing out what you already know."

I was not going to be able to avoid dealing with my relapse and the fact that sixteen hours of my life were missing. I didn't know if the police had established a time of death, but I assumed it coincided with my disappearing act. He said I could leave whenever I wanted.

Kathy said she'd be here in half an hour when I called to say I was ready to go. She sounded friendly, even forgiving. I felt hopeful. Just before she hung up I asked offhandedly, "You haven't seen my keys lying around, have you?"

"Nope."

She didn't seem nearly as curious as I was as to their whereabouts.

While I was waiting for her to fetch me, my mind wandered back to the day I met her twenty-some years ago on the tennis courts at Ohio State. Mutual friends had invited us to play doubles with them. I'd played club tennis as an undergrad at Ohio University when I'd had both arms, and I still could hold my own, although the two-handed backhand was out. My buddy and I were already on the court when the women appeared. I was mindful not to let my immediate attraction to her be too obvious. Five-eight, trim, athletic, as was befitting a woman who'd played varsity tennis and been on the swim team at Wittenberg College. Unlike a lot of female athletes, swimmers in particular, she had classic physical proportions. And a pretty face with blond hair pulled back in a ponytail. The traditional short, pleated skirt showed off a gorgeous pair of legs.

We made a good team, knocking off our friends 6-2, 6-3. Over beers afterward, she asked me about the arm. I told her about the car wreck. I didn't tell her about the drinking beforehand or what happened to the girl driving the other car. She told me later that when she first saw me, she couldn't help but notice, no one can, but by the end of the first set, she wasn't paying attention to it.

I never did stop noticing how good-looking she was. When she came into the hospital room, I felt the way I did that first day on the courts.

"You are a knucklehead," she said, handing me clean jeans, sport shirt and underwear.

"Yeah, but I'm your knucklehead."

"As I am frequently reminded."

"Have you talked to your dad?" I asked while I was slipping on my shoes.

"Oh, yes. And am reminded again why I was glad to move out of Ohio. The man won't let go. I don't think I've had a conversation with him in the last fifteen years that didn't include some form of 'When are you coming home?'"

"Be nice if he could find another woman," I said.

"Are you kidding? Sometimes I think Mom died just to get away from him."

The passing mention of death was sufficient to sweep away the elation I'd felt when she'd come into the room, replaced by thoughts of Detective Henderson and Sergeant Simpson. I was quite confident I hadn't seen the last of them.

<h1 style="text-align:center">11</h1>

I know you didn't do it," Kathy said. We were on our way to the office where I planned to pick up my car and check in with Zella, get the lay of the land, see where the MTM case stood. "God knows what you were doing in your blackout, but you don't have it in you to murder anyone. You're the guy who carries spiders outside, for crying out loud."

"There was this guy I knew in AA," I said, "killed his mother in a blackout. Did twenty years for it."

"Yeah, but was he the kind of guy you could imagine doing that? Who knows, he may have wanted to kill her for years, and it took being out of his mind drunk to be able to do it."

"I appreciate the vote of confidence. I don't think I could do it, either. I had no reason to. It's not like she was pestering me or anything. Or blackmailing me. Even then, murder is way out of the realm of what I think is possible for me. But according to Nate, the DA's office seems to think they can make a case for it. And I'm going to have to prove otherwise."

"No 'innocent until proven guilty'?" she said.

"Apparently not."

We had come to Riverside Drive. There was no gray Honda parked nearby.

"Stolen, you think?" she asked.

I shrugged, hoping someone in the office would know.

"I'll wait here; don't be too long, please." I could hear the exasperation in her voice.

"It wasn't here when I came in this morning," Carole told me when I went inside.

I called the police to report the disappearance. The woman on the desk put me on hold.

"I'm sorry, Mr. Ryder," she said when she came back on, "that car has been impounded."

My stomach lurched around. Zella came out of her office while I was staring at the phone in its cradle.

"You okay?" she asked.

"They impounded my car. They think I murdered her." I looked up. "No. That's not it! They don't really think that at all. I'm being framed."

Her eyes were narrowed, head tilted.

"Really. Nate told me that. They want to get this solved quickly and I'm the fall guy, the 'default perp.' And, I'm going to have to be my own investigator."

"Why pick on you?"

"Because I knew her."

"Wouldn't someone in her line of work have known lots of people?"

I couldn't tell if there was a judgment in her voice or not.

"Sure. I guess."

"So. Why you?"

I told her what Nate had told me about Jimmy Crawford.

"And I don't think it's just coincidental that it happened while the stuff with Mountain Timber is going on."

"You mean Mountain Timber and Mining Company is

involved in the murder of a stripper and setting you up for it? Isn't that a bit of a stretch?"

"This whole thing's a stretch, Zella. Jay and I are almost run off the road by a logging truck. We're followed by somebody who then proceeds to follow me around town. Then Jimmy Crawford tries to run me off the road. I come to the office on a Sunday morning and there's a dead girl in the parking lot. Crawford cops to this ridiculous story implicating me. Jeez. It's unreal. Surreal. My mind is in no shape to think about this stuff now. I'm going home to bed."

"Take some time off," she said. "You've been through a lot."

"Thanks. But I've got to be active, I can't be lying around with this going on."

"I thought you were going to be investigating the murder. Your mind is going to be elsewhere than here. I'm serious. Take some time. We'll talk in a few days."

I was about to argue before it sunk in. The matter was not up for discussion.

"Where's Jay?" I asked.

The look on her face suggested that was also not something we were going to talk about.

I went back outside and told Kathy the car had been impounded.

"Couldn't it be because it was parked illegally along the road?"

I raised my hand in supplication.

"Of course. Why couldn't they have just told me that?"

I felt for my cell phone, realized it was in my car and asked to use hers to call back to the police. I repeated my name to the woman who again put me on hold. When she came back, she said I'd have to speak with Detective Henderson. I got his voicemail and left my name and phone numbers, although I was sure he already had them.

"I think it's other than illegal parking," I said as I folded up her phone. "And something's going on with Jay."

"What?" she asked.

"I don't know. But when I asked Zella where he was, she just gave me this look. She didn't want to talk about it, that was clear. And she told me to take some time off. I guess I'll do some serious sleuthing."

"Do you suppose that can wait a little while?"

12

She suggested I go to bed and she'd fix something to eat later. When I woke, the sun was making its descent toward the southern tier of the Blue Ridge Mountains. Since Kathy didn't cook, I wondered what we'd be having for dinner. I made my way downstairs and through the double glass doors that led out to the deck.

A glass of wine hung in one hand as she lounged on a deck chair, long blue skirt draped over her legs, sandals dangling from her feet. An off-white sleeveless shell complimented her figure. She had a phone in the other hand. A pack of cigarettes and a lighter sat on the table.

"We're not moving back to Ohio, Dad. We have a life here. You're more than welcome to come down here. We could redo the basement for you."

I winced. She rolled her eyes.

"I understand that, Dad. We both have homes. And they're hundreds of miles apart. Dad, I don't want to have this conversation anymore tonight, okay? Call Robbie. I love you…. Yes, I'll call in a few days."

She ended the call, pulled a cigarette from the pack, and lit it, inhaling deeply.

"You know," she said, "growing up, I always thought he was the one in charge, the strong one. It's becoming clear that it was really Mom who made things happen and he's lost without her guiding the ship. Has no clue what to do with himself and thinks if I'd just come home, everything would be fine. He's not like this with my brother. Although Robbie avoids him, too. I guess it's just something I have to live with but, damn, it wears me out."

She sucked more smoke into her lungs, breathed out, stared out toward the woods.

She turned back to me.

"Now let's you and I talk."

I didn't think this was going to be a discussion about how nice the weather had been. In place of the scotch I would have liked, I went back into the kitchen for a glass of sparkling water.

"I did a lot of thinking this week, especially the past two days," she began. "I know you go to that club. You know I don't like it. I particularly don't like that you talked to one of the dancers a couple of times, but that's going to have its own consequences for you."

I felt much as an earthworm might right after a rain shower, when it comes to the surface and the birds are waiting.

"I know it has nothing to do with me, not with any shortcomings I might have, no deficits in the sexual attractiveness or availability or prowess arenas. It's your stuff. And here's the deal. As long as I don't have to hear about it—I'm okay. Really. I don't to want talk about it. It's a part of your world I want nothing to do with. I'd prefer you didn't do it. I think it reflects poorly on you. I think if you were honest in your recovery program, you wouldn't do it. But I'm powerless over you and over that behavior. I love you. We have a good life. And I want that to go on."

I thought I could actually taste whiskey in the back of my throat. I sipped my water.

"Okay," I said, not knowing what else to say.

She held her glass up for a toast.

"To us," she said.

"To us," I repeated and leaned over and kissed her cheek.

We chatted in the kitchen as she pulled some things together. The final remains of a curried chicken salad, some tabouli that was nearing the end of its lifespan, arranged on lettuce leaves with slices of bright red tomato. I opened a bottle of wine without fanfare and poured a glass for her. We'd been through the does-it-bother-you-that-I-drink business, and she accepted that it didn't. That said, at times like these, I was glad she didn't drink hard liquor.

When we finished eating, she suggested I go back on the deck and relax. Five minutes later she came out wearing a short white satiny robe and, apparently, nothing else, carrying a glass of wine in one hand and a coffee cup in the other.

"Regular or decaf?" I asked.

"Regular."

"You know it will keep me up late."

"I'm counting on it."

She slid her chair next to mine as we sipped our drinks. A chill descended as the daylight disappeared.

"Shall we retire for the evening?" I suggested.

"Oh, let's finish our drinks, shall we," she said, crossing what were still, at age forty-two, terrific legs, making sure to lean forward as she picked up her glass. After draining the last of her drink, she reached for my arm and led me, puppy-like, to the bedroom. There is something about sex with a long-term partner that is like aged wine, with subtleties unimaginable in younger vintages. Our stamina was a product of pure desire rather than great physical ability. She died several little deaths, while resurrecting me repeatedly. If my life had ended at that moment, the undertaker would have had to tame the smile on my face.

"Not bad for a couple of old-timers," she said. Holding

each other we began to laugh, laughter that comes with physical exhaustion when there is nothing to stop what, in public, would be perceived as unseemly or insane.

My body woke at its accustomed time with no regard for the exertions of the past couple of days. Kathy didn't stir as I ran my fingers through her hair. I went downstairs to start the coffee and put some water on to boil. I walked to the road to fetch the newspaper, hoping there would be nothing in there about me.

The front-page headline bellowed, SENATOR'S TAXES SCRUTINIZED. I scanned the story as I walked back up to the house. The Senate Ethics Committee was looking into suggestions that our own Malcolm Simmons may have underreported income from his family's timber and mining operations.

Kathy was just sitting down at the table on the deck with a steaming mug of tea. I dropped the paper in front of her as she took a cautious first sip.

"I believe they're trying to get us to back off the lawsuit," I said. "If our case goes forward, all the ethics stuff about Simmons sitting on the committee that deals with the Forest Service is gonna come up. No wonder they've got trucks trying to run us over and people trashing the office."

"And following you around town," she added.

"And that. Kind of primitive, but I guess their style is physical intimidation. You'd think they'd be more about trying to tie this thing up in court."

I went inside, fixed a cup of coffee, and rejoined her on the deck.

"I'm still bugged about a connection to The Doll House," I said. "Or maybe there is no connection, just a coincidence these things are happening in my life at the same time. I suppose that's what I've got to find out. And soon, before they have me roped and tied and ready for the branding iron."

She went up to pack her bags for her trip to Charleston, and I turned on the small TV in the kitchen to keep me company while I fixed a second cup of coffee. I was heading for the deck when I heard the familiar voice of Malcolm Simmons. I turned back to watch the senator as he excoriated the liberals in Washington who would do anything to tear down a man of God who had gone to that city to uphold family values on behalf of the good Bible-believing folks of North Carolina.

My righteous indignation matched the senator's. I would find out what was going on, who was setting me up and why, although I had no idea how I was going to go about it.

Half an hour later, Kathy tossed her things into the back of the Infiniti, ready to head to South Carolina for a two-day-plus conference on physical fitness for young people, one of those pointless events required of a manufacturers' rep for playground equipment companies. We necked a little in the garage before she said she better get going. I followed her down the drive and waved her away.

I had reached the back deck again when the front door bell rang. The other shoe was about to hit the floor, and I wouldn't have to worry about what I was going to do next.

13

A short man in a blue police uniform stood in the doorway. He wasn't smiling. "Mr. Ryder?"

A taller, similarly outfitted man stood next to him. An APD car was in the drive. I didn't hear all the words that followed after I acknowledged who I was, although "murder" and "Miranda rights" were clear enough. He told me I could call my lawyer once I was downtown and booked. When he clacked one handcuff around my wrist and the other on a belt loop, I was afraid I might throw up. The men were courteous, talking quietly as if the whole thing was as embarrassing to them as it was to me. When we got into town, I kept my gaze down.

I was processed, feeling like an animal transformed from a living being into something of an altogether different kind of matter, much as a pig becomes sausage. They allowed me call to Nate's office before I was escorted to the jail. Katrina, who as paralegal, secretary, and office manager, kept his practice going, was appropriately solicitous, but my attorney was not available. Lawyers.

The holding cell is non-discriminatory. Regardless of the nature of one's alleged offense, you hang out with everyone else arrested in the recent past who has not been released on bond or moved to more permanent quarters in the stories above. When I arrived, early in the day, the drunks were sobering up and the marginally insane reasonably subdued. The color was gray, matching the prevailing mood. Gray walls, gray ceiling, gray floors, gray concrete benches along the sides of the room. Disinfectant had been liberally applied not long before but had lost the battle for dominance over the smell of urine, feces, and the funk of people who live outdoors. Coping with the smell, trying not to gag every two minutes, helped keep my mind off my emotions, which were running along the humiliation-outrage spectrum.

My new associates were generally impressed that I was charged with murder, murderers apparently being an elite of the incarcerated class. On the other hand, being a lawyer tended to undermine my standing, as it was universally understood that lawyers were responsible for the rest of them being here. To hear my fellow jailbirds, it was their attorneys who were the responsible parties for whatever crime they'd been accused of, since they hadn't committed whatever acts were being alleged and it was only due to the malfeasance of counsel that they were not out on the street. Being without a limb did not go unnoticed, either. One of the wits among them said that a lawyer like me gave new meaning to the expression, "one-armed bandit."

Regardless of their general aversion to my kind, a couple of the men consulted me about their cases. When informed that I was not a criminal lawyer, they took it as if I was shirking my responsibility to my new homeboys.

"Get me out of here, bro," I said to the Big Man, facing him in the visitation room.

"Working on it, my man."

"The jailhouse gossip has it that I murdered my girlfriend. Jimmy Crawford's making a big deal of knowing me and me telling him I wanted to get rid of her. Pretty much what you said he told the police. Everybody in the holding cell knows the story."

"Crawford still in the tank?"

"He's up in general population. They must be expecting him to be here for a while."

"Maybe yes, maybe no. Here's something that has to have you wondering about the workings of the universe. You know Victor Chavez?"

"Heavy hitter in the Latino community?"

"That's the one," said Nate. "With grandiose notions for that community and his role in it. Has a little fiefdom there across the river. He's been appointed Jimmy's attorney. According to a source in the Public Defender's Office, the way that came about was extremely irregular."

"Meaning?"

"Meaning rather than being a random assignment, somebody suggested Victor. Victor's done public defender work before, but it seems someone higher up in the criminal justice system wanted him to be working with Crawford."

"How higher up?"

"D.A., judge, I don't know. Somebody who can influence the Public Defender's Office. Also the appointment happened unusually fast."

We looked at each other through the wire-mesh window.

"Just makes you wonder, you know," he mused.

"Yes, it is interesting, Nate. But right now, it's hard for me to concentrate on much other than getting out of here. When's that gonna happen?"

"I think we can get you out on bail tomorrow. We'll give the judge the usual upstanding community man, no previous record, no indication of potential harm to the public, unless they produce a list of other women you're likely to want to bump off. You're going to have to put up your house for the bond."

"Kathy'll love that."

"The D.A.'s probably going to ask for bail of a million dollars. I'll argue for two-fifty. Unless you have twenty-five to fifty large laying around, the house is probably all you have for collateral. He's hoping to get a judgeship soon, so he thinks he's gotta show he's tough on crime, blind justice, the rich get the same as the poor, you shouldn't get to walk free just because you're a white guy in a suit."

"When is it I became rich, Nate?"

"You are one of the haves in the have/have not equation, my man. Unlike Crawford."

"So I may be a sacrificial lamb to some make-believe idea of justice?"

"The judge will feel he's got to set a reasonably high bail. That's the bottom line. Kathy may not be happy about it, but I don't guess she's happy about any of this."

I wanted to say that she seemed happy enough the night before but restrained myself.

When he stood up, his figure filled the window. I had to lean forward and look up to see his face.

"Unless something comes up," he said, "I'll see you at the hearing tomorrow."

He was gone before I could say anything else.

I had another day to look forward to living with the righteously indignant rage of a bunch of men who believed they were pawns in the game of life. I put my name on the list to use the jailhouse phone, hoping Kathy would have her cell on. She wouldn't be happy about having to put the house up for collateral, but I wasn't going to run off. The money was safe, even if one of the contingencies that would ensure getting it back was my going to prison.

After stripping, showering, and donning the off-white jumpsuit of the semi-permanent county inmate I was moved to the deluxe accommodations of the jail proper, sixth floor south, since I would be the guest of the county for at least another day.

14

She answered on the second ring, and before she could finish saying "Hello" I blurted out, "I'm in jail."

"I know. Nate called. About putting the house up for collateral." A pause hung in the air, pendulous as a nursing cow. "I've worked up a great tirade of indignation and justification. But my guess is you're beating yourself up pretty well without my help, so I'll just get to the point. I don't want you coming home. I could deal with you going to that club, even talking to one of the strippers. But you were trying to make a date with her. That's why they've arrested you. Because you did more than talk with her at the club."

"I know there is no way to explain this that can mitigate—"

"Mitigate? Don't use lawyer jargon on me, please. You were seeing a teenage stripper."

Put like that, it doesn't sound good. I wanted to challenge "teenage." I wanted to say "seeing her" overstated what had actually occurred. I wondered where she was getting her information.

"I suppose I should have some compassion here, although I'm not sure what for. So you had a seizure. I can imagine your brain going, 'Oh, shit, this won't look good when Kathy comes home.' BZZZZZ! Overload! I really don't want to talk about it.

Although, of course I am curious about what is going on that someone murders a stripper and dumps her body in your parking lot. I don't believe for a minute that you killed her. But I do believe you are a first class jerk. And I don't want to be around you. Not now. I might have to kill you if I was."

I wanted to raise my voice back at her. I wanted to be outraged and self-righteous. I felt foolish and guilty, and terribly sad. And I didn't want to cry; I got that vulnerability was not a good characteristic to display on the sixth floor south.

Among the mortifications of incarceration was being escorted from the jail to the County Courthouse the next morning, my hand cuffed to my escort's wrist, wearing the county issue jumpsuit with INMATE stenciled across the back and front, a twenty-first century unisex version of the scarlet "A." Apparently, I wasn't a flight risk since they didn't put leg shackles on me.

The District Attorney took the opportunity at the hearing to grandstand about the mighty and the low, asking why Mr. Ryder should be treated differently than poor Jimmy Crawford, the man who had directed the police to me, now having to remain in jail because he could not make bond on a piddling drunk and disorderly charge. As Nate predicted, the D.A. asked for a million and the judge ordered a quarter of it. We were out of the courthouse by ten-thirty and agreed to meet back in the coffee shop in the basement of the old building. Nate went off to do the bond work while I was escorted back to the jail to change clothes and claim my personal effects.

15

The headline screamed at me from the newspaper rack outside the courthouse.

LAWYER ARRESTED IN MURDER OF DANCER

My picture was next to the story. I fed the machine two quarters and took a copy into the small café. My attorney was easy to spot, seated at a four-top in the middle of the room. I dropped the paper in front of him and went to get a cup of coffee, served in a white ceramic mug reminiscent of old AA meetings in the days before Styrofoam.

"Keeping it for your scrapbook?" he asked as I pulled up the chair across from him.

"Yeah. To remind me of the good old days. At least I'm sober."

"Yes. And that brings up a point, Mr. Ryder. Where were you on the night of June fourteenth?"

Like a witness being interrogated, no social amenities, right into the cross-examination.

"That does seem to be a relevant concern," I answered.

"You're going to have to do better than that when you're on the stand, Counselor."

"The truth is, Nate, I don't know what I was doing. I was in a blackout from about eleven-thirty or so Saturday morning until three-thirteen Sunday morning."

"Three-thirteen. You seem to have that time nailed."

"It's what I woke up to. Big red numbers on my clock-radio."

"The reason I ask that this morning is because your pal Jimmy Crawford is sticking to his story that you were out at the club that night, asking to see Tiffani, saying you had to do something about her, or something to that effect."

"I was in a blackout, Nate. I could have been there. But I didn't kill her."

"Of course you didn't. You don't have it in you. Me, on the other hand ... it's a good thing I stopped drinking when I did."

He grinned.

"You wouldn't kill anybody, either," I said.

"Don't be so sure. At any rate, there are these calls on your cell phone. They have the appropriate warrants, if you're concerned about the niceties of the law."

"I only know about one call. I presume you mean her calling me about a date. It was about playing tennis. I started to call her back, but hung up."

He nodded. "There's that. And then it seems she called you again. Wondering where you were and why you hadn't called. The way I hear it, she was frantic, something to the effect of, 'Where are you? Are you okay? Please call me.' Supports the idea that you were being bothered by this woman."

"Okay. Two calls. Does that seem like sufficient harassment for me to kill her?"

"So she wasn't frantic over the possibility of a tennis date. What was it?"

"Nate! I'm telling you, I don't know," I spit out between clenched teeth, afraid if I opened my mouth everybody in the room would hear me. "Although, the second time I talked with her—second and last time, by the way—she did say something about leaving this town. I thought she was just fed up with the whole exotic dancing scene."

"Stripping."

"Yes. Stripping."

"But maybe it was something else."

I stood with my mug in my hand.

"I need a refill," I said, chewing off my words. "Want anything?"

He handed me his mug. "Black. And if they have one of those crullers, bring me one."

I hooked a finger through the cup handles and walked back to the snack counter. It was operated by a self-help organization for blind people, and I was always impressed with what they could do without being able to see. Handling bills required honor on the part of patrons, but I'd never seen anybody try to scam them. It was in the courthouse, after all. I got a small tray to put everything on, having honed my one-handed carrying skills over the past two decades.

"Jimmy Crawford," I said when I returned.

"Jimmy Crawford what?"

"I don't know, exactly, but he's all over this, isn't he? The first time I saw Tiffa—Debbie—at The Doll House, he claimed to have seen her dance in Atlanta. She denied it, but he was adamant about it. Almost got himself thrown out that night over it."

"And now he's locked up and gets Victor Chavez specially assigned to him," Nate said.

"And claiming I made some incriminating remarks that only he heard, I suppose."

"Is it possible she was running from someone down there, in Atlanta?" Nate asked.

"If Crawford was telling the truth, and she was trying to be anonymous, it would explain why she didn't want to admit to having danced there."

He dipped the cruller in his mug and took a bite. I sipped my coffee.

"Still doesn't explain why someone would want to implicate me."

"Gotta hang it on somebody. And here you come, blundering in, actin' the fool. Going out there Saturday night, like saying, 'You looking for somebody to go down for this, here I am.'"

"You're so charitable."

"Hey. Charity ain't gonna get you off the hook here. And it would be nice to know if you really were out there and how else you spent that sixteen hours."

3:13 came back to me. I cradled my head in my hand and closed my eyes. I saw her face—what was left of it—on the pavement. The edges of my mouth pulled in, my chest hurt.

"You okay?" he asked.

I sat silent for a minute, looking around the room at the lawyers, and sheriff's deputies, and judges, and the accumulated detritus caught up in the stream of justice.

"Not going to have another seizure, are you?"

I shook my head. "Just replayed Sunday morning in my head. I gotta go get some air."

He stood up with me and we walked outside.

"It's getting to me, Nate."

"What?" he said. "Girl you liked found dead in your parking lot? You suspected of murder. Thrown out by your wife. What a pansy."

"Yeah, just an old wuss, I know."

"You better get used to this shit, Counselor, 'cause it's gonna be all over you before the fat lady sings."

We headed for Nate's car.

"So, the deal is, I've got to find out who's screwing with my life and why. And according to you, I'm not going to get much help from the people we pay to investigate these things."

"Looks that way. But you are a highly skilled investigator, licensed by the State of North Carolina. Even got a gun, as I recall, although as a felony suspect, the authorities would probably take a dim view of you carrying it. And like I said earlier, Dominic might be available for some assistance."

Dominic was Dominic Hayes, a guy who did investigating for Nate, also a licensed P. I. Unlike myself, he was not restrained from carrying a firearm.

"What are you smiling at?" Nate said.

"Oh, just the idea of me carrying a gun around."

"Yeah, well, remember, this whole thing started because someone got shot dead."

<h1 style="text-align:center">16</h1>

"Where do you want me to take you?" he asked as we approached his Jaguar coupé. Early in our friendship he explained that one of the dilemmas of his work was dealing with people who would not have confidence in a person in his position unless he demonstrated that he was successful—the right car, well-tailored suits, big house—and conversely, having to contend with those who thought all that stuff was evidence that he had sold out. Luxury being more congenial than poverty, he opted for the former.

"I'll need a car since mine seems to be temporarily unavailable. That place over on Coxe Avenue would be okay."

As we drove, he asked if I thought Jimmy Crawford was the killer.

"Kid's a crackhead," I said. "They're a notoriously unpredictable species. If he did it, it wasn't his idea. She did dis him at the club, but I don't think he'd have killed her because of it."

We were taking a shortcut through a part of town I didn't know well but where Nate received and returned occasional waves from people out on the street. I imagined he had represented some of them, certainly enough of them to be known and have unimpeachable street cred.

As we approached the rental agency, he said, "What's your

plan?"

"I suppose I should have been working on that while I was in the slammer, but somehow my creative juices just weren't flowing. Know what I mean?"

"I can imagine."

"I need to find out what I was doing the rest of the day Saturday and early Sunday morning. Be interesting to know when I bought the scotch, and if I drank it somewhere other than at home.... And find out where Debbie came from."

"Got anybody else on your short list?"

I must have had a strange expression on my face.

"Possible suspects," he said, as if I was impossibly dense. "Anybody else you can think of who might be involved in this?"

I hadn't thought of him since the morning we'd gone to the office to fetch my car. I didn't want to think of him this way now.

"Well?" he asked.

"Jay."

"Jay? That intern of yours, kid from that hippie college. What's up with him?"

"I don't know. But on the day after the offices were ransacked, he came in early, earlier than he usually did. The cop who investigated— guy named Hammer—thought it was interesting enough to ask Jay about it. I came to his defense and Hammer jumped all over me. Zella and I exchanged glances, like we also thought it was interesting but we let it go. Neither one of us said anything about it after that. The next day I went in early and he and Carole—"

"Your office manager."

I nodded.

"They're standing at the file cabinets looking like they just ate the canary."

"Maybe they're having an affair."

"Doing it standing up at the file cabinets?"

"Little kissy-face maybe. Just an idea. Why don't you ask him?"

"If he's having an affair?"

"Why he's coming in early. If he's got a good explanation, it could ease your mind, you could check him off your list."

"That would certainly be the direct route."

We pulled up in front of the car-rental office. I was about to step out of the Jag when I said, "And then, of course, there's the green Buick."

"Ah, yeah. The green Buick," he repeated. "When did you say you first saw it?"

"The day Jay and I were in the forest checking out the MTM business."

"Had you seen the girl..."

"Debbie."

"Debbie. Had you seen her before then?"

I had to think for a few seconds. "No. I didn't see her until the night I picked up my tennis racket. I didn't know who she was, at the time. Just a really cute young woman."

We both pondered the implications.

Before I'd gotten both legs out he said, "And then there's Kathy."

I looked at him as if he'd spoken Swahili.

"You know they questioned her," he said.

"When?"

"This morning. She came back to town after you talked to her from the jail."

"She was in Kentucky when it happened, for God's sake."

"Says she. Just like you were at home."

"You don't really think it's possible that Kathy killed someone, do you?"

It was absurd.

"Or had her murdered. How many people in that courthouse

this morning have done things to which people have responded, 'I can't believe he'd do a thing like that.'? People do unbelievable things. That's a fact. And another fact that may help you understand the reality of things is that you are under arrest for murder."

"Well, it's still ridiculous. And dragging Kathy into it smacks of harassment."

"Why wouldn't she be a suspect? She had motive. She apparently had the opportunity."

"What opportunity?" I asked, skipping over the motive part.

"I understand there's a lot of time the night and morning of the murder when she has no more alibi than you do. Maybe the two of you were in cahoots," he said.

"Come on, Nate."

"Just letting you know the kind of things I imagine are going through the D.A.'s mind."

"Come on. Kathy?"

He shrugged.

<h1 style="text-align:center">17</h1>

The lone clerk was attending to another customer when I walked in. He said he'd be right with me. My mind started churning as I waited. It was hard for me to believe that the police wouldn't investigate. As Nate pointed out, I tended toward naïveté in my idealism about the justice system. In real life, evidence got covered up or manipulated or manufactured or lost. Bad guys got let off, good guys got screwed. People with money and influence seemed to get away with whatever they felt like doing. Jay's rants about corporate corruption were not without foundation.

Although I was, as Nate reminded me, a licensed private investigator, I had no real experience in the crime game. The few private cases I'd had were standard extramarital affairs, following wayward spouses until they incriminated themselves, situations in which a telephoto lens was a more useful tool than a Smith & Wesson .38.

When the agent finally got to me, I asked him for the sportiest thing he had. It was a little two-seater roadster. I said I'd take it, thinking I deserved it; it's not every day you have to clear yourself of murder. When he hesitated, I told him not to worry, I'd had twenty-four years of experience driving with one hand. Most people drive with only one anyway, using the other for their coffee or cigarette or cell phone. When the transaction was complete, I drove to the mall for a new cell phone to replace the one the cops had, the one with the incriminating messages.

Twenty minutes later, I was headed north on the Blue Ridge Parkway, not remembering how I'd gotten there, like I'd been on autopilot. A subversive thought insinuated itself into my mind. I could just keep going, all the way to end of the Parkway in Pennsylvania, and nobody would know. It was a week-to-week car rental. They wouldn't miss me at the office or at home. I wondered how far I could go, how I could change my identity.

Halfway up to Mount Mitchell, I stopped at an overlook. The view was the kind they put on the postcards you can buy at the Visitors Center. Unblemished powder-blue sky above; a full spectrum of greens below. Reality seeped in as I gazed at the vast expanse of valleys and hills spread out before me. This was my home. I wasn't going to run off, and the longer I put off my own search, the more time someone else had to make a case against me. I filled my lungs with clean mountain air and aimed the little car back down the way we'd come.

Courtesy suggested I call before going out to the house while self-righteous indignation shouted, It's my house, too, dammit! When I got to the bottom of Cove Road, I relented and called from my new phone. There was no answer. Pulling into the drive, I saw that her Infiniti was gone, but inside there were dishes in the sink, newspapers on the kitchen table, her stuff in the upstairs bedroom. I gathered my necessaries: clothes, the Perry Mason book, my laptop. I considered snooping for hotel receipts. Just thinking about it felt like an intrusion, and they wouldn't tell me what time she'd checked out anyway.

After stopping for some basic food supplies, I drove to a new extended stay motel on Tunnel Road, just on the outskirts of downtown. The room was clean and commodious if not luxurious—a double bed, writing desk, a table for eating, a kitchenette with microwave, stove and oven, coffee maker, everything you'd need in your home away from home. Except your wife, your stuff, your own life. I set up the laptop and sent an email telling everyone my new cell phone number.

Standing on the narrow balcony, I gazed into the middle distance, like some long-ago emperor surveying his city, knowing the barbarian hordes are just over the horizon. I was listening to traffic pass on the nearby interstate, inhaling exhaust-tinged late morning air, when I heard an insistent, unfamiliar sound. It took a few seconds for me to figure out that it was my new phone.

"That was quick," I said to Zella.

"When I saw your email, it reminded me that I'd wanted to call when you were, hmm, free, as it were."

"You mean, as in not behind bars."

"Yes, that. I wondered if you'd like to come out for dinner."

To go to Zella's on my own had been unthinkable until this moment. It was a boundary we'd established years ago, a way to prevent anything remotely questionable from arising between us, an honoring of my marriage and the sanctity of her widowhood.

"This is unprecedented."

"These are unprecedented times," she said.

"When?"

"I know your calendar is probably crowded these days, but I was thinking about tonight."

"Yeah, I'll have to check with my social secretary and see if I can clear a space. Oh, here she is now. What time?"

"Six-ish?"

"Apparently I'm free then. You want to tell me what this is about?"

"We'll talk when you get here."

Another mystery. I was getting my fill of these but assumed it would bear in some way on my present precarious condition. A noose was tightening around my neck, and I needed to get some slack.

$$18$$

The litany of ritual readings at the noon meeting was familiar—and a comfort while everything else in my life seemed up for grabs. The speaker was a woman I'd seen at several meetings who had twenty-five years of sobriety, telling us what it had been like, what happened, and how it was now. Predictable. Familiar. Even the bad coffee in Styrofoam cups was a comfort.

I returned to the motel to work on a plan of action, but my mind kept wandering to the upcoming dinner date. I was fidgety and realized I hadn't had any exercise in days, no workouts in my basement gym, no long hikes, no tennis. I decided to take advantage of the motel pool, taking pad and pen with me. Four young women sunbathing in skimpy bikinis all smiled at me. I smiled back. It was a tossup, who had the harder time not staring: them at a one-armed swimmer, or me at the expanse of exposed skin. I laid the pad on a table and jumped in, hoping the cold water would calm my libido.

After ten minutes of laps, I moved to the table to begin working on strategy. One of my pool neighbors sat up and fiddled with her top. This was not going to allow for focused work. I returned to the room.

When I closed my eyes in the shower, I saw Kathy. I turned off the water and draped myself in a towel. Before I reached the bed, my legs began to shake. I staggered across the room. I began to cry; my chest heaved. I was afraid the sounds might attract attention from the next rooms or passersby. I started throwing pillows around. It may have been two minutes, it may have been ten, but eventually I ran out of steam.

My mind drifted. It came to rest back on Kathy. I was sure we'd weather this as we had previous storms. She'd left me twice before because of my drinking. I understood why she left. I wasn't sure why she came back.

The still-strange sound of my new cell phone awakened me. I had no idea how long I'd slept.

"Are you coming?" the voice asked.

I had to scan the room to remind myself where I was and who was expecting me.

Zella's townhouse was in the area built up around an eighty-year-old resort hotel and country club, a part of town inhabited by few dark-skinned people. Years ago, when she'd moved in here, I'd asked why she had come to this particular area rather than one that might be more welcoming. "Because I can," she'd said.

She was at the door as I walked up the sidewalk.

Zella was a stunning woman, an inch or two taller than me, who might have weighed 140 pounds and carried it regally. Her complexion was an amber ale, reflecting her ancestry. Her hair, once perfectly jet black, was now seasoned with gray. I had been infatuated with her the moment we met in Raleigh fifteen years earlier when she hired me onto the legal staff of the state Department of Environmental Resources. Five years later, soon after her husband died, she was offered the Director's position at the newly created Mountain Center for the Defense of the Environment in Asheville.

There was also an opening for a lawyer/investigator at the new Center. Zella told them she'd take the director position if they also hired me. It was just after I'd gotten my P. I. license, and she knew I was bored. Kathy thought it was a great idea, since it would give her an excuse to leave her corporate job and go out on her own, something she'd been talking about but holding back from. When Zella told us the Mountain Center had accepted her proposal that they hire both of us, we thought it was one of those offers one could not refuse.

She led me through a room commanded by a baby grand, on which stood a richly framed and matted photo of her late husband, then on into the dining room where the food was already laid out. She asked what I wanted to drink.

"Got any good water?"

When she returned, I could smell the scotch in her glass as she handed me my San Pellegrino. At that moment, I would have taken liquor if offered. We sat across from each other at one end of the formal table.

"I'm sure you're wondering why I asked you here tonight," she said, grinning with the theatricality of the cliché. "First, I want to repeat that I know you had nothing to do with the death of that girl. I know you too well. You aren't capable of such a thing."

I remembered Nate's comments at the courthouse, about all the people there who had done things of which nobody could have imagined they were capable.

She sipped her scotch.

"The Board has asked that you be put on administrative leave for the time being, during this ... sensitive time with the MTM investigation."

I nodded. MCDE represented a consortium of environmental groups suing MTM and the U.S. Department of Agriculture, and the audiotape I'd acquired was powerful evidence. But right now, my continued involvement would hurt our case, not help it.

"With pay?"

She smiled again. "For now. Depends on how long this thing drags out."

"According to Nate, the case is on a fast track. Somebody wants it out of the public consciousness. Unfortunately, I seem to be the default suspect."

"So, are you okay with this?"

"Let's see. Don't work. Get paid. Not a bad deal. I can use the time to find out what really happened. I think I can live with that."

"And that leads into the next subject."

I raised my eyebrows.

"I'm worried about Jay."

"Since the break-in?" I recalled the silent uneasiness we'd shared when Jay said he'd been the first one in the office the day it had been trashed and the look she'd given me when I'd come to get my car. I didn't tell her about my conversation with Nate about him.

"Yes. He's often in the office before I get there. Carole thinks I'm crazy, but then she's usually there, too. He talks in hushed tones on his phone. He leaves during the day on personal business, in itself no big deal, we all do it, but he seems skittish about it, like he's hiding something. I used to be amused by his archness about corporations being Satan personified, sort of the comic relief. But I thought he actually believed the rhetoric. Now I'm wondering if it's all been for show, so we wouldn't suspect that he might be working at odds with us."

"Like a mole?

"Something like that, I guess, as hard as it is to get my brain around the idea." She sipped more of her drink and went on. "How would you feel about following him for a couple of days? Give you something to do."

I settled deep into the chair.

"I thought I was on leave."

"Technically, you are. I can't pay for gas money or anything. And if he finds out you're following him, you're on your own. Will you think about it?"

I thought about it. I felt the release of adrenaline. I was letting The Cowboy in—the part of my personality, according to my last therapist, that thrived on too much drama, too much excitement. The Cowboy would get to chase bad guys, not necessarily a healthy frame of mind. I said I'd do it.

Over sorbet and cookies, she said the next day might be good since he'd already told her he was going to have to leave the office early but would be back by mid-morning.

"One hardly gets to say this these days," I said smiling at yet another cliché, "but the game, it seems, is afoot."

Saying it, I realized it was no game. It was life and death, and I wondered if I had my priorities right, chasing Jay around instead of trying to find out who murdered Debbie.

At the door, Zella held her hand out to me, preempting the hug I had fantasized. But her smile was warm, letting me know there was at least one woman in my life who still liked me.

I didn't see the Buick and I didn't think it likely that an unfamiliar vehicle could have sat unobtrusively on the street in this neighborhood for any length of time. Nonetheless, I used evasive maneuvers on the way back to town. I checked the rear view mirror repeatedly as I circled the area around the motel to assure myself I hadn't been followed, repeating to myself the axiom that just because you're paranoid does not mean they aren't out to get you.

It was after nine o'clock when I got back to the room, too late to make an AA meeting. I called my sponsor. He reminded me of a midnight Narcotics Anonymous meeting at First Presbyterian. I got there a few minutes early, skipped the coffee, picked up the reading, "Why We're Here," and sat down. I knew I was there because I was powerless over alcohol, and my life had become unmanageable. I also seemed to have a problem controlling whatever it was that impelled me to go to The Doll House and permitted me to give out my phone number to young strippers.

19

I got up at six, worked out at the motel gym, and was at the car rental place before eight. The little two-seater was fun, but something less attention-grabbing would be far more sensible for tailing someone—especially someone I knew. The agent seemed relieved to have his sports car back, happy to rent a nondescript brown American two-door coupe.

I found a spot in a corner of the restaurant parking lot just down the road from the office, strategically positioned where I'd be able to see Jay coming to work. I slouched in the front seat, hoping my black Western Carolina University ball cap and dark sunglasses would obscure my face without making me look suspicious. I was armed with a pair of binoculars and my trusty old Nikon. It was eight-twenty.

While waiting, I called Nate's office and smiled when Katrina answered the phone. She'd been in the country for ten years and, I imagined, could speak without much accent but preferred to maintain her exoticism. Her deep voice brought to mind Mata Hari. I felt like I was involved in some kind of conspiracy whenever I talked to her. After exchanging greetings, I asked how I could get hold of Dominic and how much his services might cost me.

"Mr. Chatham said you might be calling and to tell you he

thought after the current situation is resolved, you might help him out on a case or two, so do not worry about paying for Mr. Hayes's services. I will have Mr. Hayes call you."

I gave her my new cell number and was wondering what Nate might use me for—stuff involving white people, I imagined—when I spotted Jay's Toyota coming in my direction. I watched him pull into the office parking lot.

Not more than ten minutes had passed when the Toyota came back out onto the road. I let him get around a bend before pulling out behind him. If I hadn't figured out he was taking the back route to McDowell Street, I probably would have either lost him or given myself away. Bypassing Biltmore Village, we were soon on Hendersonville Road headed to the south end of the county. As suburban sprawl petered out, undeveloped tracts alternated with mini-warehouses, used furniture stores, an adult book store and sex emporium, an old-style do-it-yourself car wash. When he turned left into a small strip mall, I turned right into the parking lot of the Holiness Tabernacle Church, a small pre-fab metal building with a spire and cross stuck on top. I angled myself so I could keep him in sight in my rear view mirror. Within two minutes, a small red convertible pulled in and both drivers climbed out of their cars. The driver of the convertible was a woman, considerably shorter than Jay, wearing a short dress. Their arms wrapped around each other in a way that suggested more than passing acquaintanceship. I could only see the woman from the rear. Not a bad view but I couldn't see her face. I assumed it was his girlfriend, Zoey. I let them enter the building before turning around to look with the field glasses.

The office they had gone into was tucked between an insurance agency and a finance company. The set of offices, also including a chiropractor and an accountant, was probably less than ten years old, in what I guessed was the moderate rent range, certainly less expensive than similar space closer to town. A small sign in the berm between the parking lot and the road identified it as the C&M Center.

Trading the Nikon for the field glasses, I took a couple of pictures, then drove a quarter mile down the road before turning around. I had just pulled over to a place at the curb from which I could maintain my vigil when my phone rang.

"Hi. This is Rick."

"Dominic."

I told him what I needed.

"Donna," he repeated back to me. "Barmaid at the Doll House. And why can't you go out there and ask her yourself?"

"I believe I'm persona non grata out there, Dom. You know, supposedly killed their top attraction. And I don't think the police would look favorably on me questioning people they might want to question themselves."

"You just want me to find out where she lives, that it?"

"And her last name. Shouldn't be too bad a gig, being the kind of club it is."

"A job's a job," he said. "I'll be out there tonight, call you in the morning."

I returned my attention to the C&M Center. Being otherwise unoccupied, my mind drifted into memory, back to when I first met Jay. He had come to interview for the internship, and I liked him right off. Nice-looking kid, few inches taller than my five-nine, slim, athletic, a shock of disheveled sandy-blond hair. He was bright, funny, and a little full of himself, as bright, funny college kids often are.

"You know," he'd said, "all the conservation and alternative energy development and lobbying with public officials is ultimately useless unless you can hit the big corporations where they notice. They aren't gonna answer to anything but legal pressure, since the only logic they understand is profit. Lawsuits affect the bottom line. That's why I want to work with you instead of with some other environmental outfit that just wants to get people to drive more fuel-efficient cars. You know, even if people got more miles to the gallon, they'd just drive more. You can tell that by the way driving goes up and down with the price of gas."

And so he went. I attributed his over-the-top rhetoric to the spirit of a rabid youngster yet to get a feel for the nuances of the real world. I knew little about him personally other than that he liked river sports—kayaking, canoeing, and the like—and was in a relationship with Zoey. The two of them were working on a movie. I wondered if that was what had brought them here this morning.

The couple reappeared half an hour after they'd gone into the building. I whipped up the glasses and confirmed that the woman was, indeed, his girlfriend. I snapped a few more shots. They repeated their lovers' ritual, got in their separate cars, and headed north, back toward town. Finding out what went on in the office they'd been in would be more productive, I decided, than following them back to town. I pulled into one of the parking spots they'd vacated and took a chance that, in this small city, I wouldn't be recognized by anyone inside.

20

An astonishingly good-looking woman greeted me. She was seated at a desk, obliquely behind a flat monitor, a headset resting on a nest of blond hair. She smiled in a way that called for one in return.

"May I help you?"

"Since the name on the sign at the street and on the door are the same, I assume you are the business that owns this property."

"Yes, we do," she said, smile intact.

"I'm looking for some commercial rental space."

"I'll see if Mr. Manetti is available. Can I tell him who is inquiring?"

"Bob Mitchum," I said.

Giving no sign the name meant anything, she spoke softly into her headset, then to me.

"Mr. Manetti will be with you in a moment."

She motioned to some chairs around a glass-topped coffee table. Behind her, in the open room, were four or five desks, all unattended. Two walled-off offices filled the rear. The walls were naked, the coffee table unburdened by reading material; the whole place appeared as if the office outfitters had just delivered it.

A man about my age, a little shy of six feet, came to greet

me. He had dark hair and a sallow complexion. By the look of his biceps and barrel chest, he spent time in a gym. He and Jay seemed an unlikely fit.

"Mr. Mitchum?" he said, extending a hand.

"Bob," I said, reaching out to reciprocate.

His grip would have been painful to a hand not used to doing the work of two.

"Tim Manetti," he said as he released the pressure. "Come on back."

The office was modest, maybe twelve by twelve. A chrome and glass table served as a desk, its surface pristine except for a telephone and a few "missed your call" notes falling neatly in a small cascade near his right arm. The walls continued the minimalist décor of the outer room. It didn't look at all like the office of someone who spent much time here. In addition to a black leather executive chair, there were two matching chairs triangled to the table. He motioned toward the general area of the chairs as he walked behind the desk.

"Bob Mitchum," he repeated as he took his seat. "Like the actor."

I nodded.

"Don't make 'em like that anymore."

"Movies or men?" I said.

"Both."

I nodded. He sat back, hands clasped behind his head, a self-satisfied pose.

"What happened to the arm?"

I made the guy for a salesman. They're the ones who know to get the awkward stuff right out on the table, don't let any of that nervous energy get in the way of the transaction.

"Car accident."

"Bummer."

"You adapt."

"Still…. Well, Charlene says you're looking for office space."

I said I was an editor who had worked at home until a recent divorce and now needed work space outside of my condo. He asked where I lived. I took a chance and made up a name.

He nodded. "Nice place."

He could have just been being conversational. Or he was full of crap. I believed the latter.

"C&M isn't really in the real estate business," he said. "We only own one other building in town and it's not offices. But I think the guy in the end unit, the accountant, may be leaving soon. Maybe the end of next month. I could give you a call."

"So, what else does C&M Productions do, if real estate isn't your business?"

He smiled, like that's what he really wanted to talk about.

"Entertainment. Clubs. Movies. That kind of thing."

The word "movies" landed heavily. I wondered how Jay would be involved with this kind of guy. It could be what was making him spooky at work. "Movies. Sounds like fun," I said.

He shrugged. "There are some fringe benefits," he said, lifting his chin in the direction of the space outside the office, his eyebrows rising.

"Looks like you've just moved in," I said.

"Yeah, we're just getting set up."

"I won't take up any more of your time. If I haven't found any space to rent by the end of the month, I'll get back to you."

He handed me a card: TITO "TIM" MANETTI – PRESIDENT – C&M PRODUCTIONS, with an address and phone number. No email address or website, which seemed unusual for an entertainment business in the twenty-first century. Of a piece, however, with the absence of a computer on his desk.

We stood and shook hands, this time avoiding a power play. I smiled at Charlene and thanked her as I passed her desk and got a smile in return.

"Nice to meet you, Mr. Mitchum."

I was surprised my name had registered with her and wondered what her job required other than to sit and look good.

Back at my home-away-from-home, I called the Chamber of Commerce to ask what information they had on C&M Productions. I was surprised to hear they were paid-up members. The Chamber had no other information than what was on Manetti's card except that they'd been members less than a month. I opened the laptop and Googled "C&M Productions." There were several listings for that name including a company that provided ambient music and one that did wedding DVDs. Nothing that looked like Manetti's outfit, which was consistent with the absence of a website on his business card.

I knew it was too soon in my digging to expect the couple of shards I'd dug up to resemble anything recognizable. I had acquired more questions and no answers. What was an "entertainment and movie" business doing with a shell of an office and nothing on the web? What were Jay and Zoey doing there? I was pondering the possibilities when my phone rang.

21

Without a word of greeting, just a voice of cool efficiency, Zella said, "MTM wants to meet."

I didn't know what to say and waited for what was coming.

"They wanted to meet today. I told them that wasn't possible. They think they're inviting only me, but I want you to come along."

"Aren't I on leave?"

"You're also still on the payroll. My guess is they think we're in a weakened position given your recent unfortunate ... mess. They won't expect you. It'll put them off balance."

"Will Forest Service people be there?"

"They didn't say. But since it's them calling the meeting and not the feds, I doubt it. I imagine their idea is to have a 'just among us friends' kind of chat. The woman I talked to got impatient. I could tell she was thinking, 'Who do these people think they're dealing with?' She supposed it could wait until tomorrow. Which means they're feeling pressure to resolve this thing, maybe before the press gets a hold of it and Senator Simmons's name gets splattered across the front page again. I told them tomorrow at three would work."

I asked if Jay had gotten back to the office. He had.

"I think I'll follow him tonight. Might shed some light on

what he was up to this morning. I'll fill you in tomorrow."

We agreed to meet downtown at two.

Standing on the balcony, I again surveyed my realm, watching traffic on the freeway, the comings and goings of people in the plaza below, sensing my own insignificance, about to slip into terminal self-pity. I called Charlie Eagleston. Charlie had made a fortune in a dot-com enterprise a few years ago and was more or less retired, one of those whose life situation irked me until the stock market began to head south. Schadenfreude.

"I wondered what was going on when you didn't show up Saturday. Then I saw the article in the paper. Nice picture."

"Thanks, Charlie."

We met at one-thirty, split the first two sets. He had just gotten warmed up and his natural superiority overwhelmed me 6-1 in the third.

"I think I'm out of shape," I said, as we shook hands at the net. "I'd like to do this more regularly again. Especially since it appears I might have the time for a while."

We made a date for Saturday.

"Of course, I am at the mercy of outside events."

"We're never at the mercy of outside events, Rick. Only certain of our behaviors depend on external circumstances. Most of it's all internal."

"Easy for a retired millionaire to say."

"How do you think I became a retired millionaire?"

I was simultaneously disappointed and relieved when Kathy didn't answer either the home phone or her cell. The Infiniti was not in the drive, but her stuff was still there. I wondered what she was doing about her business. In the bedroom I grabbed a black, long-sleeved Western Carolina pullover and a pair of black slacks.

I scanned the bedroom to see if there was anything else I needed. As I glanced at the bedside stand, I remembered Kathy asking me if I'd thought about carrying the gun. I thought about it. Sitting on the bed, I opened the drawer and felt a moment of panic. I pulled the drawer the rest of the way out, dumping the contents onto the bed. A small box of tissues, hand lotion, lubricating gel, a small vibrator, nail clippers, an Anne Rice paperback. Box of .38 Super cartridges. No gun.

I couldn't imagine her carrying it. She hated the thing. It was a big deal every year to get her to come to the range with me. Surely she would have told me if she'd moved it. I sat for a while letting whatever wanted to enter my consciousness come on in. I remembered the day I came home and disarmed the alarm only to find that I had armed it again. At the time, I assumed I'd punched the numbers in wrong, even though that wouldn't really explain what happened. As far as I knew, nothing else in the house was amiss, and I hadn't thought about it again. Until now.

I wrote a note.

Hi. I came home to get some more clothes. While I was here I discovered the gun is no longer in the drawer. It's got me weirded out. Please call.

After a pause, I added, I miss you.

At the motel, I put on the nighttime sleuthing outfit, hiking boots, and black ball cap. At four forty-five I was back in the restaurant parking lot waiting for Jay to emerge from the office. This time when he left work, he headed north, up along the river.

22

I lost him in a series of S-curves paralleling the river and picked him up again not more than ten seconds before he turned onto a side road. The small sign informing us that we had entered another county reminded me of my felony-suspect status, since I wasn't supposed to leave Buncombe without permission from the D.A. A quarter of a mile later, he turned up to the right. I knew the area, the subject of a recent clear-cutting controversy. Nothing illegal, but owners of nearby property were unhappy about what it had done to the value of their land. Jay and I had come up here to see if we could help the neighbors protect some of their holdings from a similar fate. Half a mile up, there would be another old logging road leading to the area of devastation. I saw him make the turn.

This was a dirt road when I was last out here. The gravel now covering it looked as if it had recently been put down. I stopped before I got to the crest of the ridge. On the other side there would be an old cabin, one of those dwellings caught up in family feuds and left to die. The road would go on through the valley and up over the next rise, eventually making its way to the northwest area of the county. There would be acres of denuded forest spread out like a huge, ugly brown carpet. I backed around, left the car parked along the side of the road and slipped into the woods.

From among the trees, I saw the old log home. I remembered it as being at risk of collapse if you gave it a few sturdy kicks. There had been no glass in the windows, the roof line sagged, small trees grew among the pine needles and oak leaves on the roof. The land around the house had been thick with brambles and scrub growth. Now it looked as if the grounds had been recently sodded and the house itself was almost completely rehabilitated. Building supplies were stacked nearby, and it appeared that two guys were replacing a window casement. There were five vehicles parked around the cabin: Jay's Toyota, Zoey's convertible, a newish BMW sedan, and two pickup trucks. Two large motor coaches sat alongside the road across from the dwelling. I had seen something like this before in a rundown section of Asheville a few years before. An old house had been refurbished, and the lawn was almost preternaturally green. It had been a movie set. The logical conclusion was that this was the set for Jay and Zoey's "project."

Jay, Zoey, and a man in a suit were walking from the cabin to one of the motor coaches. I moved as quietly as the Indians I'd learned about as a Boy Scout, making my way through the woods until I was directly behind the motor coach the trio had entered.

Voices leaked out a window. I got up against the skin of the coach. The conversation was about money. The hum of a generator muffled much of what was said. I heard the woman.

"They're into a whole other thing. I don't even want to talk about it, he made me so mad." Laughter. "It's not funny." The voice moved away from the window, ice cubes clanked, voices overlapped. The next voice I heard clearly was Jay's.

"... him out of the way, it was easy to get into the files. Carole's got a lot of the stuff on computer but I don't want to mess with that. Tracks and ... It'll come together, don't worry."

"Little late in the game, isn't it?"

I didn't hear a response.

"You got the permits?" the businessman asked.

"Everything's on go. They're delighted to have us out here."

"Cabin gonna be ready?"

"Yeah," Zoey said, "but it's a good thing we decided to do interiors somewhere else. It looks good from the outside, but the place is really not habitable."

Again there was no audible response. I heard a door close and voices moving away from me. The stuff about "him being out of the way" and Carole having a lot of stuff in computer files seemed to confirm Zella's and my fears that whatever Jay was doing was counter to the interests of the Mountain Center. I wondered how Manetti was involved. It didn't seem like the kind of cinema his outfit would be into—if they were really into movies at all.

Dusk began to settle. I didn't want to be skulking around in the woods in the dark so I slipped back the way I'd come. Heading down the hill, just before making the turn onto the paved road, I saw the green car to my right, aimed in the direction I was going to turn. I wondered where it had picked me up. Maybe from the office. Maybe it had been watching me watching for Jay. It felt like I was in some game, the rules for which could only be discovered as you went along, like Alice after she fell down the rabbit hole. I wondered if the driver knew where I was staying and felt it was important that he not—some desire for a private life, maybe, since the one I used to have had been blazoned across newsprint throughout the region.

The clock on the dash showed 7:40. The phone let me know I had missed three calls, one each from Nate and Zella, and one from a number I didn't recognize. They could all wait.

The eight o'clock meeting had already begun at St. Marks when I arrived. My sponsor came up to me while I was at the coffee mess fixing a cup of decaf.

"How's everything?"

"Four days sober."

"Good for you. Let me know if you need anything."

We headed to a couple of folding chairs. I knew I would get a lot of support and encouragement at the after-meeting gathering at the Waffle House but I skipped it anyway.

Back in my room, I listened to the messages. Nate said he heard I'd connected with Dominic. Zella reminded me of our meeting in the afternoon. The third voice was unfamiliar.

"Hello, Mr. Ryder? My name is Dee Dee Mankin. I got your number from a friend. She said you might be able to help me find my daughter."

23

I looked at the phone wondering how this person got my number—especially as I'd only had it a day. Who even knew I was a private detective? It was not something I advertised. The little business I'd had was all word of mouth, typically preceded by a call from some friend of mine. I know someone who I think could use your services. That kind of thing. I'd get their number and call them. I wasn't listed in the phone book. Didn't have a website. No shingle hanging out anywhere. I hit the button to call the last number received.

A woman said, "Hello."

"Ms. Mankin? This is Rick Ryder returning your call."

"Oh, thank you so much."

What with Dee Dee's crying jags and digressions into the personality defects of her estranged husband and all his low-life family, it took me ten minutes to get a nickel's worth of information. Pamela Mankin, Dee Dee's daughter from her second marriage, was nineteen. Dwayne Mankin had adopted her when he had become Dee Dee's third husband. The girl had been getting into trouble ever since she'd been in middle school, and Dee Dee wondered if the scumbag Dwayne had sexually abused her. She'd run away from home twice in high school, once getting as far as

Marion before returning on her own. They'd had a fight two weeks ago about a boy Pamela was seeing. She'd gone off that night and hadn't returned. After three days, Dee Dee called the police, who told her there was little they could do, since the girl was legally an adult and there was no evidence of a crime, but they would keep her name. I knew the routine. She had also talked to a sheriff's deputy she knew who said he'd be on the lookout for the girl. Dee Dee was afraid her daughter had gotten hooked up with a bad crowd and may have left the area again.

"By bad crowd, you mean drugs?"

"Yes. She's ... had a problem with them since high school."

"Any arrests?"

"A couple of times she was at parties where there'd been a lot of drugs, and the police had been called, and she was charged with possession of marijuana."

"What else did she use?"

"Use?"

"Drugs. Other kinds of drugs."

"Oh! Nothing. I mean, I'm not aware of anything else. I mean, she's not a real bad drug addict or anything."

I wanted to say, Oh, she's one of those good drug addicts. Instead I said, "I'm sure the police told you that if she's found and is unharmed and doesn't want to come home, that's her right."

"Oh, I know all that. I just want to know she's okay."

I knew that was a lie. If Dee Dee found out where the girl was, she would hound her to come home until the girl either relented or found a better hiding place. I asked her if she knew about my own situation. She did.

"And you're okay with a suspected murderer looking for your daughter?"

"Oh, you didn't do it," she said, as if the notion was too ridiculous for consideration.

"I'm doing everything I can to prove that, Mrs. Mankin, since not everyone is as confident about it as you are. And that's my priority right now. I can give you the names of some other—"

She assured me that, based on the reference she had gotten, I was the one she wanted working for her. I explained my fees; she didn't flinch. She gave me her address. I told her I'd be out sometime in the morning to get a picture of the girl and pick up my retainer.

I realized I was grinning, like the kid who has just been told by the coach that he's going to start in the big game. My mind wandered into the plot of how I would approach the case of the missing daughter before I caught myself. I was going to go to prison if I could not get myself cleared of murder, and here I was thinking of spending time wandering around after some rebellious teenager who was mad at her mother. And playing sleuth for Zella, although the comments I'd heard about me not being in the way, something about the files, certainly made that personal and justification enough to pursue. And I couldn't help thinking it was somehow related to the rest of my "situation."

Sitting on the motel bed, flicking through the zillion channels on the TV, I was reminded why we didn't bother to get cable at home. I picked up the paperback I'd gotten at the hospital and rejoined Perry Mason as he tried to outsmart D.A. Hamilton Burger. Maybe I'd be inspired.

The phone woke me up. I couldn't remember where I was. The room lights were still on. The alarm clock showed 6:30.

"Ryder. Dominic. I got your information. Lady's name is Donna Pavone. Lives at New Bridge Apartments, unit three-oh-two." He added a phone number. I wanted to ask him if he knew what time it was, but guessed he did.

I thanked him and was about to click off when he chuckled.

"Oh, by the way, you were right about it not being a bad gig.

I guessed he had worked his way into some fringe benefits from Donna.

My whole body ached, including my left arm, from which I'd been separated for twenty-plus years. Phantom feelings, I was told. I often got them after playing tennis, as if the missing limb was worn out from helping me with my backhand. I soaked in the tub while I ran through an itinerary for the day.

If I was going to meet Zella at two, I'd have to be at Donna's by noon, late enough for her to have gotten some sleep after Dominic left, but before she'd leave for the Doll House. I could call her, but I counted on it being harder for her to shut the door in my face than to hang up on me. That left enough time to see what was up with the Mankin family. It was too early to go out there just yet, but another ache motivated me to get moving. It hurt not being welcome in my own home.

24

I saw no green Buicks lurking about when I left the motel. Armed with a cup of coffee and a sweet roll from the Downtown Bakery, I ignored the "NO FOOD OR DRINK" sign at the entrance to the municipal botanical gardens and found a creek-side bench. When I'd finished my breakfast, I walked a path through rhododendron thick with white blossoms, fading mountain laurel, and a plethora of wildflowers of whose names, in spite of repeated attempts to learn, I remained ignorant. In the peaceful stillness, I thought about why I was taking on this case. The best I could come up with—besides the pure drama of it— was that it had something to do with Debbie, another lost young woman. On my return to the parking lot, I automatically scanned for a big green sedan.

The Mankins lived in a modest two-story frame house set just below a ridge line in the far northwestern part of the county. From the porch, they had an unobstructed view of farm land in the valley on the other side of the road. When I pulled up, a woman who had been leaning over a fussily manicured garden bordering the front walk straightened herself up and turned to face me. I pegged her in her mid-thirties, meaning she'd been a child mother if Pamela was her own nineteen-year old daughter. At eight-thirty on a weekday morning, she was in full make-up and a party dress. She ungloved a hand as I approached.

"You must be Mr. Ryder. I'm Dee Dee Mankin."

I told her "Rick" would be fine.

"Sorry to bother you," I said, imagining she was getting ready to leave.

"No, no. It's fine. I'm so glad you came."

In the house, kept dark as country people without air conditioning do, she directed me to the living room where I sat in an upholstered chair. She left the room and returned with a clutch of photos. A flow of tears had already begun before she handed them to me. On the sofa across from me, she crossed her legs. I thought the flash of thigh was not inadvertent. In addition to nice underpinnings, she had a pretty, though overly made-up, face. The pictures, a mix of studio poses and snapshots, presented a Dee Dee clone, especially the posed ones. I wondered how conscious the mother's efforts to recreate herself had been.

I took two of the pictures with me: a head shot that was taken for her senior yearbook, and a more informal one of her in jeans and a T-shirt leaning against the split-rail fence that bounded the front yard. I also took a check. In the memo area, Dee Dee had written "to find my daughter." I wondered if she thought paying to find runaway children was tax deductible.

"I meant to ask you, Dee Dee. Who referred you to me?"

"Carole Batson. She works with you at that environment place? We go to the same church. She speaks very highly of you. She said you were on vacation, so I really didn't want to bother you, but she said she thought it would be okay."

"It's kind of a working vacation, actually. It'll be fine."

As vacations go, this would be no trip to the beach. Besides living in a geographically remote area, folks around here had a reputation for being skeptical of outside authority. People weren't any more likely to talk to me than they would a city police officer or a sheriff's deputy who wasn't kin. But you never knew. There might be someone around who liked the girl and didn't want to see her get hurt, didn't like the kinds of activities she could have gotten herself mixed up with, or was just helpful rather than secretive by nature.

Although convenience stores had largely replaced the old country stores, they were still places where information was exchanged, where gossip was a kind of currency, often as valuable as cash. At the first one I came to, a half-mile from Dee Dee's place, I got a bottle of water out of the cooler and picked up a candy bar. The clerk—late teens, early twenties I guessed, a contemporary of the Mankin girl—was in a conversation with a customer, a woman, some years his senior. I realized, as he was ignoring me, they were flirting. She became aware of my presence and stepped aside so I could lay down my purchases, along with a twenty-dollar bill. The clerk looked at me, scanned the two items and said, "Two-oh-seven." I pushed the twenty toward him and he rang it up. I pulled out the casual picture of Pamela and put it on the counter.

"Either of you seen her around recently?"

They both looked at it quizzically.

"No," I said. "I'm not the cops. I'm working for Mrs. Mankin."

The young guy shook his head.

"You know her?"

He shrugged.

"Come on. Her home is just up the road. I know you know who she is. I'm just wondering if you've seen her recently. Her mother hasn't."

The woman leaned over to look at the picture. "It's Pam Mankin, isn't it?" she said.

I nodded.

They shrugged in unison. I supposed it was possible the girl hadn't been out this way since she'd left home. I handed the clerk a card with my new cell phone number written on it while giving my change a nudge in his direction.

"If you see her, give me a call. You could also tell her her mother is looking for her. But I'm sure she knows that."

The Starbucks effect had rippled out past the confines of the city, a coffee shop-slash-used book store having washed up in a small strip mall on the four-lane, just before it peters out into two. It called itself New Country Café and Readery. The barista, a pleasant looking woman wearing a floor-length skirt and peasant top, was about my age. I introduced myself and explained who I was looking for as I showed her the pictures. She called into a back room.

"Mickey? Come out here a sec."

She told me her name was Taylor, and we shook hands before a man a few years older than the two of us, gray hair pulled into a ponytail, came through a beaded curtain. Taylor showed him the photos of the girl.

"Isn't she the one who came in with that bunch when we first opened?" Taylor asked. "Kind of punk kids. Piercings all over. Tattoos. Girls wearing low-rise jeans with thong panties you could see when they bent over. You remember them, I know."

The man's cheeks colored. "I always thought they were high. After a few times in here they started getting rude with other customers so I had to ask them to leave. I thought we might have to call the cops, but they had some choice words to leave by and never came back. Didn't sleep well for a couple of nights, afraid they might try to get revenge or something, but nothing ever came of it."

The information didn't help much except to confirm Dee Dee's suspicion that her daughter had gotten hooked up with a bad crowd. I thanked them for their time and ordered a coffee to go. They said they'd keep their eyes and ears open and encouraged me to stop back.

Outside, I looked at the newspaper rack. The headline on the front page blared out at me so I paid the machine fifty cents and read the article.

Senator Pays Back Taxes

Senator Malcolm Simmons (D-NC) paid $177,500 in back taxes yesterday. In a statement distributed by the senator's office, he claimed that the non-payment was unintentional and was the result of differing interpretations of tax laws. Senator Simmons' payment comes a day after it was announced that the Senate Ethics Committee is investigating allegations that the senator had not paid taxes on income from Mountain Timber and Mining Company for several years. The company has been owned by the Simmons family since the late 1800s when it was founded by Sen. Simmons' great-grandfather.

The Senator had made it to the front page without the help of the Mountain Center for the Defense of the Environment. It seemed more than coincidental that news about the Senator's taxes, the ransacking of our offices, and a request by MTM lawyers for a meeting had all occurred within a few days of each other. I dropped the paper on the passenger seat and headed back toward town, hoping to find Donna Pavone at home.

25

It wasn't hard to find 302. The apartments were a half-mile closer to town than the Doll House and consisted of six buildings, modest in the extreme, on land that had been clear-cut a decade or so ago. There were no visible amenities, not even shrubbery to soften the look and feel of the place. The only evidence that people actually lived here, other than the mostly older and shabby cars in the parking lot, was a scattering of bright red plastic toys, tractors, bikes, jungle gyms, wading pools—the detritus of young families living life on the margins but determined to occupy their kids' time, if not their minds.

Donna opened the door just enough for me to catch a glimpse of the shirt that covered her to mid-thigh. If I hadn't wakened her, she hadn't been awake for long. Her face was void of expression for a split second until she recognized me.

"Hi, Donna. I wondered if I could talk to you for a couple of minutes."

The shirt's shapelessness could not conceal the outline of her figure. Without makeup and the artificial light of the club, she was softer, prettier, more like the mid-thirties I figured her to be. Her head came around the edge of the door like a turtle's coming out of its shell. She looked quickly left and right, then whisked me inside.

"What do you want?" It was more of a challenge than a question.

Behind the bar, Donna gave off an air of sexy self-assuredness. Here, her eyes wouldn't hold mine. She was shaking. The room was spare: a couch, two upholstered chairs, a coffee table, unframed prints on the walls. It was uncluttered and smelled of orange-scented cleaner.

"I was hoping you could tell me something about Debbie."

"I can't talk to you. They can't know you were here."

"Who are they?"

She narrowed her eyes and tilted her head as if she couldn't quite understand me. She presented the classic appearance of a habitual cocaine user. Spastic twitching, furtive head movements as if constantly looking for something. It was hard to know if her fear was grounded in reality or came from using too much of the drug for too long.

"They must have something to do with the club," I said.

"Please leave."

"I don't think they've followed me today. I'm pretty sure they haven't figured out where I'm staying, don't know where to pick up the scent."

"Still. You can't be here."

Remembering Sunday morning, I realized her overwrought state could be equally due to drug-fueled suspicion and the reality of what "they" were capable of.

"Can you at least tell me—"

"She lived with Angi out at Meadow Glen, on the east side. That's all I can tell you. Please don't tell anybody you've talked to me. Please," she begged, sounding like a kid who'd gotten in trouble at school and was afraid her parents would find out.

She went to the front window, drew the drapes apart two

inches and scanned outside.

"Can you tell me if I was out there on Saturday night?"

"Yes," she said, not looking at me, keeping her eyes on the parking lot.

"Did we fight, did I threaten her?"

"I don't know what you said, but she was crying when you left."

"Do you know about what time that was?"

"Please go."

Now she was crying.

I had nothing more to say and was halfway out the door when she stopped me.

"Talk to Marilyn Morgan. She lives out on the East River Road in a trailer park."

"Marilyn who?" I asked, turning back to her.

"Morgan," she said, looking me in the eye as if she were asking me something. "Please don't tell her you've talked to me."

I assured her I wouldn't and was going to ask if she had a phone number for Marilyn when she stepped up to the door and pushed it shut. But I was making progress. I had two leads, the roommate and the Morgan woman.

The clock on my cell phone reminded me it was time to shift gears and get up to running speed for the meeting with the MTM crowd.

26

I was already in a booth at the Downtown Bakery when Zella walked in. She got several nods of recognition. Those who didn't know her tended to react as if they were seeing someone they thought they'd seen on the cover of People magazine, someone they thought they should know. She was wearing a long sari-style dress in black, bronze, gold and orange.

"Tina Turner," I said as she sat.

She cocked her head.

"Tina Turner. Dress is longer than what she prances around in, but you've got the legs."

She smiled. Not blushing. She was used to this kind of thing.

"Maybe I should get up on the lawyers' table and break into 'Proud Mary.'"

"That would be an attention-grabber. Not that you need one."

"Actually, I'm hoping you'll be the one drawing their attention."

"Thanks. I've gotten more than enough the past few days."

A wide smile overtook her face.

"It seems like the senator may be getting more than he wants, as well," I said, putting the newspaper on the table between us. "Think this and today's meeting are connected?"

She scanned the article.

"If our lawsuit ever gets to trial, the media will have a field day. All the more reason for them to settle it quickly and for us to push for everything we can get out of them."

Her smile was infectious.

"So, wanna hear about Jay?" I asked.

Of course she did. I told her about the visit to C&M Productions and to the cabin in the woods.

"And you think this is the movie Jay and his girlfriend have been working on?"

"It sure had a movie-set feel to it and they talked about shooting interiors. The last time I mentioned it to Jay, he was real skittish, like he didn't want to talk about it at all. And then there's the meeting with the guy from C&M Productions, Manetti. There's a real sleazeball. I got the impression the only movies he's interested in are the adult entertainment kind. But he could be looking for legitimate pictures to invest in, like organized crime does. Hell, he might be organized crime for all we know."

"You think Jay and his girlfriend would go to the mob to finance a movie?"

"Maybe they don't know he's organized crime. Maybe he's not organized crime. I'm just saying, Manetti could simply be an investor to them. And maybe Manetti's got nothing to do with it. But then there's the stuff about someone being out of the way and them having access to computer files. I can't help thinking I'm the one who's out of the way and it's the Mountain Center's files they have access to."

"So, say Jay is some kind of—what was your word? Mole? What kind of a movie would they be doing?"

"Maybe some kind of fluff piece on the timber industry. You know, how it's been a way of life in the mountains for generations, been the source of income for numberless families. Like the one living in this little cabin right here."

"It just doesn't sound like Jay," she said."

"Remember," I said, "you were the one who said he was acting weird and wanted me to follow him."

"Yes. I know." She paused. "Are you going to go back out there?"

"In a day or two. The guy in the suit seemed to give off a sense of urgency, but they weren't ready to do any shooting yet."

"Keep me posted," she said. "I need to know if I should put Jay on a leave of absence, too, if he's involved in something that could hurt us."

I assured her I would. When that seemed to be the end of that, I told her I'd been retained on a private matter. Her eyebrows rose.

"Seems like you'd want to be spending as much time as you could finding out who killed the girl if, as you say, the police aren't going to do it."

"You haven't been reluctant to ask me to do things for you."

"For the Center."

"My point is—"

"I get your point," she said. "What's so interesting about this case?"

"I'm not sure. Maybe it's a chance to help a young woman, maybe make up for what happened to Debbie."

"You think you had something to do with that?"

"No. No! Come on."

"I meant, do you feel responsible somehow for what it is you want to make up for?"

"I know I didn't have anything to do with Debbie's death, but maybe I can help keep something bad from happening to Pam Mankin."

"Your P. I. license still current?"

I pulled my wallet from my hip pocket and asked her to hold

it while I rummaged through the sections, finally extricating two pieces of paper.

"Here. And a permit to carry my thirty-eight, although the gun itself seems to have gone missing."

Saying it, I realized I hadn't reported the disappearance, still waiting to hear from Kathy.

"Missing?"

I explained about looking for it and remembering the incident with the front door alarm.

"You think someone broke into your house to steal a gun?"

"Sounds far-fetched, doesn't it?"

"Who knew you had it? Besides Kathy?"

I thought about that, who-all I might have said something to about owning a gun. There was Nate, of course. Then I felt sick.

"Jay," I said.

"Jay?"

"Yeah. After we ran into that guy in the forest, the one we have on tape, he asked if I ever thought about carrying a gun on the job. I said we really weren't doing cops and robbers here, and my experience taught me the presence of a gun often produces more guns. That seemed to be the end of it."

"You think Jay might have stolen your gun?

"I'm just saying he knew I had one."

"So, what are you saying, Rick? There's a lot at stake here, you know."

"Yes, there is," I said, trying to keep my voice under control. "The future of the southeastern forests, for one. My freedom, for another. Not to mention the fact there is at least one killer running loose, and other people's lives could be in danger. I get it. If Jay has anything to do with this, I think we should let him stay out there without him thinking we know anything so we can see who and what he leads us to."

"Okay. You're the detective. But if I think the lawsuit is in jeopardy, I'll have to do whatever is necessary to protect our interests."

"I hope that's what I'm doing now."

We walked the two blocks to the offices of Mountain Timber and Mining, Inc., located at the top of the old Carolina Mountain Insurance Company building on Pack Square, the heart of downtown Asheville.

"You know," I said while we were riding the elevator to the top floor, "Sam Simmons, Malcolm's grandfather, founded Carolina Mountain Insurance and built this building. They have a very cozy relationship with the senator, too. Someday, stuff is going to come out about them, like it's beginning to ooze out about MTM."

When the elevator doors opened, we were ushered into a room that seemed to deliberately mimic a stereotype—dark wood, legal tomes lining the walls, leather chairs. A pitcher of water and two glasses marked our places at the end of an enormous table.

As soon as our escort left, three men entered the room. Two of the men were in black suits, white shirts, and conservative ties. The third was jacket-less, wearing pants attached to red suspenders. He introduced the taller of the two suited men as Arthur Pitts, the other as Steve Kerrey. He looked at me and said he was Harvey Feldstein. Zella had apparently already made his acquaintance. They gave no indication my presence surprised them.

Feldstein thanked us for coming on such short notice and launched into a monologue about MTM's commitment to the environment. Zella held up a hand, palm outward, interrupting the man.

"Let it be stipulated that MTM is committed to the environment. What is at issue is not anyone's commitment to the environment, but how that commitment is manifested. It is our clients' contention that, regardless of how you feel about the environmental benefits of clearing standing growth from public lands, it's illegal."

"Mrs. Jefferson," the tall suited man began as Feldstein handed me a black folder. "Your action involves the relationship between the Department of Agriculture and our corporation." The cynic in me thought he was given this part in the show because he was African American and would, therefore, be more simpatico to Zella. He continued. "There are differing interpretations of the law. We would like to spare your clients, the public, and ourselves undue expense merely to parse the fine points. Our offer is outlined in the proposal Mr. Ryder is holding, with no suggestion that either Mountain Timber & Mining or the Department of Agriculture have done anything outside of the law. And we reiterate our commitment to the law as it applies to federal lands."

"Mr. ... I'm sorry, I've forgotten your name."

"Pitts. Arthur Pitts." If one can be said to have a glare in one's voice, Arthur Pitts had it.

"Mr. Pitts. Our clients are not interested in monetary gain from this lawsuit. They want you to refrain from violating the law. We are aware that you can make this an expensive proposition. And we understand you'd like to make this case go away."

Feldstein started to speak and again Zella's hand went up.

"We'll take your offer back to our clients. They'll decide how they wish to proceed. Thank you, gentlemen, for your time." Without forewarning, she stood. I followed her cue. She reached her hand to the Messrs. Feldstein, Kerrey, and Pitts in turn, giving each a firm handshake, as I did in her wake.

"We'll get back to you," she said as we walked out of the room.

When the heavy outer door closed behind us, I turned to Zella and gave her a high five. "Way to go."

"Oh, I don't know. They're probably in there right now talking about the bitch and the token white guy and figuring out how much more it's going to cost to bury this thing than they'd planned on. It's only round one."

The descent of the elevator left me lightheaded. I was still woozy as we stepped into the daylight and I saw the familiar Buick parked at the curb, as if a concierge had called down to have it waiting. As I walked toward the car to get a look at the driver, it pulled away.

"I guess this answers the question, 'Do they want me to know I'm being followed?'"

"Why would they want that?" Zella asked as we headed back toward our cars.

"Intimidation. If they can't get us to drop the lawsuit through negotiation, maybe they can scare us off. Or maybe they just want to know what I'm up to and don't care if I know or not. But being there, outside the office building, makes it pretty clear that MTM is behind it."

"I thought you'd assumed that all along."

"I've got to start taking notes," I said. "I forget what's been going on. I had begun to think C&M Productions was behind it. But that's ridiculous. It started back before I ever knew anything about Manetti and C&M, before they knew me. I think."

"As you're so fond of saying," she said as we approached her car, "more will be revealed."

A cold wind was coming up off the river. The temperature had dropped ten degrees while we'd been in the meeting. We were in for a change.

27

If the man in the Buick was following me, he was now keeping out of sight. At the motel, I changed into my country sleuthing outfit—jeans, boots, a plain light blue T-shirt, and the WCU cap. I grabbed a light windbreaker and headed out to the northwest reaches of the county. A light mist had turned into a steady drizzle by the time I reached the New Country Café. Taylor was straightening up behind the counter when I walked through the door.

"One for the road," I called.

"Nasty day to be out roaming the hinterlands," she said as she placed the cup in front of me and slid a small pitcher of cream and the sugar bowl my way.

"It is. Duty calls."

"Glad you stopped by. You remember that bunch we were telling you about, had to throw them out of here?"

I nodded, and Taylor leaned forward confidentially, her elbows on the counter.

"One of the girls was in yesterday by herself. Name's Justine. She's cleaned up. When I asked her where the rest of them were, she said she wasn't hanging around with them anymore, they just got her in trouble. She was about to get kicked out of school and figured that's not what she really wanted. I asked her about the Mankin girl. Justine said she's hanging out with an older guy named Harney. That's kind of a familiar name out here. There's a Harney Branch, Harney Creek, Harney Road, anything you can drive on or fish in, they got one with their name on it. I gave her your number, but she said why didn't I just tell you when I saw you again. Doesn't want to get involved. Can't say I blame her, people could make life tough for her if they wanted to."

"Did she say where this Harney guy lives?"

"She didn't know for sure, said he's the kind of guy moves around a lot. It's not much to go on, I know."

"More than I came in with," I said. I thanked her and told her to tell Mickey "Hi" as I headed into the afternoon gloom. I reconnoitered the area for a while, noting three more small stores within a mile radius of Dee Dee's house.

When I put my water and candy bar on the counter of the first one, the clerk said, "You that guy looking for the Mankin kid."

I admitted I was, silently acknowledging the speed with which the rumor mill operated.

I placed her in her mid-forties. Attractive face, hair that may have been naturally blond at one time pulled back in a ponytail, a physique that might have gotten her on the cheerleading squad thirty or so years ago. Dressed much like me, in jeans and a T-shirt. She looked like she'd be fun to hang out and drink beer with.

"Yeah, she got hooked up with kind of a wild crowd. I heard her mother was looking for her. She paying you?"

I smiled.

"That's like her. Won't come around herself and say, 'Have you seen my kid?' Too good to come down here, I guess."

I didn't bite. She rang up my stuff. I put a five on the counter, waiting for what more she might have to say. She gave me my change and nothing else.

"Know anything about a guy named Harney she might be

hanging around with?" I tried.

"Lotta Harneys out this way, mister."

"So I hear."

"If you want to give me a twenty, I'll keep a look out for her, too."

"My reputation precedes me."

She smiled. I pulled out a twenty and handed it to her with one of my updated cards.

"You're the guy they're sayin' killed that dancer, aren't you?"

I nodded.

"Well, if you didn't do it, you must have pissed off some serious people for someone to try and pin it on you."

"What it seems like," I said, wondering if there was a message in there for me.

A teenage boy was behind the counter at the next place. Pimply kid, unkempt greasy hair falling into his face, jeans, Metallica T-shirt with a four-inch tear on the right side. Shook his head when I showed him the photos.

"Don't know her?"

Another shake.

"Never seen her?"

Another shake.

I figured him to be about Pamela's age, would have gone to school with her. Hell, he might even be living with her.

"You're lying, you little shit. Take another look."

He looked down, said, yes, he guessed he had seen the girl before but not in the store. My twenty would be wasted here so I thanked him and left without buying anything. If he'd gotten the word that I was paying for the possibility of information, he'd be pissed. Served him right.

My mood reflected the weather. I was getting discouraged

when I went into the last store on my list. Big older guy. Wearing bib overalls over a white T-shirt. Brown hair pulled back in a ponytail like the woman in the first store, a Harley tattoo on his right bicep. I introduced myself. He said his name was Ronnie.

He nodded in recognition at the pictures.

"Haven't see her lately," he said. I was surprised when he went on. "Used to come in here with some lowlifes from up Jackson's Branch. Pretty girl. Always wondered what she was doing hanging out with them. Well. That's not hard to guess. I mean, sorry, I know this is hard for her mama. But I do believe they cook meth up there. That's the rumor, anyway."

The guy struck me as someone who'd know if a rumor like that was true or not.

"Guy name Harney involved?"

He smiled. "Been doin' your homework. Yeah. Zeno Harney."

"Zeno?"

"Yeah. Family name. Goes by Cujo."

"Like Steven King's mad dog?"

"The one. Guy's pretty crazy. Meth doesn't help."

"You think she's a volunteer out there?"

"You mean, are they makin' her stay there? Nah, I don't think it's like that. I think she ran away from home and ended up as far from her mama's kind of life as she could possibly get."

"Sounds like I need to go out to Jackson's Branch."

"I'd have some backup, it was me goin' out there."

"Something you'd be interested in doing? There'd be money in it."

"No, thanks. Those characters don't play by any rules. Bad as crack dealers in town."

I waited a minute, hoping he might have a suggestion. It didn't come.

I could just tell Dee Dee what I'd learned, that Pamela was

staying with some meth-heads on Jackson's Branch. She could do whatever she wanted with the information. But I thought I should at least try to see the girl. I gave Ronnie my card and my standard inducement, asking him to ask the girl to call me if he saw her. Now I needed to find someone to go out to Jackson's Branch with me.

Sitting in the brown coupe, I ran through possibilities. Ronnie had been the most forthcoming of the store people, and I guessed I'd gotten as far with him as I was going to. I'd gotten the message that asking the law for help could just get me in more trouble. Taylor and Mickey seemed to be the most interested in helping. Like me, they weren't from around here, but being new to the area and entrepreneurs, they may have done some homework before they set up shop, might know some other people to talk to. I had to switch the wipers on full as I pulled out of the little store's parking lot, heading back to the four-lane. The café was dark when I went by.

The Buick wasn't in sight after the eight o'clock meeting at St. Mark's. Even so, I took a roundabout way back to the motel. Everything was familiar when I stepped into the room. The chairs, the bed, TV set, table with the place to hook up your laptop. I'd seen it all before when I traveled for the state. I could be anywhere; Raleigh, Charleston, Atlanta, Chicago. Anywhere. Generic living. My breathing got shallow and my chest hurt. I forced myself to take deep breaths, did some calisthenics, hopped in the shower, and came out reasonably refreshed. With a Braves-Mets game on the TV to keep me company, I thought about what I'd do the next day.

I wanted to talk to Jimmy Crawford, but he was in jail. Angi, the roommate, seemed the next logical step. I made the same assumptions about her that I had about Donna. Work late, sleep late. I could go out there before noon and maybe go back out to reconnoiter Pamela Mankin's part of the world if nothing more compelling arose.

The ballgame wasn't exciting enough to keep my attention. My mind kept wanting to make up conversations with Angi and they kept leading to what I'd been doing Saturday night. I wasn't sure I wanted to know. I picked up the Perry Mason book.

I sat straight up. The clock read 3:13. I was covered in sweat. Something bad had happened. I didn't know what, only that whatever it was, it was going to get me, too. There were tubes stuck in my arms. I tried to shake them loose. I tried to call for a nurse but nothing came out of my mouth.

I was sitting straight up, sweat pouring off me. The room was dark. I snapped my head to the side to see the clock radio. It read 1:32.

28

It didn't require Carl Jung to figure out what was going on in the dream. I was scared shitless. What had I been doing Saturday night? Was I going to go to prison for murder? Had I screwed up my marriage for good? I threw on some sweats and headed to the motel gym. Forty-five minutes later, I'd had another shower and was back in bed.

The phone rang at seven-thirty. Charley wanted me to play doubles at nine-thirty. I could make the eight a.m. meeting at St. Luke's, get in a couple of sets, and still be out at Angi's before noon. We took two sets out of three from a couple of guys I knew in passing from the courts, and I was headed for the east side at eleven-ten.

Meadow Glen challenged my idea of how strippers lived. A mix of garden apartments and townhouses, swimming pool, tennis courts, clubhouse. The lawn and shrubs were well-trimmed. I flashed my I.D. to the woman who opened the door designated "Manager." It worked.

"Apartment twenty-one-oh-four. Wasn't that a terrible thing happened to that girl?"

I agreed it was. Before she could continue a conversation, I asked for directions.

My hand was poised to knock on 2104 when I noticed the door wasn't fully closed. I rapped lightly with my knuckles.

"Angi?" I called into the space between the door and the jamb.

I called again and got the same response. I pushed the door open with my elbow and stepped into the living room. It looked like the same people who had trashed the Mountain Center offices had been here. A low moan coming from a bedroom sent a chill down my back. I headed toward the sound, hoping the mayhem I'd seen in the living room hadn't been played out on another human being.

From the bedroom door, I saw the girl lying on her side, tied to a ladderback chair, duct tape over her mouth. There was a red mark on the side of her face and her left eye was swollen shut. A wave of nausea started up my gullet. It settled down when I turned away. After a couple of deep breaths, I went to her, knelt down and pulled the tape off her mouth as gently as I could.

"Angi? ... Angi?"

She had a pulse and she was breathing. Another low moan came, an involuntary sound. I pulled out my cell phone and punched 911. My inclination was to undo the rest of the tape, but I caught myself. I didn't want my fingerprints all over the place, and I wanted the cops to see her as I found her. Although there'd be some uniforms here momentarily, I put in a call to Detective Henderson, leaving a message for him to get back to me.

Two squad cars pulled up almost simultaneously, before EMS arrived. They were curious about my presence. Name plates identified them as Officers Wyatt and Young. I gave Wyatt my identification.

"Ryder. Aren't you the guy they got for murdering that other girl?"

"I am. And this woman was her roommate."

"And what are you doing here?"

"Trying to prove my innocence."

"Yeah. This'll help."

"It's how I found her," I said. I didn't care for the sarcasm, but I let it pass.

The other cop was tending to Angi, removing the rest of the tape, confirming signs of life. She hadn't come to by the time the ambulance arrived. They figured she had a concussion at least, loaded her on a gurney, and headed off to the hospital.

"Know any next of kin?" Wyatt asked.

"I didn't even know her. I came out here to ask some questions about her roommate, try to get some idea of who's trying to frame me for the murder. I don't know her last name."

"Office manager will, probably has an emergency contact, too."

My phone rang.

"Ryder. Henderson."

"Detective. Thanks for calling back. I'm in the middle of a situation here. I'll let your colleague tell you more, but the bottom line is, I'm in the apartment of the late Debbie Douglass, came out here to talk to her roommate. Found the girl unconscious, taped to a chair. Apartment trashed. I'd guess someone was looking for something."

Wyatt watched me talk to the detective.

"Where's the girl now?"

"In an ambulance on the way to the hospital."

"Who else is there?"

I told him.

"Let me speak to one of 'em."

I handed the phone to Wyatt, who described the scene and told how I had explained my presence. Wyatt asked if they should book me, at least for illegal entry. I glared at him. Henderson must have said no, and the cop gave me back the phone.

"Know what it means to impede an investigation, Rick?" Henderson said.

"I didn't impede, Detective. I didn't have the chance."

"You're out there on pretty thin ice. I'd think you'd want to stay squeaky clean."

"I do, Ted." I felt my hand clench. "I also understand you guys don't have much investment in looking beyond me for a murder suspect."

"Are you questioning how we're conducting our investigation?"

"Just trying to save my neck."

He had some other words of caution, although by then I was so mad I didn't really hear them. I slapped my phone closed.

"You're free to go," Wyatt said.

Go where? I wondered. The person who potentially had the most information about Debbie was indisposed. The other lead I'd gotten from Donna was Marilyn Morgan. I was almost afraid to find her.

29

The green sedan appeared in my rear view mirror when I left the Meadow Glen parking lot. I began evasive action, going to the west side of town, doubling back twice, taking alleys and side streets. By the time I was back across the river, it was no longer in my sight.

From my home-away-from-home, I dialed the phonebook listing for an M. Morgan at Lot twenty-eight, Riverbend Mobile Home Court. No one answered. I ate a peanut-butter-and-jelly sandwich on the balcony. I wanted to be home on my deck, listening to the creek meander down the hillside. I wanted to talk to Kathy, tell her what my life was like, see those sexy legs.

Lying down on the bed, messing with the remote, my eyes began to feel as if a hypnotist was working on me. When I opened them again, the clock showed 5:00. I debated the pros and cons of calling Kathy, gave up the discussion and dialed home. The machine kicked in after the sixth ring. My voice answered. Apparently I still lived there. I couldn't think of a message that wouldn't sound whimpering or groveling. I didn't call her cell phone.

The day was gone. I treated myself to dinner at a Thai restaurant. It was an easy walk from there to First Presbyterian.

When the eight-o'clock meeting was opened for discussion, I

said, "I'm Rick and I'm an alcoholic. I'd been sober for ten years up until a couple of days ago. If you read the local paper, you may know something about that story. It doesn't really matter. What matters is that I am sober and at a meeting and I know I can stay sober again, one day at a time. What I need to do is to look at my part in what is going on, to do what I can about what I can, and let go of the rest. There's probably a topic in there somewhere. Thanks for letting me share."

Not ready to face a motel room, after the meeting I went with a group to the Waffle House, sipped decaf and listened to people talk about how much better their lives were now than when they were drinking. I wasn't convinced that my life was all that much better, but I did know if I started drinking, it would get worse. I also knew it could get even worse if I never took another drop.

At the glass door to the balcony, I watched the rain and the sparse Sunday morning traffic drifting by. My cell phone rang at seven a.m. sharp. I got excited thinking it could be Kathy returning my call until I remembered I hadn't left a message.

"Yo, my felonious friend."

"This better be good, Nate. It's too early for bad."

"Seen this morning's paper?"

"Haven't been out of the room."

"I'll narrate. Headline: 'Immigration bill passes—Simmons's switch crucial in fifty-one-to-forty-nine vote.' Got your interest?"

"Since I understand he's been opposed to that bill all along, yes, I'm interested."

"Indeed. Story goes on to say how surprised observers are about his shift. The senator says he has heard the voice of his constituency which includes a significant Latino population that has been pushing for support of the bill. So, I'm thinkin', who is the most significant voice of the Latino community hereabouts?"

"That would be Victor Chavez."

"Got your early-morning thinking cap on. And in what regard has Señor Chavez's name come up in relation to you?"

It took a few seconds to withdraw it from the memory bank.

"He's representing the man who has implicated me in a murder case."

"You must have gotten a good night's sleep."

"And...?"

"Yes, of course," my lawyer said, "that is the question, isn't it. I know you've got a hectic schedule these days, but I thought it being the Sabbath and all, you might have time for a cup of coffee."

I called a nurse I knew named Bruce F. from AA who worked at the hospital. I asked him if he could find out what happened to a young woman named Angi who was sent to the ER yesterday around noon, badly beaten up, and could he get her name. I was stepping out of the shower when the phone rang.

"Angi Dillingham," Bruce said. "Admitted to ICU, regained consciousness, but has some serious internal injuries."

"How hard will it be to get into ICU to see her?"

"Probably not going to happen. They keep it pretty tight up there, immediate family."

"What if I was her uncle?"

"What if her real uncle's there when you show up?"

"Oh. Yeah." I thanked him and said I might see him at a meeting.

I got a paper from the rack outside the motel office. There, in the same place the story of my arrest had been two days before, was the report of the Simmons vote, including a quote by Victor Chavez extolling the virtues of the senator. Strange bedfellows, indeed.

Someone was vacating a parking space ten feet from the bakery's front door. Although it would be just a quick dash from the car, it was raining hard enough to warrant an umbrella.

"So what's the quid pro quo?" I asked as I was taking my seat at the table Nate had claimed by the front window. He was in his Sunday best, unlit stogie held firmly between his teeth, raincoat and hat on the seat next to him. I sat down with my coffee and a cinnamon scone. We clacked mugs, toasting our health.

"You mean what's the senator get for at long last hearing the voice of his Latino constituency, since we know that up until now he's been the great defender of a lily-white America? The obvious question for those of us in the know is, does this have anything to do with Chavez's appointment as counsel for Jimmy Crawford?"

"How would the senator be involved in that?"

"Indeed," he said. "I think that's something an unemployed lawyer-slash-investigator might want to look into."

"On administrative leave, Nate. Not unemployed. I'm still on the payroll."

My absentee arm ached, probably due to the weather. I swirled the coffee in the mug, pondering implications.

Nate sucked on his cigar for a few seconds before asking what else had been going on. I told him about talking to Donna and finding Angi.

"You were there?" he asked, eyebrows raised.

"That's what I'm telling you, Nate. It was a very thorough trashing," I said, "very much like our offices. Although at Angi's, they were less restrained. Tore the covers off chairs and the couch, pretty much emptied cupboards and cabinets and closets."

"Then you might find this other article interesting," he said, opening the paper to the "Mountain Neighbors" section.

I read the headline.

EXOTIC DANCER ASSAULTED

LINKED TO MURDER OF DOLL HOUSE EMPLOYEE

"Probably ought to buy your own copy," he said as he handed me the paper.

The article got what happened right.

"I wish they hadn't put the part about her going to the hospital in there," I said.

"Why? Because they'll find her and do something bad to her? If they wanted to kill her they would have done it at her place, don't you think?"

It seemed reasonable.

"What do you make of it?" he said.

"It would seem like they were looking for something."

"Like?"

"Don't know. Not money, I wouldn't think. I guess the girls, one or both of them, could have been involved in drug stuff. You know, got fronted some dope and never paid up. That kind of thing."

He sat, his head moving slowly, like a bobble-head doll. He took a pass on my offer to refill his coffee while I was getting more for myself.

"Sure would help if I could talk to Angi," I said when I got back to the booth. I told him of my call to the nurse I knew.

"You really want to get your tits in a ringer."

"Somebody's going to have to talk to her."

"You do know about things like impeding an investigation, don't you, Counselor?"

"Henderson used those exact words yesterday. Said he thought I was on thin ice."

"As my young nephew would say, 'Duh'! You do realize you are a suspect in a murder investigation. This is not just another opportunity for you to demonstrate that you're one of the good guys. My God, man, you're dealing with seriously bad people here. Somebody wants to hang you for a murder. They kill young dancers and trash their apartments—and your own offices. Henderson's right. You go messing around with potential witnesses, you're gonna piss people off. And not just the police."

"And what are they going to do, Nate? Kill me? If they did, then somebody really would have to investigate, which, according to you, no one wants to do. As long as I'm out here taking the fall, everybody else is in the clear."

He rolled the cigar stub around in his mouth.

"As your lawyer, the less I know about what you're up to, the better. I don't want to have to answer questions like, 'Mr. Chatham, were you aware that your client was in the apartment of the victim at or about the time the apartment was vandalized and the woman living there was beaten to the point of having to be hospitalized?'"

"But if I can't talk to my attorney...?"

"I'm not going to presume to tell you what to do or not do. Wouldn't do any good if I did. Just try to exercise a little discretion. Don't make my job of defending you any harder than it is."

"I'll keep that in mind."

"Appreciate it if you did."

He asked if I'd spoken with Kathy. I told him of my phone call the night before.

"And why didn't you call her cell phone?"

"I didn't want to hear her not answer."

"If I was you, I'd suck up to her pretty good."

He looked at his watch and said he had to get going, was taking his wife to church. Like me, he was an atheist, said he didn't see how a loving God could let whole races of people be treated like crap for centuries and let their adversaries get away with it. But, where he lived, it's what people did, just part of life. Show up, sing songs, give 'em money. Don't make a big deal about it.

I stayed in the booth, nursing my coffee, thinking about the rest of the day. I realized I hadn't told him about Jay. Or Manetti, or my foray into the forest. I wondered if it was just an oversight on my part or if there was something about it all that I thought I should keep secret.

30

The one-handed-umbrella-opening maneuver is not very difficult, but it wasn't raining hard enough to bother with it on the way back to the car. Sitting behind the wheel, I considered my options. Early in recovery, I followed the "ninety meetings in ninety days" suggestion. Since then, I'd rarely been to one on a Sunday. I called the AA hotline and was told there was a ten o'clock at the Seventh Day Adventist Church on the south side of town, then joined a small group at Denny's for brunch.

Afterwards, sitting in the restaurant parking lot, I called the M. Morgan number stored in my phone. A young voice answered, "Morgan's." I hung up. It sounded like a girl, but could have been a pre-pubescent boy. Now wouldn't be the time if I wanted to talk to her while she was alone.

I didn't feel like driving around the boonies looking for Jackson's Branch in this weather. The motel room held no attraction for me. It was still early in the day, and I hadn't accomplished anything, had just talked, and listened to people talk. I wanted a drink. I'd just been to a meeting, hanging around recovering people like you're supposed to do, and I still wanted a drink.

It had been suggested—repeatedly—in my work in therapy over the years that I was an angry man. Angry at my workaholic, binge-drinking father who died before I could prove myself to him. Angry at my controlling, social worker mother, typical of women living with workaholic, alcoholic men. Angry at myself for repeating my father's workaholic, alcoholic life, and for losing an arm along the way. Who wouldn't want to drink?

I called my AA sponsor.

"It's crazy, Jim. I'm angry at people who are dead."

"So, what's new, Rick? This is old stuff. What's bringing it up for you today?"

"The weather's lousy, for one thing."

"Maybe you've got SAD, that seasonal affective disorder thing."

"That happens in the winter, Jim."

"So, what else?"

"Well, for starters, there's a dead girl and I'm suspected of murdering her."

"You pissed off about that?"

"Of course I am!"

"You're yelling at me."

"Sorry." After a pause, I added, "And Kathy's gone off."

"Gone off?"

"Out of town on work."

"You've been abandoned once again."

"Do I sound like I'm feeling sorry for myself?"

"A little. Can you change your mother and father? Or Kathy, for that matter?"

"Yeah, I get it."

"What can you do today?"

"If I don't get my ass in gear and find out who killed the woman, I'm going to prison."

He didn't say anything for about five seconds.

"And what can you do about that today?"

I thought about it.

"I don't know."

"Maybe you just need to let it alone for a while. Give yourself a break. Take the day off."

It was such a reasonable suggestion. No wonder I hadn't thought of it.

After we said goodbye, I felt my anger settle around The Doll House. They killed Debbie. They put Angi in the hospital. They set me up. I was sure that whoever was behind The Doll House was behind all of it. And all this happening right when things with MTM were coming to a climax, when we were on track to nail the timber company. I hated being pulled in two directions. It felt as if the senator was just as tawdry as the lowlifes at The Doll House, and while I'd never been an altar boy, I had tried for years not to get mixed up with sleaze like them. Until now, when they were coming at me from all directions.

And I hadn't even thought about all the questions I had to answer about Jay. Maybe I would take the rest of the day off, go to the movies, go out to dinner, maybe make another meeting, watch a ball game on TV. Not work. Let it be. Tomorrow, I'd go out to The Doll House. That's where the work had to start. I knew it was a questionable choice when I decided not to tell Nate about it.

31

At seven-thirty a.m. the sky above the hills facing me across the interstate was the color of corn silk. The day before I'd hung out in a couple of bookstores instead of going to the movies. In Blue Ridge Magazines and Used Books, I found *The Novels of Dashiell Hammett* for four dollars. My spirits immediately soared and I spent most of the rest of the day immersed in the book, maybe not overjoyed but at least distracted by the exploits of Sam Spade in *The Maltese Falcon*.

I didn't know when management types went to work at a strip club, but doubted anyone would be there before nine. A call to the hospital revealed that Angi Dillingham was still in ICU. I ate at a downtown place that made its own sausage and served eggs from free-range chickens. Another day without my name in the newspaper. Or the senator's. It was mid-morning when I headed out to the club.

Halfway between downtown and The Doll House, my cell phone rang. It was Katrina from Nate's office.

"Mr. Chatham says, quote, 'Get your ass down to Henderson's office ASAP.' End quote."

Her thick Slavic tones were ominous. I took the urgency of the message to mean either I'd been exonerated or things had taken a turn for the worse, the latter being more likely. I was glad I'd indulged in a big breakfast, thinking it might be my last meal for a while.

Having become something of a fixture at police headquarters, I was allowed to see myself up to the Senior Detective's office. Beyond the open door, the Lieutenant and my attorney were laughing. It's always better when they are in a good mood, police and lawyers. Henderson stood and signaled me in. I took the chair catty-corner to Nate's, the detective sitting behind the desk. I opened my eyes wide, beseeching.

Henderson began. "A couple of boys were fishing along the river bank a quarter of a mile or so up the road from your office, near where that little riverside park is. Know the area?"

I said I did.

"They came upon a bundle of clothes in the brush near the water's edge. Curious, as young boys are, they investigated, pulled the bundle apart. Pair of shorts, T-shirt, bra, panties, tennis shoes, socks. Girl stuff. What was more interesting was what had been rolled up inside all of this."

I don't know why, where it came from, it just occurred to me.

"A gun," I said, immediately realizing the implications, that this might be taken as evidence that I actually knew what was there rather than having taken an intuitive stab at it.

Henderson nodded.

"And how did you know that?"

"Just a guess. You've obviously brought me down here because you think it may relate to the murder. If the murderers threw the clothes away, why not get rid of the gun at the same time."

Henderson nodded again. "That's our bet," he said, as he reached down to get something off the floor, coming up with what looked like clothes rolled up as one might put them in a bag to take to the pool or the gym. "This is how they found it, they said."

He unrolled the bundle, laying the clothes on his desk. My breath caught when I saw the pink CHARLESTON, SOUTH CAROLINA shirt on top of the pile. I thought I might be sick. When the only garment left was a pair of panties, he made a little drama of unrolling them, revealing a revolver.

"Recognize any of it?"

My chest began to quake. I put my head between my knees to keep from passing out.

"You don't have to say anything," Nate said.

"It's okay, Nate, I'd like to get this thing solved, and the more information they have, the better." Turning back to the detective I said, "Yes, I've seen the shirt and shorts. It was what she was wearing when I saw her in the sporting goods store, before I knew who she was. I was surprised when I saw her dancing the next day. The gun also looks familiar, like one stolen from my house last week. A thirty-eight?"

"You had a gun stolen from your house?" Henderson asked, in that tone parents use to let you know what just happened was unimaginable until you told of it.

I related the incident of the fouled up alarm pad, then finding the revolver missing.

"You just discovered it missing. And you think it's related to how your alarm key pad was a week ago?" the Detective reiterated. "And you didn't bother to report it when you did notice it was gone?"

"And here's the even stranger part of it," I added. "Whoever took it didn't bother to take the ammunition that was in the drawer with it."

"Meaning what, you think?" Nate asked.

"That they didn't intend to fence it or even use it very often."

Nate asked if it was loaded. I said it was.

"Without getting into whether I give that story any credence, we're thinking it's the murder weapon. Same caliber, a thirty-eight.

One round fired. Ballistics is working on it." We sat with that a few seconds before he asked, "Could someone have taken it without stealing it?"

I looked at him dumbly for a couple of seconds, like he had said something in a foreign language that was vaguely familiar.

"You mean Kathy?"

"She had access to it, knew where it was."

"Come on," I said, working to keep my voice under control. "I know you've talked to her, but do you really think she murdered Debbie?"

Henderson shrugged. I looked over at Nate. He was shaking his head, ever so slightly.

"Or had someone do it," Henderson added.

"You don't believe that," I said.

"Rick," the detective said, still sounding like a father talking to a wayward son. "I'm a cop. I believe anything that fits the evidence."

"Are you going to arrest her now, too?"

"Nah. Not yet. One per family's enough for now."

"Cute. But why not? What do you have on me that you don't have on her?" I asked, not because I wanted them to arrest Kathy or thought they ought to. It just seemed no more reasonable to have arrested me than it would be to arrest her. Unless there was some other motive for arresting me, something unrelated to the murder of a twenty-one-year-old stripper.

"Well, since you ask," Henderson said, "there is something I want to clear up, something you said in the hospital. You said the last time you saw the victim was Tuesday night."

"That's right."

He nodded an affirming nod. "It seems there are people who claim to have seen you at The Doll House about eight o'clock Saturday night."

"Who's saying that? Jimmy?" I knew it sounded defensive. It

was.

"And Tom Longo," Henderson said.

"The guy Jimmy works for."

He nodded again. "And a couple of guys who I.D.'d you from a photo."

"You know as well as I do, Ted, if you give someone a picture, ask him if he's ever seen the person, he knows he's supposed to have because you've asked the question. And if it happens to be someone whose picture has been in the paper recently, they very likely could remember the face, but not know from where..."

Henderson signaled for me to stop.

"All right, Rick. I'm just asking you to rethink this."

"Are you taking me back into custody?" I asked.

"Nope. Really just wanted to see if you could identify the clothes."

"And the gun?"

"Nah. That was a surprise, kind of a bonus."

We were silent as we left the courthouse. I waited for a lecture.

"Anything you want to tell me about Saturday night?" my lawyer asked.

It was unseasonably warm for early June. Not yet noon, and it felt like it was already in the mid-eighties. We moved into the shade of the huge old magnolia on the courthouse lawn.

"I was in a blackout, Nate. It's possible I could have gone out there. I don't remember. That's why they're called blackouts." I didn't tell him what Donna had said.

"According to my source," he said, "Debbie's supposed to have left the club about one-thirty Sunday morning."

"Who's saying that besides Longo and Jimmy Crawford?"

"Don't know. The good thing is, I don't believe Henderson puts too much stock in what The Doll House people say. That's why you're still a free man. Apparently, nobody's been interested in the toxicology screen they did at the hospital, either, because nothing's been mentioned about alcohol. It could get messy if that gets out."

"On the other hand," I said, "it would lend credibility to my story of a blackout. If, in fact, I was out there that night."

"Oh, yeah, that's a good defense. 'Your honor, I was very drunk. Exceedingly drunk. Drunk enough to be in a blackout. I cannot be held accountable for what I might have done.' That gonna be how you beat this rap?"

My gaze wandered off somewhere in the middle distance. I thought about what I was going to do next.

"What are you up to now?" Nate asked.

"Nothing you want to know about."

"I won't lecture you with 'This is serious business here, et cetera, et cetera, et cetera.' And I will pray to whatever powers keep the universe together that you don't do something egregiously stupid. More egregiously stupid than you've already done. I think Henderson doesn't believe you committed murder, or you'd be back in the slammer, especially after you went out and saw the roommate. On the other hand, he's not going out of his way to exonerate you, either. If you give them any more ammunition, none of us will able to save your ass."

I felt like I was back in eighth grade and had just been chewed out by the assistant principal.

32

My phone was ringing when I got back to the car. I fumbled to answer it before it switched to voicemail. Just made it.

"They just moved the Dillingham girl out of ICU," Bruce said. "She's in room 441 in the west wing. Thought you'd want to know."

I thanked him and adjusted my itinerary accordingly.

A middle-aged woman was sitting in one of the two aluminum-framed, vinyl-cushioned chairs when I walked in. The woman in the bed was younger, her face still puffy. She appeared to be asleep.

I took a chance and said to the seated woman, "Mrs. Dillingham?" She looked a few years younger than me. Pretty, but too much makeup, looking very tired. The dress she wore showed a lot of leg.

She smiled up at me. "Yes. Luella."

"Hi. My name's Ryder." I flashed my I.D., hoping it would work as well as it had out at Meadow Glen. "I'm a detective. I need to ask your daughter a few questions."

Some internal flood control mechanism gave way, unleashing a torrent of tears onto her face. Her sobbing was close to a wail. I wished I hadn't come.

"Oh, God, what now, Mama?"

The mother and I looked at the bed. Angi was still on her back, eyes closed.

A nurse appeared. Looking at me, she said, "Who are you?"

"I'm a detective."

"Can't you people let her rest for a while?"

Angi tried to lift herself up. "Who the hell are you?" she said.

"He says he's a detective," Luella said.

"Aw, shit," Angi said, letting herself fall back.

"I'm sure he's here to help."

"I can ask him to leave," the nurse said.

"No, it's okay," Luella said.

"Who put you in charge of my room?"

"You'll have to excuse her, Mr....?"

"Ryder," I repeated.

"They've got her on a lot of drugs..."

Angi worked her way up to a fully seated position.

"Now I recognize you. The guy with one arm. You used to come in the club. Oh, Jeezus, shit. You're the guy they say killed her."

"Mr....?" the nurse said.

"Ryder! Rick Ryder."

"You killed her?" Mrs. Dillingham said, eyes wide open.

"No, I did not kill her, but I would like to find out who did. That's why I'm here." I turned to Angi. "I'm the one who found you at the apartment, who called the police. I'm not the killer."

The nurse disappeared.

"They hurt you pretty bad," I said.

"No shit, Sherlock."

"Angi!"

I laughed. "I deserved that."

A slim smile slipped onto Angi's mouth. Luella maintained her glare. Our brief silence was interrupted when the nurse reappeared, now accompanied by a security guard.

"You folks need some help here?" the borderline-geriatric guard asked in his most officious voice.

"It's okay," Angi said.

Luella's eyes were wide open. "But what if he's the killer?"

"He's not the killer. Are you?"

"Nope."

"How does she know that?" Luella asked, looking at the nurse and the security guy.

"It's okay," Angi repeated.

"You sure?" the rent-a-cop asked.

"Yes!" Angi yelled.

"Okay, lady. Just doing my job."

"You see how she is," Luella said, absent any of the signs of the distress that had recently wracked her body.

"You see how she is," Angi said.

I tried to ignore their Ping Pong game.

The guard had slipped out, leaving the nurse behind.

Angi looked at her. "You can leave, too."

The nurse gave a huff almost under her breath, almost soft enough to not be heard, and walked out.

"Do you know why they trashed your place and, uh—"

"Beat the shit out of me?"

"Yeah."

"I wish she wouldn't use that language. That's not how she was brought up."

Angi rolled her eyes and shook her head. "They were looking for something," she said.

"Do you know what?"

She took a sip of water from the plastic cup on the bedside stand.

"Not exactly. Debbie ... she was my roommate." I nodded. "She came from Atlanta, you know, running away from this guy.

She had something she said would protect her. I never knew what it was. Or where it was. Not that those assholes would believe me. They wanted me to tell them where it was. I couldn't. I kept telling them that. That's when they finally taped my mouth shut. They were pretty mad they couldn't find it."

"And you don't know what this ... something she had was?"

"Unh-uh. Like I said, it was something that would protect her, like insurance, she said."

"What do you know about Debbie's life before she came here?"

"She'd ... God ... Her life was more fucked up than mine, if you can believe it."

"You see what I mean," the mother said.

"Yeah, well. It has been messed up."

I was afraid Mrs. Dillingham might unleash another tsunami. Instead, she restricted herself to a few loud sniffles.

"She'd been dancing in Atlanta for this guy who'd been her stepfather before him and her mom split up. It was fucked up..."

"Angela!"

"Well, it was. She ran away from her mother to go live with this guy..."

"Guy have a name?" I asked.

"Archie, Arlo, Arno ... something like that. So she goes to live with him, 'cause he was her stepfather, or had been. And pretty soon he's got her dancing for him."

"How old was she then?"

"Like fifteen, sixteen."

"And she's dancing for him?"

"Like I said, it was fucked up. Anyway, this guy, guy who was her stepfather, he's got like something over her, some way to make her work for him. Then she began planning her getaway."

"Do you know the name of the place where she danced for

this guy?"

"No, she never said. Excuse me, I've gotta pee."

She slid out of the bed, still wearing the hospital-issued gown. I tried unsuccessfully to not glance at her backside as she made her way across the floor. She limped and walked with an arm pulled up against her side, grimacing.

When she was in the bathroom, Luella said, "I don't know where she learned to talk like that. She surely didn't learn it from me."

I wanted to ask what she might have learned from her mother that had led her to her career choice. Instead, I said, "Probably picked it up in the workplace."

Angi was halfway back to the bed when she stumbled. I was close enough that I could grab her elbow and keep her from falling, although she was leaning far forward.

"Angela! Cover yourself!"

I wondered how much of this was an act for my benefit. Surely the woman was aware of what her daughter did for a living. When Angi was settled back in the bed, I asked her what she knew about Saturday night.

"It was fucked up from the beginning." She turned to glare at her mother, daring her to say anything. "I drove us to the club about five-thirty—I always drove since Debbie didn't have a car. Tom was in a shitty mood. He thought we should have been there earlier, though I didn't know why. It was the time we always got there. He said I was being bitchy. I know I can be, but I didn't think I was then." She grimaced and shifted on the bed. "After my first set, he came into the dressing room and asked if I was sick or something. Then he told me I could go home, said there was obviously something wrong with me, my set sucked. I couldn't understand why he was saying that. I felt fine. I thought I danced okay, got the usual tips. He asked if I'd been using crack again, which was a laugh since most of the girls did and they got it from him—I did when I was using. But I haven't had anything for two weeks now. I even thought he was really pissed off because I wasn't doing it anymore."

"You know all of this wouldn't have happened if she didn't do, uh, that for a living."

"Yeah. And ask her why she's had four husbands. She just shakes it for one guy at a time. I do it for a room full of 'em. Same thing, though. Gettin' 'em to give you money."

"You see?" Luella said, fighting tears of anger … or self-pity. I ignored her.

"So, you left the club early?"

She nodded.

"How was Debbie going to get home?"

"Tom said don't worry about that, he'd be sure she got a ride, he'd drive her if he had to."

"Was that unusual, for him to drive dancers home?"

She snorted.

"Nope. Especially if he was trying to get in someone's pants. That's actually what I figured was going on. He was setting it up so she'd have to ride with him."

"When did you hear about what happened?"

"Tom called early Sunday afternoon and asked if I'd heard. I couldn't believe it. It made me really want some crack. I almost called that asshole, Jimmy."

Mother gave a loud exasperated sigh. Angi and I ignored her in unison.

"Jimmy," I repeated.

"Yeah, a guy hangs around the club, does some odd jobs, thinks that ought to be a ticket into our pants. Like Tom. He's a creep. But he's usually got some rock or can get some."

"I've met the guy. Tom say anything else?"

"Not much. Wasn't it shitty, you know, like that. He said I

could take the day off if I wanted, maybe a coupl'a days." She gave another snort. "Be a while before I get back on stage."

"Will you?" I asked. "I mean, go back to work there?"

"What else am I going to do?"

I wanted to scream at the girl, or have her mother scream at her. *Don't you know these are the people who had Debbie killed, who put you in the hospital?* But I didn't know that either, just had a strong belief it was true.

She closed her eyes. "I'd like to sleep now."

I asked if it would be okay to come back.

She nodded. "Do you think you can find out who did it?" she asked, eyes still shut.

"I'm gonna go at it like my life depends on it." I looked down at the mother as I was leaving. "Nice to meet you, Luella."

She looked up at me, her eyes like those of a little girl who had lost her way home, hoping someone would help her.

When I got to the hospital lobby, I saw Henderson and a uniform at the information desk. I redirected myself to the gift shop, hoping I hadn't been spotted. I had a small stuffed bear sent up to Angi's room. I didn't sign a card.

33

Half a dozen cars dotted the parking lot at The Doll House when I pulled in, prominent among them a new Mercedes roadster and a white Cadillac convertible. I knocked hard on the front door, there being nobody with large, tattooed arms standing nearby to let people in. A minute later, I gave a louder bang. That achieved a "hold your horses," and, in another moment, Jimmy Crawford opened the door. I don't know who was more surprised.

"What do you want?"

I looked back at the lot.

"Where's your truck?"

I could tell by his eyes he was going to lie.

"In for repairs."

"I thought you were in jail."

"They bailed me out," he said, with a nod toward the interior of the club.

"They?"

"Sally and Big Tom."

"The owners?"

"Yeah."

I chewed this around in my brain like a dip of tobacco. In itself it wasn't necessarily significant—why wouldn't they bail out a part-time employee? Then again, why would they?

"That's who I'm here to see," I said.

He was silent as he led me toward the main room. There was music, the kind they played at night although several decibels lower. I saw the girl dancing as we walked toward the edge of the stage. She was down to a G-string and was being watched by a man and a woman. She looked like the girl who had come on stage before Debbie that first night I saw her dance, Terri or Shari. She'd seemed young then and appeared even younger close up. I looked over at the couple who were watching her. The man turned toward me. He seemed familiar, but the stage lightning made it hard to see clearly. We were of less interest to him than a nearly nude dancer.

"Audition," Jimmy said.

"I thought she already worked here," I said.

He shrugged.

"What's her name?"

"Shari."

As he led the way past the stage, I felt a chill. Sadness descended on me like a winter storm. We went past the shop with its cornucopia of sex goodies to an office at the end of the hall. Jimmy knocked lightly on the partially opened door. A good looking middle-aged woman pulled it the rest of the way. I was operating out of a paranoid notion that, since my picture had appeared in the paper, everyone knew what I looked like. She gave no indication that my face was familiar. Instead, her expression was a question mark. Jimmy filled the gathering void.

"Sally, this here's Rick Ryder, the guy killed Debbie."

This was not the way one wants to begin a conversation. A burly man, six-feet-plus, maybe two-fifty, came up behind the woman.

"What the hell you doing here?"

"I'm investigating the murder."

This seemed to confuse him.

"The police already been here."

"I figured that. But, as Mr. Crawford said, I'm the one they think did it. I didn't, and I'm trying to find out who did. Since you folks probably knew her as well as anybody, I thought you might be able to shed some light on things."

He hesitated, like an actor not quite sure of his next line.

"Yeah, well, couldn't tell 'em much. She danced a regular night. Then left about one-thirty. That's all I know."

I had to be careful here. If they knew I'd been talking to Angi, they could decide to visit her in the hospital. Might anyway. "How'd she get home?"

Jimmy was still standing next to me. I thought I could feel his body stiffen.

"I don't know. I don't keep up with their comings and goings. I assume another girl gave her a ride."

I did a quick scan, looking at the eyes of the three people in the room.

"Nobody saw what car she got in?"

Nobody said anything.

"Listen, buddy," the man I assumed was Tom Longo said, the register of his voice dropping, the volume rising. Like the MTM-guy out in the forest, this man was used to getting people to do what he wanted by puffing himself up. "We've been through this with the cops. Debbie was my most popular dancer. I don't like she's gone. You were out here that night, arguin' with her. There are people think you did it, that you needed to get rid of her, that she was complicating your home life. Now, if you don't get outta my face, I might decide to take justice into my own hands."

I couldn't tell if it was frustration or defensiveness. Or both.

I slipped into my best lawyerly persona for dealing with irate opponents.

"Okay, Mr. Longo. I assume you're Tom Longo?"

"What if I am?"

"I did talk to Debbie the couple of times I was in here. She was a nice girl. She didn't deserve to die. And believe me, I didn't have anything to do with her murder, so I'd like to find out who did. I don't mean to get on your nerves, Mr. Longo, but, you know, the police, well … they want to solve their case, so they.... Well, let's say they have different priorities. Not to say they won't do the best they can, but I really want to find out who killed her, since I didn't."

I knew he was lying about the circumstances of Debbie's departure from the club that night but didn't know what other role he may have played in her death. He couldn't appear to know too much, but he also had to seem sympathetic to someone wanting to find the truth.

The energy in the room dissipated a little.

"Sorry," he said. "It's very disturbing. And lousy for business, you know. People don't like to hang out where people are getting bumped off."

This was an interesting point of view, since no one had suggested she was killed at the club. I also wondered if the reverse wouldn't be true, that people would come out here just to see the place "where that girl who got killed danced."

"I understand she danced in Atlanta before she came here," I said, turning to look at Jimmy Crawford. "That right, Jimmy?"

A look went between the two men.

"You know," Jimmy said, "I was beginning to think maybe she was right. It wasn't her I saw dance there. Some'un looked a lot like her."

He looked back at his boss. So did I.

"You don't know where she danced before she came here? She didn't give a reference?"

Longo laughed.

"References?" He grinned. "We don't ask where these girls

have been, what they've done. We do a criminal background check. As long as there's nothing serious—felonies, prostitution, that kind of thing—we go by audition. It's all based on talent. This isn't like being a doctor or lawyer or working for some big corporation. Turnover's pretty heavy. Cost of doing this kind of business. Some of these girls use drugs. Lots of 'em have financial problems. Some of 'em fight. It's a hard fucking business, man. I admit that. But we try to run as clean a place as we can."

I didn't know what all he was trying to convey to me. When you work with liars as much as lawyers and snoops do, many of whom are your colleagues, you come to recognize something in a person's eyes just as they are about to hand you some bullshit. The question was, what exactly was he bullshitting about? If Angi was to be believed—which I did—Debbie had danced in Atlanta. I believed Jimmy had seen her there. Why didn't they want me to know this?

"How did Debbie get along with the other dancers?" I asked, thinking a resentment factor may have been involved, that it was that simple, and there weren't any other conspiracies.

Sally said, "I'm kind of a sorority housemother here. These girls make their money by getting men to pay attention to them. Women, too, for that matter. They're competing for attention. The more attention they get, the more money they make. Debbie was good-looking and a good dancer and she didn't do drugs. She showed up on time. Within a few days, it was clear she had something the other girls didn't have. Presence, they call it in show biz."

"Didn't she replace Angi as the top-billed dancer?"

"You think Angi killed her because of that?" Sally asked in a voice suggesting that was just the silliest thing she'd ever heard.

I was tempted to remark that, given the way she looked in the hospital, there were people just as upset with Angi as they were with Debbie. But then they'd know I'd seen Angi, and I didn't want them to know that, at least not right now.

"I'm looking for any possibilities," I said. "Somebody's trying to set me up. I don't know if it's because I'm a good patsy or if somebody's out to get me personally, if her murder was a way to get to me, not just to do away with her."

I heard the coldness of "do away with her" as it came out of my mouth. People in this room knew more than they were letting on and I knew I'd never get it out of them. I needed to talk to someone else who was in the club that night to find out if I had really been here, and, if so, what happened between Debbie and me. I wanted to know where she danced in Atlanta and was clueless as to who might be willing and able to give me that information. I thanked them for their help, all of us knowing none had been given. While turning to leave, my attention was drawn to a group of a pictures on one wall, a dozen or so very attractive, well-endowed women in the company of Tom and Sally, all the photos having some variation of "thanks" written on them.

"Real pros," Tom said, catching the drift of my gaze. "Penthouse models and such. Now, those girls know how to put on an act. Debbie might have made it that far if..." His voice trailed off as if he'd forgotten what he'd been talking about.

"Yeah, if," I repeated. I was looking at a framed certificate hanging in the midst of these celebrities. I stepped towards it. It indicated that business license fees had been paid to the city. The name it was issued to was "C&M Productions DBA The Doll House Lounge." I recalled the face that had turned toward me as Jimmy and I passed the stage and knew why it was familiar.

The music had stopped. Another woman came into the office. Pretty, a nice figure under a snug T-shirt and short skirt. Black hair. I thought she must be the woman who'd been auditioning the girl. She walked with a slight limp and used a cane. We glanced at each other and she quickly turned away as if she might catch something by looking at me. I moved on to the door, turning back just as I reached it.

"By the way. I know you don't want me to find out what happened that night. But I will."

I don't know why I said it. Just wanting them to know they weren't off the hook as far as I was concerned.

Manetti was talking to the young dancer as I walked past. She wore a short robe that she didn't bother to pull closed. He glanced in my direction, giving no indication he recognized me.

Back out in the daylight, I pulled out my cell phone. I had two messages. When I was in the car, I glanced in the rear view mirror and saw the green Buick looking back at me.

34

The bile of self-righteous indignation roiled in my stomach. I wanted to grab the tire iron out of the trunk, smash headlights and windows, bash metal, scream at the driver. Recovery taught me to accept my powerlessness over people, places, and things, but I was afraid that what I couldn't control was going to land me in prison for something I hadn't done. I let my anger settle on Manetti.

After some deep breathing, I listened to my messages: one from Zella, the other from Dee Dee Mankin. Zella wondered if I'd found out any more about Jay. I told her voicemail that I didn't have anything to add since our last conversation, but I'd try to see what he was up to tonight. Dee Dee wondered what I'd found out about her daughter. When she answered the phone, her anticipation was so intense, you'd have thought I was Ed McMahon calling for Publisher's Clearinghouse. I told her my investigation had generated information leading me to believe her daughter was still in the area, and I would check it out the next day as long as nothing unexpected came up. I inferred from her voice that her gratitude could easily manifest in sexual favors. It is a sad reflection on my state of being at the time that I allowed myself to consider the possibility.

I called Manetti's office, knowing he wasn't there. After Charlene told me he wasn't in, I asked when he was expected.

"He should be in after lunch. Would you—"

"And when would lunch be?"

"Would you care to leave a message for him? He can call you when he gets in."

"No, thanks. I'll try him later."

The Buick followed me out of The Doll House lot. At this point, I didn't care if he knew where I was going but I played dodge 'em with him just for the hell of it. I got a traffic light between us, doubled back on myself, and was off the main road before he could head in my direction. When I stopped at Pete's Greek Diner for an early lunch there was no sign of him.

My sponsor came up to me after the noon meeting and asked if I wanted to catch lunch. I said I'd already eaten and had some business that needed tending to.

On the south side of town, I pulled into the C&M Center parking lot, noting the Mercedes roadster near the entrance to Manetti's office.

Charlene was wearing the same friendly smile she'd had on the other day.

"Mr. Mitchum," she said. "Bob."

My smile was the genuine article.

She spoke discreetly into her headset, looked up and said that Mr. Manetti would see me in a moment and I should have a seat. No reading material had appeared on the glass-top table amidst the three leather chairs. I closed my eyes, opening them when I heard footsteps. When I looked up, he was smiling and holding his hand toward me like we were old friends. I stood, ignoring the outstretched arm.

"Apparently this isn't a social call," he said without losing the smile. "Come on back."

I wondered if he now knew who I was. They would have told him at The Doll House that Rick Ryder had been there, but he may not have connected me to the name.

When we'd taken our respective seats, he said he imagined it wasn't office space that brought me back.

"I'm Rick Ryder, Tim."

"Yeah, I was beginning to think I recognized you from the club. So, you weren't looking for office space when you were in here before, were you?"

"No. I was trying to find out what Jay McIntyre was up to with you."

He laughed.

"So, you know Jay," he said.

"I do."

"Friend of yours?"

"He is."

"So, why don't you ask him?"

Good question. I didn't answer, just looked at him. I wondered what I really expected to find out.

"Well," he said, "it's kind of, you know, confidential. As in, none of your business."

His expression hadn't changed, still the same grin.

"That girl, what's her name, Zoey. That's it, cute name. Cute girl. If you know Jay, you must know her. Don't you think she'd look good without any clothes on?"

My eyes narrowed. I could feel blood pound in my temples. I wanted to reach over and throttle him but held my seat.

When I didn't respond, he said, "That it?"

I said, no, that wasn't it. There was more.

"It's like this, Tim," I said. "I've been implicated in the murder of a young girl, a girl I'm pretty sure you knew, Debbie Douglass. I'm convinced her murder has something to do with people from

Atlanta, of whom you are one. You and that damn green Buick keep popping up in my life, and I want to know why."

The feigned warmth dissolved. I shivered.

"I want to know why you're having me followed. I want to know what you had to do with Debbie's murder." I was surprised my teeth didn't chatter as I said it.

He leaned toward me. I had to fight the inclination to lean backwards, away from him.

"Did it ever occur to you that you might not be the only one who wants to find out what happened to her, that there were other people who cared about her and who maybe aren't satisfied with the story the police have cooked up?"

"You're full of shit, Manetti, and I'm gonna get you before this is over."

"Get out of here, Ryder, you one-armed hack, before I call the police and tell them you've been here trying to intimidate me with some crap about a murder investigation. And I don't expect to see you here again."

He had awakened The Cowboy. Me intimidate him? Well, okay.

I stood and stepped up to the glass-topped table, grabbed its front edge, lifted it up, and pushed it toward him.

"Yeah," I said, "but it's one damn good arm."

He jumped back as the table fell to the floor with a loud crack.

A stream of epithets followed me as I walked away. I smiled and nodded at Charlene on my way out. Manetti had almost caught up with me when a black Lincoln limousine pulled up outside the office. Manetti stopped. I kept moving.

I was in my car when I heard him yell, "Get that son of a bitch." I saw the chauffeur in the rearview mirror headed my way as I backed out. I shifted fast and took off, wishing I could stay around to see who was in the car, or at least get the license plate.

An adrenaline hangover and the misery my arm would feel in

the morning would be payback for my impulsiveness. I wanted to tell someone what had just happened, but my boss, my lawyer, and my sponsor would all give me feedback I didn't want to hear. And I wasn't prepared to deal with the disappointment of Kathy not answering one more time.

My right arm shook. The non-existent left one ached with sympathy pain that I tried to shake off.

Questions swirled around in my head. What were The Doll House people covering up? What were Jay and Zoey were doing with Manetti? If he made movies, they would not be the G-rated kind. Surely, Jay and Zoey wouldn't be involved in something like that. Maybe it was blackmail, maybe Zoey had once danced at The Doll House. I did think she'd look good with no clothes on.

After my heart rate returned to near-normal, I thought about the possibility that Manetti might press charges against me for assault and destruction of property. No doubt he had a few reliable cops in his pocket, but I could probably count on him not wanting the authorities looking too closely into his activities. I drove on toward town and hoped he'd write the episode off as just part of the overhead of running a sleazy enterprise.

35

Clouds gathering in the west suggested that our respite from the rain would be short-lived. It had been a busy day already and I could have justified knocking off. Instead, I stopped by the room for my foul-weather gear, then went to the car rental agency. I would need a different vehicle for snooping out in the country. I'm generally opposed to SUVs on principle, but a fairly new all-wheel-drive Ford Expedition was all they had that met my need for maneuverability in the boonies. The clerk was even less happy about a one-armed man driving this car than he had been about letting me behind the wheel of the little convertible. I had to play the 'Americans with Disabilities Act' card on him.

At the New Country Café, Taylor had a cup of coffee for me before I reached the counter. I sipped it and allowed it was pretty good.

"Jamaican Blue."

"Expensive stuff to be giving away, isn't it?"

"I just made a small pot. What's the point of owning a coffee shop if you can't drink the good stuff? And I don't give it away to everybody. You still looking for the Mankin kid?"

"I am. But I'm not sure what my next move is."

"What about the fire department?"

I was interested.

"They know a lot about what happens around here. It's in their best interest to know who's who and what's where."

"Aren't they volunteers? Show up when there's a fire?"

"Mostly. But there're a couple of old guys who hang out at the firehouse. Retired. You know, need a place to be and feel useful during the day. One of them has started coming in here. He can't believe he's paying almost two bucks for a cup of coffee, but even the convenience stores are selling what they're calling gourmet stuff, and ours is better, he says. That's what you call a major endorsement."

"Think he'd be at the station now?"

"Probably. Name's Bobby Headley. I think he may have been a sheriff's deputy back in the day, until he got fed up with the politics of it. Nice guy."

"Should I use you as a reference?"

"Fine by me."

The fire station was three-quarters of a mile on out the two-lane. There was one car in the parking lot when I pulled in. I walked into the garage.

"Anybody home?"

"In here," a voice called from a small office. A nice-looking older man sat behind a desk.

"Bobby Headley?"

"I am. How can I help you?"

I introduced myself and told him about Taylor down at the New Country Café suggesting I talk to him. When he stood to shake hands, I could detect no excess baggage on his six-foot-plus frame. He appeared to be in his mid-60s and was wearing a pair of blue jeans and a white T-shirt emblazoned with "Erwin High Warriors." His open smile and salt-and-pepper hair—heavy on the salt—gave him the appearance of an old movie actor, like Gary

Cooper or John Wayne. His grip was firm with no attempt to be overpowering.

"Those folks may be Yankees and all," he said, "but they're nice people. Make a good cuppa Joe, too. Whatcha need?"

I explained about the Mankin girl.

"Yeah. Heard you were pokin' around out here. You're the guy they're makin' for that stripper killer, huh?"

"That's me."

"Understand the Crawford kid's messed up in it somehow."

"He's the one fingered me. I'm not sure why."

"Kid's a piece of work."

"You know him."

"Oh-yeah. 'Nother local boy makes bad. I don't know what's happening out here. Got more churches you can shake a stick at, and more dope dealin', thievin', you name it."

"Got any idea why they might take his word against mine ... other than I can't prove where I was at the time the murder supposedly occurred? And I did know the girl. And apparently I'm the owner of the weapon used to kill her...." I paused as he raised his eyebrows. "Doesn't sound good, when you put it all together, does it?"

"The wheels of justice," he said with a shrug and a smile.

"Well, enough about me. Know anything about meth cooking out on Jackson's Branch?"

"I know where it's supposed to be goin' on. Out to the old Harney place. Zeno Harney—'Cujo,'" he added with a snort— "inherited it a couple o' years ago, and it's been nothin' but a hangout since. All kind of stuff goin' on. Supposedly got into meth about six months ago. We try to know where all the meth cookin' is happening, 'cause sooner or later one of those places is gonna blow up. Sheriff's been out there, says he didn't find anything. Probably went out with his sy-rene blastin', give 'em a chance to clean up the place. There's usually not but one operatin' at a time, and they move around. You can't hide the stink that stuff gives off, so the neighbors catch on pretty quick. But it's been quiet out there for a while."

"You suppose people are living there, in the place they cook the stuff?"

"Prob'ly. You thinkin' of goin' out there?"

"I thought I would. Don't know what else to do."

"Want company?"

"Don't you have to man the fort?"

"Oh, we got a back-up system. I ain't around here twenty-four-seven, you know. If you want, I'll drive, make it kinda' semi-official."

He called somebody, said he was going to be away from the station an hour or so and he'd transfer the calls over. We got in the old red Jeep Cherokee that served as the chief's car.

Jackson's Branch was off Shady Cove Road, a mile off the two-lane. A half-mile up, after the road turned to gravel, sat a ramshackle cabin. There was an equally rundown pickup truck in the yard. We pulled up next to it and walked up on the porch, where an old washing machine and a couch occupied pride of place.

The front door was open. Bobby knocked on a screen door held semi-upright by one hinge.

"Anybody home?"

After calling twice more with no response, we went on in.

"Some people might think this constitutes an illegal entry but I believe there are some fire safety issues here," he said. "Could probably have the place boarded up as uninhabitable."

Food wrappers and uneaten carry-out and fast food were all over the living room and kitchen. Not a whole lot of dirty dishes, probably because they were never used. The place stank, but of stale and moldy food and clothes, not methamphetamine being cooked. Shirts and pants, bras and panties, were strewn everywhere. I poked around a little to try to get a sense of how long it had been since someone had been here. There was a partially eaten fast-food burger and a few fries that didn't seem like they'd been sitting around too long. The Chief agreed they were probably not more than a day old, two at the most.

"I don't think they've moved out," he said.

We walked on through and out the back door. Bobby pointed to a fifty-gallon drum.

"That's ammonia," he said. "Gotta have it to make meth. A dead giveaway. It's what makes it smell so bad."

"I don't suppose they can be busted for having an inordinate quantity of it sitting in the backyard."

"Actually, there are laws about having the ingredients to make the stuff. A good lawyer can fight it, though it's pretty hard to come up with a reason for having that amount of ammonia."

"Housecleaning," I said.

"Housecleaning? Not much of that going on around here."

"I heard about it at an NA meeting a while back," I said. His expression shifted, the narrowing of his eyes hardly noticeable. "I'm AA. Every now and then, I take in a Narcotics Anonymous meeting. Pretty much the same thing for an addict. Anyway, this woman, probably mid-thirties, says she claimed she was in the home-cleaning business, that's what she used all the ammonia for. It got her off once, she said, but then she was busted when she'd just cooked up a batch. Neighbors smelled it, like you said, hard to hide. She said she thought her conviction also had to do with the fact that she wouldn't put out for the deputy sheriff."

"Wouldn't be surprised," the chief said. "That's a sad commentary, isn't it?"

An old springhouse sat at the edge of what had once been a

cleared yard. Except for a footpath to the outbuilding, the yard was overgrown, briars starting to reclaim lost territory. The building was padlocked. The chief pointed to a corner of the roof, where a line was attached.

"Power," he said. "I imagine this is where they do their cookin'. Be interesting to see what's in there, but I'm afraid if I break it open, they'll know someone's been pokin' around and they'll pull up stakes, and it'll take another while to find out where they're at."

We turned back toward the house as the wind kicked up, pushing black clouds across the sun. Back inside, I poked my head into one of the two bedrooms. It looked like an extension of the living room, but with more clothes and less food. I wondered how many people hung out here and what all they shared.

The other room was padlocked like the springhouse.

"More supplies, I imagine," Bobby said.

We rummaged around some more, found an electric bill for Zeno Harney, which didn't tell us anything we didn't know. The afternoon was almost gone. Although it appeared I'd found where the Mankin girl was staying, I felt the press of other matters. Clearing myself of murder was still high on the list.

Fat raindrops slapped against the windshield on the way back to the station. A few minutes into a silent ride, he asked, "What happened to your arm?"

"A combination of factors, really."

"Yeah?"

"Youth and stupidity. And alcohol."

"Dangerous mix."

"Sure was for me. A car wreck. I was twenty. I was drunk." We were silent until I added, "I killed a girl."

"Explains the AA business," he said.

"It took me a while to get there. The judge in my trial said he thought I got what I deserved and put me on probation instead of sending me to prison. I punished myself for a lot longer than he could have put me away. It took a lot of years living around people who didn't think I was as bad a person as I thought I was."

When we pulled up to the station, he held out his hand.

"Thanks for the tour," I said.

"More fun than sittin' round here, fillin' out reports, waitin' for somethin' to happen. I'll give you a call if I hear of signs of life out there. If they're cookin', I wouldn't go in there alone."

I thanked him, said I hoped to hear from him and maybe I'd see him out at the café.

"And good luck with the murder rap," he called as I was walking away.

A crack of lightning lit up the countryside, followed abruptly by a great crash. Rain obliterated the road's guidelines, forcing me to ease off onto the shoulder. Images from twenty-five years before and another rain-soaked road flooded my mind. Sitting with my eyes closed, I heard the squeal of tires, the sickening sound of metal crunching metal, sirens. I didn't often think of that episode and I wondered if my search for Pamela was an attempt to balance the books.

After some deep breaths, I lost myself in the sound of the rain beating on the car.

36

By the time the rain let up enough for me to get back on the highway, my thoughts had wandered again to Manetti and how he might be involved in whatever Jay and Zoey were working on. When I saw the sign for Alexander Road, I didn't have time to slow down before making a hard left in front of a car coming at me. He honked and gave me the finger, but I ignored it. The road cut across the northwest rim of the county, coming out by the river back toward the east. I thought I knew how to navigate so I could wind up on the other side of the valley from where I'd seen the movie set—what I assumed was a movie set—the other day.

As I approached the area, I detected a glow through the fog and rain. Cresting the rise, it was as if I'd come across a carnival in the middle of the forest. Towers of light created the illusion of daylight ahead. A group of motor coaches like those I had seen two days before were parked in horseshoe formation with the old cabin at the open end of the U. A bunch of panel trucks were lined up along the newly graveled road. Dozens of people milled around seemingly unaffected by the weather.

I turned around and aimed the Ford back up the hill, idling for a moment while I considered getting out and going down for a closer look. My decision was made when headlights approached from the perimeter of the activity. Security, I imagined, coming to check me out. I didn't know how they felt about strangers on the set and I didn't want Jay to know I was onto him. Heading back up the slope, I was glad I had chosen the all-wheel drive vehicle. When I reached the main road I turned right to go back the way I'd come. Headlights appeared in the rear view mirror. The rain was coming harder and I had to turn the wipers on double-time.

As I leaned into the dim light reflecting off the fog, I wondered what was going on. If they were worried about someone driving onto the set, why wouldn't they have security up at the main road? I was also aware of how foolish it was to be driving an unfamiliar, unwieldy vehicle on a winding mountain road in the rain with one hand, a nightmarish scenario of the kind I imagined the rent-a-car agent feared. When I came to a cut-out, I pulled over. Nothing passed on the road. The headlights I'd seen were probably those of the vehicle turning around at the top of the ridge crest before heading back down into the valley, not someone chasing me.

I was letting The Cowboy take over. I sat for a few seconds, regaining my breath and my composure. I'd been doing a lot of that lately.

I called Zella and told her what I'd seen.

"Maybe they're doing a propaganda film for the timber industry, for MTM, specifically. A kind of Little House in the Mountains kind of thing, some heartwarming story about a family struggling in the Appalachians. A timber company comes along and graciously offers to pay them to remove some trees. They even cut some up for firewood for the poor folks. I don't know. And there's the whole matter of Manetti. I still wonder if he's funding them, although I can't for the life of me figure out why he would."

After a moment's silence, she asked, "Anything else?" She was a good lawyer. Keep the conversation going, you never knew what might come out.

"Yeah. Why haven't we heard anything about this? I mean the public. You know they've had to get permits. The neighbors certainly know something's up. Those lights are visible in that whole area of the county and into the next. And why nothing in the paper or on TV news? Usually movie makers want all the publicity they can get. It doesn't make sense."

"Does seem strange," she agreed. "So, what's next?"

I said I didn't know and I'd check in with her the next day.

Thunder crashed as lightning lit up the sky. My phone rang simultaneously with my starting the car. I heard the beep indicating a message had been left on voicemail.

37

It was Kathy. I was back in my motel room when I checked the message. I couldn't decide if she sounded more businesslike or urgent-but-controlled. I called.

As she was talking, I could see her standing upright as a poplar tree, her face as firm in concentration as the faces on Mt. Rushmore. Like the last time we talked, there was no, "Hi, hon, how've you been," no endearing words, just a straight launch into a cold speech.

"Someone called an hour ago, just before I called you. He said he wanted the material. He said you might be so foolish as to put yourself in jeopardy, but he doubted that I was willing to do so for some stripper." Her voice carried little inflection, and I knew she was keeping a lid on a cauldron. "What the hell's going on, Rick? Let me in on it. I'm a big girl. I can take it."

I had the good sense not to remind her that she had thrown me out, making it difficult to keep her abreast of current events. I gave her a *Reader's Digest* version of the story—what I knew of it.

"Apparently, Debbie—the deceased—had something she thought would keep people in Atlanta from messing with her. She misjudged them. Somebody wants me to take the fall for her murder. I've got nothing to do with any of it other than knowing the girl."

"What people in Atlanta?"

"People she used to work for, as I understand it, one of whom had been her stepfather."

"So she was killed because she had this ... whatever it was?"

"That's what it seems like. It's the only explanation I've found. Except Jimmy Crawford's claim that I did it because she was becoming a problem in my life."

"Don't the police know this, about this strange something?"

"I don't know. They should, if they really wanted to know about it and weren't intentionally ignoring it."

I told her of Ted Henderson's comments to the effect that this was about what evidence they had—a gun that came from our house, my knowing the girl, testimony that I had been seen and heard at the club the night she was killed and had said that I was going to have to "do something about her," the phone call from Debbie when I didn't show for a date, my inability to account for sixteen hours during which she was killed.

There was silence. I fought the urge to fill it.

"You can't believe how mad I am at you right now," she said, quietly. "I don't think you can grasp it. You have this way of living in denial of how the rest of the world works, and you have an image of yourself as this nice guy, and you don't get it when people see another side of you."

I wanted to defend myself. She went on before I could gather my wits.

"I want you to come home. I'm scared. I am really scared and mad as hell. I don't know who I'm more mad at, you or these ... murderers. That's what they are, isn't it?"

"Yes," I said, grateful for the opportunity, "that's what they are."

"You'll stay in the guest room."

"I figured that."

It was a strange sensation. I was happy I was being let back into my own home. More than that, I was needed.

"Call the police," I said. "I'll be there in half an hour."

"They said not to call the police."

"Yeah, well they would, wouldn't they?"

I packed up my stuff, checked the bathroom and under the covers, scooped up what remained of the complimentary toiletries. One could wind up in worse places, I thought, then realized that I still might.

Apparently, "they," whoever they were, knew that I hadn't been home, despite my convoluted commuting to and from the motel. I decided not to check out, hoping to put them off my trail as long as possible. My nemesis was not apparent in a quick look around the parking lot. Even so, I drove evasively, a circuitous route that involved twice doubling back on myself until I was satisfied that if anyone had been following, I had lost them before turning onto Cove Road.

I parked next to the squad car in the driveway. Lt. Hammer and Kathy were just inside when I opened the door. He stood aside as I went to stand next to my wife. She put an arm around my waist. I reciprocated.

"That was quick," I said to the detective.

He was expressionless when he turned, a cop look. I thought they'd just ask her go to the police station to make a statement. Maybe my case was getting more attention from downtown than I'd been thinking.

"A threatening phone call does seem like it might bear on a murder investigation … if there was a call," he said. "Problem is, we've got no actual record of it."

"Come on," I said. "There has to be a record." Just ask the NSA to provide it, I thought, though I had enough wits not to say it aloud.

"Maybe so, but we haven't got it. Anyway, if there was a call, it could have come from you."

My grip on Kathy's midsection tightened.

"You mean, we might have concocted this whole thing?"

"Anything's possible. We have to consider all the angles, Mr. Ryder, you know that."

I realized the depths to which the authorities seemed to be willing to go to deny any scenario other than the one in which I was the villain.

"Shall I come down and take a lie detector test, Lieutenant?" Kathy asked quietly, though with an undertone of snarky anger in her voice—the kind of tone she usually reserved for me.

Good move, I thought.

"Nah, nah. Your report'll be in the record. So, what'd the caller say? What's supposed to happen next?"

I realized I hadn't bothered to ask the question.

"I told him I didn't have any fucking idea what he was talking about and hung up on him."

"Maybe they were just shaking the tree, you know, see what falls off," I said.

"Let us know if you hear from him again. Wanna tap on your phone? Ma'am?"

"Like in a kidnapping?" Kathy said. "No, thanks. If they call again, I'll let them talk to Rick."

The lieutenant thanked Kathy for her time, nodded his head to me and said, "Mr. Ryder." As he went out the door, I thought he seemed a softer, gentler kind of Hammer.

Kathy and I still had our arms around each other's waist, my grip now relaxed.

"You're not out of the dog house," she said.

"I realize that," I said, my hope for a quick reconciliation dashed for the time being.

"Do you have any idea what I'm up against?" she asked.

I could not find an appropriate response.

"I don't think many women have this experience. There's not a lot to go on. I don't have a twelve-step group to go to, one for the wives of suspected murderers. Now this detective shows up and doesn't believe me. Or at least gives the impression he doubts what I've said. Not you, Rick. It wasn't your story he was questioning—although I understand that's at the crux of the thing for you—it was mine. It was personal."

We had stepped apart to face each other. I remained mute, avoiding defensiveness.

"Let's go out on the deck. I'm having a glass of wine. I'll fix you some decaf if you like."

I said I'd like that. The last storm had moved out and left a clear sky behind. It was cool along the mountainside. A light breezed tickled the surrounding foliage while the creek mumbled lightly to itself.

It was approaching midnight when she asked, "How is it you decided to strike up a relationship with a stripper?"

There was no way I would come out of this looking good, but I tried not to shave the truth. I started with the tennis rackets, went on through our two conversations at the club, the invitation to play tennis, my decision not to follow through with it, and the more consequential decision to stop in the bar, "to have a Coke and watch the Open."

"And you expect people to believe that you had no sexual attraction to that girl, that you didn't want to get into her pants? She was just this charming young woman?"

"That's not what it was about," I said.

"What exactly was it about then?"

"I don't know. She was fun to talk to..."

"Naked."

"Not quite naked."

"Come on, Rick. This particular girl might have been somehow different, brighter, funnier, whatever, than some of the other girls, but she made her living taking off her clothes and getting men to respond to her sexually."

"A living she was trying to get out of."

"Like the whore who's going to give up the business as soon as she has enough money saved? I'm sure you never thought for a minute that you would ever get in her pants. Just don't try to deny that you thought about it and that a part of you would like to have been able to. I have fantasies, too, Rick."

"A part of me fantasized about having sex with her. There. Okay?"

"Okay. And I had a two-night fling with a man in Charlotte. There."

I jumped up and down. Literally. It was either that or throw up.

"That's what all of this has been about," I yelled. "Hasn't it? You ... you just ... just wanting to justify your own behavior."

The lid was off my not not-very-tightly-screwed-on reservoir of self-righteous indignation.

"Yes, well, a part of me knew it was wrong."

I started to laugh. I wanted to yell more, scream, accuse, go all the way over the top. All I could do was laugh. Then, as if infected by me, she began. She stood up and put her arms around me. We laughed and sobbed and kissed each others' faces and held onto each other for dear life.

"What a fine couple we are," she said.

My assumption of amnesty was premature.

38

In spite of our embrace, I was still in exile. I slept—badly—on the futon in the den and rose with the sun. The cats showed up for breakfast by the time I had retrieved the daily paper. After a cup of coffee on the deck, I carried a pot of tea upstairs just as Kathy began to stir. She wore an old pair of cotton shorty pajamas, her hair was undone, she wore no makeup. A bittersweet feeling slid around me. She opened her eyes and smiled. The bitter went away.

I poured while she was in the bathroom and sat next to her while she drank. We avoided any mention of the previous night's conversation. I asked her if she wanted to go to find Marilyn Morgan with me.

"I was thinking a couple might be less threatening than a man alone showing up unannounced on her door step."

"You want to get me involved in this?" she said.

"You are involved in this, whether you want to be or not. They've involved you."

"Yes, well, I don't want to be, thank you. This is your mess."

I assumed that was the end of that and went down two flights to the basement gym, where I worked up a good sweat over the next half-hour. When I resurfaced, Kathy was on the phone in the living room.

"When was the last time you saw a doctor, Dad? ... Well, you're not dying.... Because I know you're not.... Dad. I'm not coming to Ohio now. Call your doctor if you're sick.... I don't know. I think I'll have some work up there soon. I'll come by.... No, Dad. For a day, maybe stay overnight.... I have a life, Dad, and it's not in Ohio.... Dad, I love you, but I have to go. I'll talk to you soon.... Yes, soon.

"Men," she said as she hung up the phone.

"Can't live with 'em..." I began.

"Don't tempt me." She wasn't smiling.

In the shower, I thought about what she must be going through. The two most important men in her life shared a penchant for self-destructiveness. Her father had been a serious drinker most of his adult life. It got out of control with the big stock-market downturn in the late '80s: he wrecked his car, broke a couple of ribs, and became addicted to the painkillers he was prescribed. When Kathy's mother died after a short, brutish battle with brain cancer, he seemed to give up entirely. Kathy wasn't sure if he quit his job or got fired, but pretty soon he was staying around the house all day, most of the time in his pajamas and bathrobe. Although he still drank some, he did get off the prescription drugs—only to replace them with a neurotic hypochondria. She told him, in no uncertain words, that she was tired of taking care of two boys.

I finished showering and dressing and found her on the deck, dressed in lightweight tan slacks and a white top embossed with spring flowers. Her feet were bare. I fixed a cup of coffee and joined her and the cats.

"You know," she said, "before Mom died, she told me she had often wished she and Dad had been more like partners instead of each having their own separate lives. Of course they did some things together, parenting, the club, that kind of thing, but he had his work and she had hers. They each handled their own money, had their own hobbies, hung around with their own circle of friends. She said it was the alcohol, of course. He was so often off in his own world."

Her gazed drifted off into the woods somewhere as she petted Wilbur who had graced her by hopping into her lap. I wondered where we were headed.

"So, I think I'll take you up on that offer to go see the woman," she said. "See how a real private detective works."

"We can take a shaker of martinis with us, pretend we're Nick and Nora Charles," I said, hoping to lighten her mood.

"We'd have to trade the cats for a dog, though, wouldn't we?"

"Okay. We'll just be us."

"When do you want to go?" she asked.

"I thought I'd call, and if an adult woman answers we'll just go on and hope she's alone. That the child who answered when I called before will be in school."

My cell phone rang before I could tap Marilyn's numbers into it. I didn't recognize the number.

"This is Bobby Headley," the familiar voice said after I'd said "Hello." "From out—"

"Yeah, Bobby. What's up?" I asked, assuming it was news about Pamela Mankin.

"I know it's a little early," he said, "but I just got a phone call from a guy looking for his lost dog in some woods above Leicester, near Little Sandy Creek. Know the area?"

"Vaguely."

"Guy came across something I thought you might find interesting. Got time to come out?"

"This is very mysterious, Bobby. Want to give me an idea what he found?"

"Oh, just come on. I'll meet you at the station."

I wondered if he was concerned about the security of the

phone call. I wondered if he'd found Pamela—or where she was. I wondered why I was about to go out there and check on someone else's missing adult child when I should have been trying to find whoever committed the murder I was charged with.

Which was Kathy's response when I told her we'd have to postpone our mission.

"I think," she said, "it has to do with the fact that whenever you're investigating the murder, you're forced to look at your own behavior and how you got into this mess. When you're out looking for this girl, you're just the good guy."

It didn't sound like an accusation, just an observation.

I was so lost in idle speculation about what some guy found that was so interesting but couldn't be mentioned on the phone that I almost passed the New Country Café. Fortunately, no one was close behind me when I hit my brakes and made the hard right into the parking lot. Taylor was behind the counter.

"Thanks for suggesting I talk to Bobby Headley," I said.

"Thought he might be helpful," she said. I stopped her from pouring the dark-roast into a mug. "To go, if that's okay. I'm on my way up to see him again right now." I laid two bills on the counter, and said to give my regards to Mickey.

Bobby and I loaded ourselves into his Cherokee and headed away from town.

"What's the big secret?" I asked.

"Oh, just wait."

Since it was clear we weren't going to talk about what we would find at our destination, I asked if he'd heard any more about Pamela Mankin. He said all he'd heard was that nobody was cooking, everybody was laying low. There was a lot of noise in Raleigh about the meth problem and law enforcement folks were being pressured to show some results in the war against it.

We turned onto Caney Fork Road and past a sign telling us we'd entered the Little Sandy Creek Community. Half a mile further along, a man was standing at the side of the road.

"That's our guy," Bobby said.

Bobby introduced him as Harold Snyder and me as an interested party. Harold directed us into the woods where we could see a trail of crushed foliage and undergrowth. Just as we lost sight of the road above, we saw red metal. There had been a half-hearted attempt to camouflage the small truck with brush and branches. It looked like whoever had done it had been in a big hurry or didn't much care.

"It's like I found it," Snyder said. "Haven't touched a thing. Just got close enough to make sure no one was inside. That's when I saw the blood."

It was all over, on the seat, the windshield, the floor. The license plate was gone from the back bumper. Bobby pointed out the VIN number on the dash.

"Now, how stupid is that," he said, "not scratching that out?"

"I always say," I said, "never overestimate the intelligence of your average miscreant. That's why most of them are miscreants. They can't figure out how to do anything right."

"Recognize it?" Bobby asked.

"The truck? I think so. It looks like the one I saw Jimmy Crawford driving," I said.

"How many times you seen it before?"

"Twice. Out at the club. Three times, actually. The first time, he was trying to run me off the road with it."

"Yeah. Well, it's his all right. Aren't many people out this way wouldn't know it."

I told him he ought to call Ted Henderson.

"He's honchoing the murder investigation," I said. "What

investigating they're doing, anyway. I get the idea that he'd like to be more aggressive, but someone's in his way."

"I'll tell him we'd been working on the Pamela Mankin case when Harold called me."

"How you going to explain why Harold called you and not them?"

"I know Henderson, too. He's no fool. Knows what people out here think about the law downtown. I don't think he'll give me any crap."

On the way back to the station house, Headley told me it was lucky this particular guy had come across the truck.

"Usually folks around here, they find something like that, they leave it. It's not their business. Besides, someday they might have to do the same thing. But this guy's a relative newcomer, only been out here ten years. He thought somebody ought to know about it."

"And why didn't he call the law?"

"Ten years is long enough to know that sometimes information gets lost over there. I called you because from the description of the truck, I thought it'd be something you'd be interested in. And I thought it might be helpful if the sheriff's boys knew that other people knew about it."

"I appreciate you thinking of me. I do think this should be good for my side. And maybe help Henderson. Assuming the blood is Debbie's, they'd have to prove I was driving Jimmy's truck that night, and then why wouldn't he have reported it stolen?"

"Maybe he has."

"That would be the smart thing to do, wouldn't it?"

I thanked him again and headed home. The clear sky of early morning was giving way to storm clouds, and it looked liked the weather was going to repeat itself again.

<h1 style="text-align:center">39</h1>

I called Kathy when I got back in the Explorer. By the time I got home, she had a thermos of coffee ready for our sortie to the eastern side of the county. She drove so I could drink. It was not yet ten o'clock.

We found the Riverview Mobile Home Court off the Swannanoa River Road. Fifty yards up a winding drive, the first of the manufactured homes was visible. At number twenty-eight, we pulled into a graveled parking space. The patches of grass in the yard were two weeks past a timely trimming. A wooden deck, its planks coming loose at the edges, struggled valiantly to glorify the front of the house. Kathy stood at my side as I knocked on the screen door.

The woman who opened it was attractive, thirty-something I guessed, dark hair hanging loosely to her shoulders. Under a white blouse, a good deal of cleavage was visible even through the screen. She was sausaged into a pair of jeans and holding a glass in one hand.

"Marilyn?" I said.

"Who's asking?" The odor of alcohol wafted out on the cool air escaping around her.

"I'm Rick Ryder," I said, holding out one of my private snoop cards. "This is my wife, Kathy. I'm investigating the murder of Debbie Douglass."

"Who?"

"The dancer at The Doll House who was murdered."

"Oh. Tiffani. Yeah?"

"Someone suggested it might be useful to talk to you."

She glanced at Kathy, then back at me.

"Who?"

"I was asked not to say."

A light rain began to fall. I hoped she'd ask us in.

"I've already talked to the cops."

"I'm not the cops. And I'm worried that more people might get hurt if they don't find who was behind Debbie's death."

"They got a guy."

"Yeah. But he didn't do it."

"How do you know?"

"Because that guy is me."

She sipped from her glass.

"Come on in," she said, turning for us to follow. It was just then that I noticed the cane in the non-drink-bearing hand. My stomach lurched. I wondered if Manetti was nearby.

As we followed her through the door, I had to look over to Kathy to keep my eyes off Marilyn's behind. Inside, she walked around the small peninsula counter separating the kitchen from the remainder of the open space, what I assumed would be called the living room.

"You want something to drink?"

Looking across the counter, I saw a one-time beauty whose looks had faded in the same way the outside of her home was deteriorating, getting rough around the edges. I wondered if she'd been a dancer, too. She pulled some ice cubes out of the freezer, plunked them into her glass, then hefted a half-gallon Jim Beam bottle off the counter top, pouring enough to cover the ice.

I could smell the whiskey, felt my throat tighten. Kathy and I declined the offer.

"I got Pepsi."

I shook my head. Kathy said she'd like one, although she never would have drunk the stuff in any other circumstances. Marilyn looked at the card I'd handed her.

"That's right," Marilyn said. "Guy's name is Ryder, supposed to have killed her. Anyway, Jessica's at work. That's what you want to know about, isn't it? About Jesse?"

"I don't know who Jesse is," I said, wondering if Jessica/Jesse might have been the young girl who answered the phone the first time I called.

Marilyn came back into the larger room using her cane to steady herself. She sat in an overstuffed arm chair, nodding toward a sofa where Kathy and I took our places.

"I'm Marilyn. I'm Jesse's mother." She looked straight at me, then to Kathy. I shivered. "And we've never had this conversation."

She closed her eyes against tears that were welling up.

"You don't know who you're dealing with," she said.

I was getting an idea.

"Manetti," I said, and she nodded. "I figured that out when I saw the business license in the office."

"When was that?"

"Yesterday. When I also saw you. I didn't put it together until I saw the cane just now."

She nodded at that but didn't say anything.

"Do you know why Debbie was killed?" I asked.

"Maybe she knew too much," she said, the words barely audible.

"About what?"

She'd been sipping her drink. She looked at the glass, then downed the rest.

"Sure you don't want one?"

"Very sure," I said, although if Kathy hadn't been there, it would have been tempting.

She levered herself up with the cane and disappeared down the hallway, returning with a VHS tape in her hand. She handed it to me and signaled to a combination DVD/VCR player. It was on a shelf underneath the TV set and I imagined it was hard for her to do the bending. I turned the set on and inserted the tape.

Snow appeared. I was afraid we were about to learn something it might not be safe to know. A moment later she said, "You can fast forward a little." I pushed the arrow on the remote. There was more snow before a stage appeared. Music came on. The lighting wasn't great, but we could see a girl come out of the wings. She appeared quite young, maybe middle teens.

"That's Jesse. You know her as Shari. For her Grandmother Sharon. The old lady wouldn't approve if she was still alive." She paused, then added, "She's fifteen there."

The girl was pretty, like her mother, developed early as I guessed her mother had. She began a standard kind of bump and grind, then took off a top, leaving a skimpy bra intact.

"Turn it off," Marilyn said. "You can imagine the rest." She wept. "Fifteen," she repeated.

I glanced at Kathy. She sat without expression. We didn't speak.

After a minute or so, Marilyn said, "I was a pretty good dancer back in the day. I could have gone to a bigger city, made my fame and fortune, but I was born here. I had friends and family. The family's all dead now. But back then..."

She told us the story of how she'd had Jesse when she was sixteen, living with her parents and waitressing.

"One day this guy comes up to me out at the county pool. Says he doesn't know what I do for a living or how much I make but he can guarantee five, ten times as much to dance at a club he owns. I knew I looked good, liked to go to the pool in little bikinis. I think Jesse was four or five. I was barely twenty."

I wondered about Jesse's father, but didn't say anything. None of my business.

"The truth is, I liked sex. How I got knocked up. Liking it a lot and not being careful."

She was up again and in the kitchen. I wished she wouldn't have another. Her words were getting mushy. As if she had heard me thinking, she slammed the glass on the counter.

"That's enough of that shit for a while."

I was surprised. When serious drinkers get on a roll, there's usually no stopping until they pass out or run out of booze and can't get any more. That's how it had been for me, anyway.

"When I thought about taking my clothes off in public, I got excited. There. Now you know that about me." She had the expression of a kid who has just shown off for company at her parents' direction. Knew she did it well, but was resentful that she had to.

She opened the freezer door, grabbed more ice and dropped it into the recently rejected vessel. So much for abstinence. She turned back to us.

"Long story short. I start dancing. Making good money. Hours suck. Can't have everything. I'm dancing for these people for like ten years. It gets old. Pretty quick, actually. They give you cocaine, help you cope, you know. Help you get out there and do it night after night and live with yourself knowing what you're doing with your life. The thrill is gone like that guy sings, who's that guy?"

"B.B. King?"

"Yeah. Him." She looked at me, eyes open wide like she was surprised I'd know something like that. Kathy's hand slid over next to me. I covered it with mine.

She repeated what Angi had told me about the company-store approach to drug dealing.

"I get into them big time, don't know how I'm gonna pay 'em off. Longo makes a deal. You let Jesse dance for some videos...." She trailed off again. She was still standing in the kitchen, talking over the counter. "You know, if the wrong people had seen that thing, DSS would have had her in a minute. Can you believe that shit? You make excuses for things if you're a dope fiend. God. I gotta get loaded whenever I think about it. This is child porn, you know. Then I find out it's all over the Internet. Can you believe that shit? Yes, I guess you can. And then, to top it off, I find out the asshole's screwing her. Oops, sorry, Mrs. Ryder. Ex-cuse my French."

Her words were thick. I was hoping she'd sit down again before she fell over.

"So, I go into his office one day, tell him he's got to cut that shit out, all of it, or I'm going to the cops. I know I'll lose custody of Jesse, but maybe they'll let my parents have her. Longo walks over to his desk, like he's going to get a piece of paper, or maybe pick up his phone. Instead, he opens the middle drawer, pulls out a pistol and shoots me in the fucking knee. You talk about being freaked out."

My jaw dropped. Kathy was sobbing next to me. I draped my arm over her shoulders.

"I am screaming at the top of my lungs. They call 911. He's got connections downtown. Tells them he was cleaning the gun and it accidentally went off. Tells me they'll take care of any hospital, doctor bills. Says he'll see what he can do about getting Jesse's pictures off the Web. So, in a way, I guess I won. But Jesus. So you better watch your ass, man. They're out to get you."

She dropped her head, looking into her glass as if answers to life's existential questions were suspended in the booze.

"How well do you know Manetti?" I asked.

A shrug. "Don't really. Just started coming around a couple

of weeks ago. He's one of the owners. I'd never seen him before. It used to be that Tom and me'd do the auditioning. I know what it takes to be good. Of course, anybody really good would be dancing somewhere else."

"I don't suppose you'd let me have the tape, or turn it over to the police, would you?"

The look she gave said, Are you nuts?

"Yeah, I thought so."

"I don't want Jesse to wind up in your fucking parking lot. Excuse me."

I stood up. Kathy followed.

"Thanks for showing us that. I know it can't be easy. But it does help me understand what's going on. If you think of anything else that might be helpful, call the cell number on that card."

She looked up at me. Her voice was slurred, whether from the booze or fear or sorrow. Or all three. "These are not nice people, you know?"

I nodded. "Yeah. I know."

We were almost out the door when I remembered something I'd hoped to find out. "Do you know the name of the club in Atlanta where Debbie used to dance?"

"Club Elegant."

Lightning flashed. The thunder that followed shook the trailer, like God's own exclamation point. I thanked her again. We let ourselves out and ran to the car in the steady rain.

"You know, you support this stuff," Kathy said, looking out the car window as she said it.

"I know. It's indefensible. I don't know what else I can say about it."

"Jesus! And I put up with it." She turned to face me head-on. "You can't do it anymore."

"I know that, too."

When I looked over again, her eyes were closed, her breathing heavy. I heard quiet sobs. I wished I had the words to fix everything, to make it all go away. On the way back to the house, we drove to a spot that looked out over the Swannanoa Valley. We sat for a few minutes and watched as the rain let up, leaving wisps of fog in its wake. Lightning flashed over the far mountains.

"How many more people do you think will get hurt before this is over?" she asked.

I thought of being run off the road and followed, about Angi winding up in ICU, the terror on Donna's face. I looked at my wife. Both of us had been threatened. The people whose job it was to find out what was going on weren't doing it. Indignation was shifting dangerously into outrage. In years past, I would have drunk myself through it. Now I had to think creatively.

"Time to go to Atlanta," I said.

40

I looked at her, prepared for another verbal assault. She looked ready to offer it.

"I know you're going to do whatever you think you have to do. There's no sense fighting you about it. I do wonder what you think you'll find there." Before I could say anything, she went on. "I know, I know. You go into a situation with an open mind so you don't distort things, don't try to make things confirm some prejudgment. Have I got that right?"

I nodded.

"Into the belly of the beast, the heart of darkness, that kind of thing," she said.

"I'll go to Club Elegant, stir the pot a little, see what comes to the surface."

She shook her head and rolled her eyes. When she started the car, she fiddled with the radio for a minute to get rid of the static, landing on a Brahms violin concerto.

"You said the roommate told you that Debbie'd had to do some pretty sleazy things," she said as she was pulling back onto the road. "Do you think the material she thought would protect her was like what we just saw?"

"Could be. Say it is. An underage girl stripping. Why would

someone kill her? Who would be implicated if it's just her on tape. If she accuses somebody of making it, it's just her word against his ... or hers ... or theirs."

"What if someone else was on the tape?"

I looked over at her, not sure what she was getting at.

"You mean, if there was more than one girl?"

"Unh uh."

"Oh. Like there's something other than dancing going on."

"Uh huh."

"That could be worth killing her over, I guess, depending on who the other party was."

"Or," she added, "parties."

It was hard to think about, the sordid world I'd supported.

"Maybe you should talk to the roommate again. Maybe Debbie left some clue about where the material is that Angi just hasn't remembered or thought about. Something the bad guys didn't find. Or, maybe, did."

"I don't think they did. They wouldn't have come after you," I said. Another epiphany lit up my brain. "Maybe that's what the break-in was about."

"Break-in?"

"Yeah. That day the alarm was messed with. They didn't come looking for a gun. They were looking for the mystery material. Thought maybe that's what was going on between Debbie and me, that Debbie'd found someone to hand the stuff off to. Finding the gun was a bonus. And they think I've still got whatever the other stuff is."

"The break-in happened before she was murdered, didn't it?"

"Maybe they were hoping to find whatever it was so they wouldn't have to kill her."

"So, why didn't they search her place before?"

"Maybe they did but did it clean, so they wouldn't arouse

suspicion. Then when they couldn't find it, they decided they had to get rid of her."

"Like that wouldn't arouse suspicion," Kathy said.

"Just thinking out loud here," I said, a touch defensively.

We rode without further conversation back toward home, my cell phone breaking the silence as we turned onto Cove Road.

Nate's name showed in the window. I pushed the button to take the call. It was the man himself.

"To what do I owe the honor?"

"Well, my pale friend, I understand you saw a red pickup truck out Leicester way."

I said I did.

"Way I hear it, some local found it, called the fire chief who called you. That right?"

I said it was.

"I'm sure there's a good story there, why they call the fire chief instead of law enforcement out there and why the chief calls you before he calls the law. At any rate, seems your prints are all over the thing. Along with the girl's and Crawford's. Crawford's of course you'd expect."

"My prints? How the hell would my prints get all over Jimmy Crawford's truck?"

"I think that's the same question Henderson's gonna want an answer for."

Silence mushroomed between us.

"Crawford saying anything?"

"Can't find him."

"Now there's a big surprise," I said.

"Bottom line is, now they have physical evidence linking you with the girl and, more importantly, linking you to her blood."

"They gonna lock me up again?"

"Don't think so, but this sure feeds into their story. If Henderson was at all interested in finding somebody besides you for the killer, this doesn't make it easy for him. One good thing my friend in forensics tells me is that Jimmy's prints on the steering wheel seem to be as fresh as yours that are mostly on the shotgun side."

"So, I wasn't driving."

"Might be able to make a case, although I'm not sure how much good it does you."

"Jimmy did it," I said.

"Doesn't seem unreasonable. But if he did, there aren't any witnesses available. You were in a blackout, Debbie's ... well ... and Jimmy's gone AWOL."

"If I was in the truck, how'd I get to my car?"

"After you shot the girl, Jimmy drove you back to The Doll House."

"Quit it, Nate."

"Just trying to think like the DA. And it's really not all that bad. Still nothing to convince anybody you were the shooter. And Jimmy was the guy making the accusations against you. If the bad guys disappeared him, I'd say they're getting nervous about this thing. If they're nervous, they're likely to do something stupid."

"Like, decide I'm dispensable now?"

"Maybe. Anyway, you probably need to stay on high alert. And I wouldn't be surprised if the cops want to talk to you again."

I thanked him for the heads up. I couldn't tell him I was planning on going out of the state and might not be available if anyone came looking for me. After hanging up, I filled Kathy in on the side of the conversation she hadn't heard.

"If someone calls and says they need to see me again downtown, think you can come up with some cover for why it might be the next day before I can appear?"

"I've been living with you long enough to come up with some lawyer-like song and dance to put them off. 'I'm sorry, Mr. Ryder is indisposed.' Something like that."

"And keep your eyes out for a green Buick," I added as we pulled into the driveway.

41

There were two messages on the machine when we walked into the house. The first was from Dee Dee Mankin, asking me to call. Her voice had that "why-don't-you-come-see-me-sometime" tone to it.

"She sounds friendly," Kathy said.

"Yeah. You know how the one-armed thing gets the girls."

She smacked me on said arm.

"Better be careful, brother, or you'll be missing both of them. Then see what the girls think."

The next call was from her father. The usual. "What am I going to do with him?" she asked after she'd hung up.

"What you're doing, I guess. I live with one arm. You live with a neurotic father. Our crosses."

"Yeah, but you brought yours on yourself. I inherited mine."

"The universe is not fair, dear."

"Oh, shut up. Aren't you going to Atlanta?"

"Yeah, but I don't want to get to the Club Elegant too early. I want there to be a big enough crowd that I don't stand out."

"Oh, yeah. I'm sure there's a good time of day for one-armed guys to be inconspicuous."

I gave her a look. She smiled. She put a PB&J sandwich, an

apple, and a bottle of water in a small cooler. I hoped our full-bodied embrace at the door was an intimation of things to come.

Before leaving the area, I had some time to investigate my whereabouts during the sixteen hours that had failed to imprint on my memory. My first stop was Jackson's Sports Bar.

As soon as I pulled into the parking lot, my hand got sweaty and my stomach began churning. I called my sponsor.

"Jim. I'm about to go into Jackson's, the place where I began my drinking the night before the dancer got killer."

"And which led to a blackout."

"Yeah, that too. I got sick as soon as I pulled into the lot."

"You want someone to be with you when you go in there?"

"No. I'll be all right. But I did want to tell someone what I was up to. I'll call again when I leave."

"Good plan, Rick. Thanks for calling."

The bartender looked familiar. He reached under the bar for something before heading my way.

"I wondered when you'd come back."

"You remember me?"

"You do have sort of a distinguishing characteristic," he said. He held up a set of keys. "These yours?"

That solved that mystery.

"Thanks," I said, pocketing them. "Okay," I said, "Just tell me what happened."

According to the barkeep, I'd drunk beer steadily until mid-afternoon when I told him I was ready to settle up.

"You guys with a lot of tolerance can look pretty good," he said, "but your reaction time's still gonna be shot. You'd never have passed a Breathalyzer test. I said I'd call you a cab. Like every drunk, you argued. I told you if you didn't give me your keys, I was going to call the police and make sure they were waiting for you outside the in parking lot. You said go ahead and call the cab."

"What cab company?"

He told me. I wondered when I had come back to retrieve my car.

"We've got security cameras out there in the lot. Triple A Security's got the tapes."

I wasn't sure what good it had done, but it felt like progress. At least I had my keys back. Although they wouldn't do me much good without a car and no office to get into. I called Nate and told him what the barman said. He'd get Dom to go over to Triple A and check what they had. My next stop was AA Blue Sky Cab Company where I asked the woman in the office if she could check her records for that Saturday.

"Rick Ryder," she said, thumbing through a stack of logs. "Picked you up at Jackson's at fourteen fifty-eight—that'd be two fifty-eight civilian time—took you to the liquor store on Charlotte Street, then took you out to Cove Road."

The mystery of where the scotch came from was solved. But that was mid-afternoon. I'd reportedly been at The Doll House much later, leaving a huge chunk of time unaccounted for.

I was about to thank the woman when she said, "And then we picked you up at your place at twenty-three twenty-two—that'd be..."

"...eleven twenty-two."

"Yeah. And took you out to The Doll House."

I could detect no editorializing in her voice. They did this stuff all the time.

"Can you see when you came back for me?"

"Doesn't look like we did. But we're not the only cab company in town."

I was getting a picture of Saturday. It was still blurred and had empty spaces in it, like a Polaroid picture still developing.

I couldn't see the Buick when I left the cab stand. I took precautions anyway. At a municipal parking lot I got my ticket from the machine that raised the gate, pulled into the first open space, and waited. After five minutes, I pulled out, drove to the exit, paid my fifty cents and headed toward the self-proclaimed "Athens of the South." I thought about what the late Woody Hayes, staunch proponent of the grind-it-out game of football at Ohio State, is reported to have said when asked why he didn't use the forward pass more often. There are only three things that can happen when you pass, he'd said, and two of them are bad. I wondered if that characterized the possible outcomes of my visit to Georgia.

42

I drove southwest, picking up US 441 through Franklin. When I got to I-85 I let the onboard GPS guide me into Atlanta. By three-forty-five, I'd found a parking space along the curb, twenty yards or so past the green canopy marking Club Elegant's main entrance. Like The Doll House, it proclaimed itself a Gentlemen's Club, albeit the slick city cousin to its hick country relative. There was a smaller canopy to my left. I asked the doorman, a vaguely Slavic-looking hulk, what the other door was.

"B-I-P."

"BIP?"

"B-I-P," he repeated, emphasizing each letter.

I caught on. "Oh. VIP."

He nodded.

"What goes on there?"

"Reservations. Special groups." His accent brought to mind Katrina in Nate's office.

The place was huge, of a scale of magnitude as different from The Doll House as Atlanta itself was to our mountain town, with a cover charge to match. Tables were arrayed facing one of three stages, although the one at the front of the room was, by location and lighting, clearly the main stage. The tables were about a third full. Two dancers performed on each stage. Along one side of the room were curtained booths for more private "dances," and there was a bar along the opposite side on which two more girls danced while a half-dozen or so did lap dances. The music was some decibels louder than the last rock concert I'd been to. In the big city, rap seemed to have gained supremacy over the heavy metal and country most of the girls danced to back home. It was oppressive. The girls were working very hard. The preponderantly male audience was working just as hard to enjoy it.

Maneuvering through the labyrinth of tables, I made my way to the far side of the room and a stool at the nearest end of the long bar. After sitting for a couple of minutes, occasionally glancing at the body undulating above me, I spoke to the man on my left. In my limited experience, people at the bar in these places tended to be regulars, the novices or visitors being more likely to immerse themselves in all the possibilities provided by a table.

"Excuse me," I said, leaning toward him.

He looked at me without expression.

"Do you know when Tiffani dances?" I heard myself yelling over a bass line loud enough for deaf people to hear in their bones.

He shrugged. "Haven't seen her for a while."

"How long a while?"

"Few weeks. Someone said she left town."

The barmaid finally made her way to me, prettier than the dancer, reminding me of Donna back at The Doll House.

"What'llitbe?"

"Coca-Cola," I said, thinking to say, "water on the side," just to be a smart ass, but instead asked, "What happened to Tiffani?"

"Quit," she said, turning to get a glass, fill it with ice and spray my drink into it.

"You know why?" I asked when she deposited it in front of me. She shrugged and headed back down the bar. I turned my attention to the stripper, now naked except for long, sheer, black stockings into the tops of which folding money could be deposited. We made eye contact. I moved my head in a "come on down here" motion. She sidled my way. When she was directly in front of me, she lay sideways and raised one leg. Maybe if there weren't scores of people around, if we were at our own table, if the music weren't pounding me toward the edge of consciousness, it would have been arousing. I slipped a five dollar bill into her stocking and, raising my voice so she could hear me over the din, said, "LET ME BUY YOU A DRINK WHEN YOUR SET IS OVER." She smiled. I took it for affirmation.

She had a fine body. Mid-twenties I guessed, although it was hard to tell anymore, given the miracles of modern medicine. When the music stopped, she came down to my end of the bar.

"Be back in a minute, Sugar," she said.

Five minutes later, she was next to me in a G-string, halter, and short opaque robe. The barmaid was there promptly with a drink for the dancer and another Coke, unrequested, for me. I gave her a ten. It occurred to me I could ask if she knew a Pamela Mankin so I could charge it all off to Dee Dee, but decided I was ethically compromised enough as it was.

"Thanks, Sugar," the dancer said.

"What's your name?"

"Nicki."

"How long you been a dancer here, Nicki?"

"Coupla' months."

She was wearing too much make-up. Her eyes had the sunken, colorless appearance of a heavy drug user, the Kate Moss-heroin-addict look, all the rage among fashion models some time back. I guessed Nicki wasn't faking it. She looked tired, and it wasn't yet six o'clock. If I'd had some cocaine, she'd have followed me anywhere.

"Did you know Debbie, girl who danced as Tiffani?"

Her nod was almost imperceptible. I thought I saw fear in her dark, sad eyes.

"What happened to her?"

Her glance came at me at an angle. She shrugged, looked away and said, "I don't know."

"Who does?"

"You the cops?"

"Why would the cops be asking?"

She shrugged again.

"Would the guy who owns the place know where she went?"

"Arnie?"

"That the owner's name?"

"Yeah. Good luck seeing him."

"Why's that?"

"He doesn't talk to people. He has people who talk to people."

The barmaid came back and held up Nicki's glass.

"Buy me a drink or I gotta go," Nikki said.

"Okay. Nice talking to you. You do a nice show."

She worked up a sleepy smile and walked toward the nearest tables, hawking her wares. Two different girls had taken over the bar, strutting their stuff. I felt tired and sad, like Nicki looked. I thought about spending more money to talk to some more girls, but I knew I'd get the same answers. Either nobody knew what happened to Debbie or wouldn't tell. The end product was the same. The place was smoke-free, and I hadn't had a cigarette in years, but it was all I could think of. A cigarette. And a glass of scotch. It was time to go.

I was almost to the door when a big, rednecky kind of guy, blond, well over six feet, wearing a dark suit that didn't quite fit, dark blue shirt, and shiny blue tie came along beside me. A good ol' boy trying out for gangster.

"You been asking' questions," he said. I looked at him. He

looked vaguely familiar in the dim light. Maybe it was just the type I recognized.

"Yeah. I was looking for Tiffani."

"Tiffani don't work here no more."

"So I hear. I was wondering if anybody knew where she went."

"And who are you?"

It was the voice that did it. The same voice that had told me I was trespassing in the national forest. I wondered if he'd figured out who I was. I squinted, trying to see more clearly.

"Marlowe," I said. "Philip Marlowe."

"Why you lookin' for her, Marlowe?"

"I saw her dance a couple of times. Really good. I was hoping to see her again."

The Russian bouncer was now on his way over, not quite bounding, but moving quickly.

My inquisitor said, "Yuri, why don't you walk Mr. Marlowe here to the door. He's decided he's seen enough pussy for one night."

As we approached the entrance, my gut churned. I didn't see my whole life flash in front of my eyes, but the image of Debbie lying naked on the pavement lit up in my brain.

The late afternoon light cast deep shadows in front of the club. The door to the VIP room was set back a few feet from the door I'd just been hustled out of. My arm bent behind me, I was led into a crook in the wall that was shielded from view of the street. He landed one blow to my solar plexus, doubling me over. When the next one didn't come, I struggled to lift my head.

Yuri's attention had shifted to a black limousine pulling up to the VIP canopy. It had the rounded edges of a Lincoln. The limo driver came around to the rear passenger door. I wanted to call out, but my voice wouldn't work. We both watched the car. A passenger got out and walked under the green entrance cover. He also looked familiar. Very familiar. I groaned silently as I stretched to a standing position. I thought I might pass out. I sucked air and forced myself to exhale.

"Senator."

It was a breathless call that I doubted would be heard. The man looked toward me.

"Senator Simmons!" I called again, louder.

He kept walking toward the building. I grimaced with each breath. With Yuri distracted, I twisted sideways, sliding my left foot behind my right, pulling my arm straight down, then up, breaking his grasp and slamming him in the face in one motion. I drove my elbow into his gut. He doubled over. Holding my rib cage, I jogged to the car. I looked back when I was behind the steering wheel. Yuri was on his knees. The senator was out of sight.

<h1 style="text-align:center">43</h1>

I hadn't driven so fast since I was a teenager throwing an old VW bug around the back roads of central Ohio, trying to impress girls. When I sat erect, my bruised midsection howled. Deep inhalations that would calm me down made me nauseous. Five minutes away from Club Elegant, convinced no one was following, I pulled over and retrieved my cell phone from my pants pocket. I'd missed two calls. I ignored them and called my sponsor. The tremor in my hands made it hard to hit the little buttons.

I gave him the Cliffs-Notes summary of the afternoon.

"Are you safe, physically?"

"I think so."

"Do you want a drink?"

"No. But I didn't think I wanted a drink when I went in the bar last Saturday morning."

"What do you need to do?"

"What I'm doing, talking to you."

"Do you want me to talk you back up the mountain?"

"No, I think I'll be okay now. I'll call again if I get squirrely."

I didn't want a drink, but if there had been someone waiting in my car holding a glass of Johnny Walker when I escaped Yuri's clutches, I probably would have taken it. I wasn't cured yet. I did believe, however, that caffeine would be life-sustaining. I came across the Jumping Bean Café, got a triple latte and directions for getting out of town.

Back in the SUV I checked the missed phone calls. One was from the office, the other from a number I didn't recognize.

The office was closed but Zella was still at work. I cut her off in mid-greeting.

"It's me."

"Where are you?"

"Just leaving Atlanta."

"I won't even ask," she said. "Jay quit this morning. Just left a message on the answering machine saying he had a conflict of interest and had to resign. I called his home and cell phone when I got in and there was no answer on either."

"Making a propaganda movie for the timber industry would be a conflict of interest."

"You said they went to this character Manetti for financing? Wouldn't the timber industry fund something like that themselves?"

"Maybe Manetti is the timber industry."

"I don't get it. I thought he was The Doll House."

The image of the Lincoln limo pulling up outside Manetti's office appeared in my still-foggy brain, right alongside the one of a limo disgorging the senator at Club Elegant. Maybe I wasn't just paranoid; maybe they were all out to get me.

"There's a connection," I said. "But I still have a hard time believing that my intuition about Jay was that far off when we first took him on."

When she didn't say anything, I asked, "Any more overtures from MTM?"

"Nothing. I think they're waiting to see what happens next."

"Who's going to do the work with both Jay and me gone?"

I imagined she might ask me to come back.

"I just talked to Stephen Carlyle, you know, with Boyce Carlyle Boyce? He's going to do some pro bono for us. We'll be able to keep up with what's on our plate, but we won't be able to take on anything new."

"I know him," I said, ego deflated, knowing someone could just step in like that. "Here's something else you might find interesting. Senator Malcolm Simmons was arriving at Club Elegant just as I was leaving. Under other circumstances—like me not being a murder suspect—I might have thought nothing about it. I understand about going to such places. Why would a senator be different? Except, of course, he makes a big goddamn deal about being a pious church-going family man. The limo he was in looked just like the one I saw pull up to Tim Manetti's office the last time I was there."

"What do you make of that?"

"Not sure. Pieces of the puzzle—Manetti, The Doll House, Senator Simmons. Jay. I just have to figure out how they fit together. Maybe I'll get enlightenment on the way home."

I reached Kathy next and told her I'd gotten some information I thought was useful and I'd tell her all about it when I got home. I skipped the part about the assault.

"Was it worth the trip?"

"Yes, I believe it was."

I stayed on the interstates and used cruise control, thankful that function was on the steering wheel. My thoughts wandered, making it hard to keep my attention on the road. I tried to focus on one thread at a time, but it kept unraveling. I gave up and put some old Delbert McClinton rockabilly on the stereo. A few miles from the North Carolina-South Carolina border, the phone buzzed. I let it go to voicemail.

The sun had fallen behind the Blue Ridge Mountains ahead

of me, leaving a copper glow in its wake. For a few seconds I was able to forget what was happening in my life. I pulled into the rest stop just over the state line, lifted the phone from its cradle on the console and looked in the caller ID window. Another number I didn't recognize. There was no message.

44

My Personal Standard Operating Procedure was to ignore callers who didn't have the inclination to leave any information. Especially people the phone didn't recognize. But these were not PSOP times.

I pushed the recall button, announcing myself after the woman said, "Hello."

"This is Donna Pavone, Mr. Ryder ... from the—"

"Yes, Donna."

"I need to talk to you."

I hesitated. I thought about a set-up, but something in her voice suggested real urgency, not something made up.

"Okay," I said.

"Are they still following you?"

"From time to time. I can lose them if I have to."

"You know Devil John's tattoo parlor on Merrimon? Across from that pizza place?"

"I've seen it."

"Park in back and go in the back door. I'll be in the back room."

"When?"

"Now."

I said I could be there in twenty minutes, thirty if I thought someone was on my tail. I called Kathy, told her I was in the area and where I was going.

"Do you think it's safe?"

"Safety's relative. But yes. I do. Although I do wish I had my gun."

She admonished me to be careful. I told her to call Henderson if she didn't hear from me in a couple of hours. She said that wasn't reassuring.

I didn't think I was being followed but dodged around the neighborhoods bordering Merrimon just in case. The parlor was in a building with two other businesses at street level and offices or apartments above. There were three other cars in the small lot behind the building. A light shone above Devil John's back door. I opened it and stepped inside. It was like the sitting room of a gypsy fortune teller without the magic ball. Oriental rugs, beads, small lamps, incense. When my eyes adjusted to the light, I saw Donna, a man, and another woman.

"Rick," Donna said as the man stood, "this is John."

We shook. The man was wearing jeans and a tank top and had artwork inked onto every exposed part of his body except his face. I nodded.

"And this is Babe. Real name is Helen, but everybody calls her Babe." She was garbed similarly to the man, and almost as tatted. I nodded again.

They said it was nice to meet me and disappeared through a beaded curtain.

"They're my only friends in the world." She had on jeans and a tube top, eye-catching in spite of appearing tired in the dim light. I wanted to hold her. "They'll kill me if they know I've talked to you."

I presumed she was not referring to her friends and that she was not exaggerating for effect. I nodded again. She took a deep breath and waved her hand in the direction of an overstuffed armchair. I sat. The incense almost masked the smell of whiskey wafting off the bottle of Wild Turkey sitting on a small table next to her. She had a half-full glass in her hand and took sips as she talked.

"Jimmy's dead."

If I'd had dentures, they'd have fallen out.

"The police were out to the club a couple of hours ago. That's why I needed to talk."

I had too many questions and didn't know where to start.

"Found him out along Sandy Branch."

"Do they know when he was killed? Shot, I presume."

"Yes. Yes and no. Yes, he was shot. That medical guy?"

"Medical Examiner?"

"Yeah, him, he's working out when he was killed."

Whenever it was, I sure hoped my alibi was airtight. Ice cubes clanked as she sipped from her drink.

"I told you before that you were out at the club the night Debbie was killed," she continued. "I didn't tell you that about one o'clock, I was standing outside the back door, having a smoke, when you and Debbie and Jimmy came out. You all got into his truck. Manetti came out before you'd all driven off and saw me. He told me I hadn't seen anything, that as far as I knew Debbie left alone."

She looked around the room.

"You want something to drink, a beer...? Oh, that's right, you don't drink. First person I ever met sat at a bar and didn't drink. Coke?"

I shook my head. "I'm fine."

"So anyway," she went on, "later, after closing, Tom and Manetti and a couple of friends of theirs are sitting at the bar as I'm cleaning up. I tried to hear without them thinking I was listening, you know. I heard them laugh. One of them says, 'It's like he just falls out of the sky whenever we need him. First he shows up, makes goo-ga over her, makes plans to meet her, for Christ sake, then just when we need to finish this thing, he shows up again.' I got cold when he said 'finish this thing.' I knew without them saying what they were talking about."

"Killing Debbie," I said.

Her head dropped and she nodded. I had to fight to stay composed.

"Why are you telling me this now?"

"There's more," she said. I let her go on.

"When I finished cleaning up, I poured a drink and sat on the stool behind the bar kind of off to the side but where I could still hear. They don't pay me no attention anymore. There was a time ... well, that's not important. Anyway, pretty soon the mood seems to change. Tom's like, 'Where is that asshole, we should have heard from him by now.' Manetti's kind of quiet. Then Tom's cell goes off. He's like, 'Where the fuck you been, it's about fuckin' time,' you know, real pissed. Then he says, 'You what?' Almost screams it. Says he'll be out and for him to stay off the road. Says, 'Don't let anyone see you.' He turns to Manetti and says, 'That asshole's made a fucking mess, man. Now I gotta go get him.' He gets up off his stool and says to Manetti, 'You comin' with?' Manetti looks over at me like he'd been hoping for a chance to be alone with me but says, yeah, he'll go along. Then Tom says to me, don't forget to turn the lights out, just kind of to remind me he's in fucking charge."

"Why didn't you tell me this before?"

"I was afraid."

"Why tell me now?"

"Because there's two people dead now. Angi's in the hospital. I decided I don't really care what they do to me. You saw Marilyn, she told me, figured it was me gave you her name. So I'm probably gonna have to leave. Like leave town. Although, they found Debbie, didn't they?"

I felt a chill at the implication for her. I wondered how much bourbon she'd had.

"Be careful," I said.

She nodded. "They must've killed Debbie and Jimmy both, and now…" her voice trailed off.

"No. I think Jimmy killed Debbie and they had to go pick him up so he could get rid of his truck. And he probably began freaking out when I showed up at The Doll House asking questions. So, they had to…" I trailed off.

"Get rid of him," she said. "You might be next."

"Better keep my head low," I said, trying to sound casual, knowing she was right. I was about to go out the door before I thought to ask, "Did you ever meet my colleague Jay McIntyre?"

Donna said the name didn't mean anything. I thanked her and headed home.

45

Turning onto Cove Road, I heard a loud pop at the same time the passenger window burst and pain seared my shoulder. My hand came off the steering wheel and the SUV continued on its left turn course, cutting off a car headed towards me, coming to rest on the far shoulder. Looking back and to my right to see where the shot came from, I saw a dark car drive away. The driver of the car I'd almost collided with had stopped and was walking over to me.

"What happened, man? I thought I was going to eat my lunch there." Before I could say anything he added, "You're Rick, aren't you. Rick Ryder? I'm Andy Molinaro, moved in a few houses down from you a couple of months ago."

His face was familiar.

"I almost hit a deer," I said, hoping the blasted out window and scattered glass shards wouldn't be visible in the dark. "Didn't see you coming and just aimed this way. Sorry."

"No, it's okay. Scared the shit out of me, but it's okay. Really. Those deer, man. I've hit two of them since I moved here. You're lucky."

"I guess."

"You sure you're okay. You seem pretty shook up."

"I'll be all right. Just gotta get my breath back."

It felt like a flesh wound, but my shoulder was screaming, as if someone had dragged a burning ember across it. There was no blood as far as I could tell. If the shot had come a split second sooner it would have landed just above my heart. I didn't want to tell this guy I'd been shot. That would require some explaining I didn't want to get into with a stranger—or with the police, for that matter.

"Thanks for stopping, Andy. Sorry to scare you."

He held out his hand. I cringed when I lifted mine.

"Don't worry about it," he said.

Easy for him to say.

I let myself in the house quietly. There was a pile of blankets on the bed, in which I assumed my wife was ensconced. I went into the bathroom and shut the door. In the mirror I saw that blood had soaked through the shoulder of my shirt. I took it off. I could see where the bullet had grazed me just below the top of the shoulder. A flesh wound, as I thought. It hurt like hell and I wouldn't be able to dress it myself.

"Rick?"

"Yeah?"

"You okay?"

"Yeah. I got a ... nick on my shoulder. I'm gonna need some help."

I heard her rustling around before coming to the door.

"Oh my God!"

"It's not as bad as it looks. Really. Just messy."

"What happened?" she asked, sounding truly intrigued.

I wanted to come up with a good alternate explanation, knowing that the idea of me being shot would freak her out. Nothing came. And I'd have to tell her sooner or later. I told her.

"Shot? Shot!? What the hell?"

"I figure they I.D.'d me at the club and the guy'd been waiting for me to return home. Could have been there for hours, just sitting."

"I thought they couldn't kill you because then they'd have to do a real investigation. Isn't that what you've been saying?"

"I think I raised the stakes."

"You going to call the police?"

"No. Then I'd have to explain what I'd been doing, like going to Atlanta. Where I shouldn't have been."

She returned to bed after treating and wrapping the wound. I was headed for the door to take my place on the futon downstairs, when she called.

"Come to bed." My heart fell open. "Hold me," she said when I stretched alongside her.

"I don't think I can," I grumbled, my arm still too painful to lift. So she held me.

I woke to daylight and stayed spooning with her until I could no longer put off nature's call. When I returned, she said, "Come here." I believe the term for what transpired next is 'make-up sex.' Apparently, I'd been let out of the doghouse.

We were having our coffee and tea on the deck when the phone rang.

46

Thought you might want to know a SWAT team is gonna descend on that Jackson's Branch property we looked at."

I recognized the voice this time.

"When?"

"Later this morning."

"How come you know about it?" I asked. Before he could answer, I said, "Never mind. You think they'll be out there, the kids I mean?"

"Depends on who else knows what's comin' down. Neighbors started smelling it. Called the sheriff. My guess is, the law'll be out there about ten or so. Takes 'em a while to get all their shit together, know what I mean?"

"So, I might have time to get to Pamela—assuming she's there—before the law?"

"Might. I'd be glad to go up with you, you want some backup. If they are cookin', they're gonna be pretty freaked out, hyper-vigilant."

"But if we show up, won't it tip them off to the law coming?"

"They'll probably think we're it, won't expect anybody else to come along. That's what I figure. You got a gun?"

"Had one, don't anymore."

"I think I've got one you can have for the time being."

He said he'd meet me at the station in twenty minutes.

When I looked at Kathy, she said, "What?"

"I'm going out to Leicester. Bobby Headley thinks the kids are at the house." I didn't tell her about the SWAT team or the gun.

"You look pretty freaked out."

"Well, she might not be happy to see me," I said, hoping Kathy would take that as a reasonable explanation for why I appeared unnerved.

"Will you call the hospital and see if Angi's still there, or if she's gone, try to wheedle a home number out of them?"

My shoulder stung like I'd been hit with a swarm of yellow jackets. In the garage I swept remnants of the exploded window out of the front seat of the Ford, figuring I might have a passenger soon. A grin crept onto my face when I pictured making the walk-around of the vehicle when I returned it to the rental agency, saying something like, "Yeah, this is the kind of thing that happens when you rent to one-armed guys."

"We're gonna go on up Shady Cove," Chief Headley said when I got to the fire station, "on up to where it swings around, almost parallel to Jackson's Branch. We'll come on back down through the woods."

He drove his Jeep and I followed in the rented SUV. When we got close, the smell descended on us like a weight. I thought I might puke and wondered if the people making the stuff got used to it or were just too stoned to notice.

I pulled up behind him as we parked on the gravel road. He walked back to me carrying two guns.

"Got a preference?" I took the one that looked just like mine. I stuck it in my waistband, like you see in the movies. I didn't know where else to put it.

"If we can get her away from them, you bring her on back and get her out of here."

We headed for the trees. From the way he moved in the undergrowth, it was apparent he spent a lot of time in the woods. I followed close.

"We're gonna come in on the side of the house. You see if you can get in that bedroom window, I'll slide around to the front."

My heart beat like it had when I was running from Club Elegant. Seemed like I'd been doing a lot of that. Having been beaten and shot in the past twenty-four, I wondered how sore I'd be trying to climb through a window. Some life for a lawyer, I reflected wryly.

We stopped when we could see the house through the trees. He drew a zipper across his lips and we split up when we cleared the tree line. I moved in a crouch toward the window, feeling the ache from yesterday's gut-punch. He disappeared from view. I had no idea how I'd get in. Would there be a screen? Would the window be locked? Would there be someone waiting with a gun on the inside?

As I got closer, I saw there was a screen lying on the ground, bent out of shape. Someone had done this trick before me. The window was open. It wasn't standard twenty-first-century construction and it would be a tight fit for me. Up close, I saw the girl, lying on the mattress, wearing a T-shirt and panties. She was smaller than I expected, staring at a TV screen. The room looked as it had the other day, maybe marginally less trashed.

I took a chance and knocked gently on the window frame. It took a couple of tries before she looked in my direction. I had my finger to my lips, like I was bringing her into a conspiracy, then signaled for her to come to me. She hesitated. I got more insistent. She looked toward the bedroom door. I shook my head vigorously, now waving her toward me with my whole hand. She got up and came my way.

When she got to the window, I handed her my Mountain Center I.D. card, hoping it looked official enough to keep her attention. I stuck my head in and waved her closer with my fingers. I got my mouth close to her ear.

"The cops are coming."

She leaned back and looked at me as if I'd spoken in a foreign language.

I mouthed it again. The cops are coming, and then kept waving her toward me, hoping she'd get the idea and come out the window. From the vapid expression on her face, I could tell she'd been doing some kind of downers, maybe to counter the effects of the crank they were cooking. She instinctively pulled back when I put an arm through the window frame. I mouthed, come on, come on. She looked back at the door one more time, then leaned her head out. I pulled her toward me, trying to get her weight against me. Although she was probably five-five or six, she felt tiny. I leaned back as she came on through, then fell all the way back, serving as a cushion for her. We lay there for some seconds before I rolled her off, wondering what had happened to Bobby. When I looked up, he was standing almost over me, a scrawny kid next to him. The business end of a Smith & Wesson handgun was lodged against the kid's side.

"Here's the deal," he said to the girl. "You go with Rick, back to your mama's, or you stay here and get busted along with your buddies. You're lookin' at multiple felonies, serious time."

I stood up. I assumed her tininess was due to using hard-core speed and not eating much. She looked at least twenty pounds underweight. Her hair was dirty, although the shirt seemed clean. Underneath the grime was a pretty girl, probably a lot like her mother looked at that age. I wanted to get her some pants before we left but knew we didn't have time for that. It didn't seem to bother her.

"What are you going to do?" I asked Headley.

"I'll just wait here with my man—what's your name?"

"None o' your fuckin' business."

"Nice lad. I actually think he's one of the Williamson kids, Webster, isn't it? Webster Williamson. A kid could go far with a name like that, don'tcha think, Rick?"

The kid sneered at us.

"So we'll just hang out 'til the rest of them get here, and then we'll get the cook. You better get goin', they'll be here soon. You just keep on goin' out Shady Cove, and it'll bring you to Upland Road. Hang a left, and you'll get back to the highway."

The girl said nothing as we trudged back up to the car. Inside, I said, "You're lucky, you know. I don't know why he decided you shouldn't be busted with the others." She stayed mute. As I put the car in gear, we could hear a helicopter overhead.

She had not said a word by the time we got to her mother's house. Dee Dee, puttering in her immaculate yard as we pulled up, became hysterical.

"Oh, my God. Oh, my baby, Oh, let me look at you.... Where are your pants? Oh, my God, go inside. Aren't you embarrassed?"

I wanted to smack her.

"Oh, Mr. Ryder. How can I ever thank you?"

I thought it was an interesting question, since she'd already paid me.

"Give her a break," I said. I wanted to say, She's your daughter, not your clone.

Before getting in the car, I turned on the volume on my cell phone and checked for messages. There was one from the same unknown number from before.

"Hi." It was Angi's voice. "I think I might know where the ... stuff is. Call me. Oh, and a guy named Jay came by. He said he worked with you. He asked about the murder and why I got beat up, that stuff. He didn't want me to tell you, but...." There was a little crackling sound and then nothing.

I pushed the button to return the call and was advised that number was no longer in service. What the devil was Jay doing talking to Angi, I wondered. How did he even know who she was? Or where she was? Then I remembered, he was in training as an investigator. He knew how to find things out. I must have been doing a good job with him.

At the Country Café, I sat in the parking lot and called Kathy.

"We got her," I announced when she answered. "I guess I've done my good deed, although she wasn't happy about going home."

"It was the mother who was paying you, wasn't it? Not the daughter."

"Yeah. Still. But I think she'll avoid prison for the time being, and that's a good thing. On the other hand, I had a disturbing call from Angi."

After I'd related the gist of it, she said, "I think we need to go see her."

"I think you're right. I'm going to stick my head in the café and thank Mickey and Taylor for their help with the Mankin girl, should be home in twenty minutes."

"You look like you just won the lottery," Taylor said, as I strode through the door and approached the counter.

"Just as good. I got Pamela Mankin back home, thanks to your help."

"That calls for a celebration," she said. "What's your poison?"

"How 'bout a double latte? To go. The bad guys never rest. We gotta keep up."

I thought I should have been happier driving home. I'd just rescued a young woman. She undoubtedly would have served prison time given her prior drug arrests. But I knew life with mother would be as much of a challenge for her as life in lock-up. It might just be a matter of time before she took off again. And Dee Dee would still be clueless about what went wrong.

As I approached Cove Road, I realized I still had Bobby Headley's gun stuck in my pants. I thought about Angi and Jay.

47

When I came onto the deck, Kathy was dressed in blue jeans, a plain pullover, and tennis shoes, a set of keys resting on the table in front of her. She was smoking a cigarette, a habit that aggravated me, not because of the smoking itself, but because she was able to smoke one or two or no cigarettes a day. I couldn't. I'd tried, often, and within a week I would always be back to two packs a day. She usually had one after a good meal, although she rarely had one after sex. She inhaled deeply. I put the revolver on the table.

She exhaled slowly and said, "Where'd you get that?"

I explained.

"What are you going to do with it?" she asked. "I don't know the law about these things, but I wouldn't think a man in your situation would be permitted to have one."

"You're probably right. But I think I'll hang onto it for a little while. Little extra insurance. You look like you're ready to go find evil-doers."

"The way you described things, it sounds like Angi could be in trouble again."

Kathy drove the Infiniti out to Meadow Glen, windows down, sunroof open. I called Dominic to find out if the surveillance cameras in Jackson's parking lot had revealed anything that might help me, leaving a message when voicemail answered.

"I like this, the two of us," I said over the sound of the air swirling around us.

"I'd like it better if you weren't carrying that weapon."

"I've been shot, shot at, beaten up.... Who knows what lurks around the corner?"

"Aren't you one of those people who contends that guns beget guns?"

I wanted to protest, but she was right.

I stuck the revolver in the glove box before we went up to 2104. There was no answer to my knock. My whole body tensed, remembering the last time I was here. Then we heard footsteps before the door opened slowly. Her eyes went from me to Kathy with no sign of recognition.

It wasn't until I said, "Hi, Angi," that she realized who I was.

"What're you doing here?" she asked, looking more at Kathy than at me.

"This is my wife, Kathy. I got your message," I said. "I tried to call you back, but it said the number was no longer in service."

"Yeah. Ran out of fucking minutes. You wanna come in? It's still kind of a mess."

She looked tired. Her hair wasn't filthy, but it didn't look like it had been washed that morning. The jeans and T-shirt she was wearing did nothing to disguise the figure that had been her meal ticket for the past couple of years.

Things had been picked up off the floor, and the place had been vacuumed, but not much had been put away, still lying out on tables in the living and dining rooms. There were two suitcases standing near the door.

"Going somewhere?" I asked.

"After what happened to Jimmy, I'm not staying in this town. And that green car keeps coming around. I was just getting ready to call a cab to take me to the bus station."

"Where will you go?" Kathy asked.

"To my mother's."

We didn't say anything.

"I know. But I don't have anywhere else to go. I thought about selling whatever I could from here, like a yard sale, and going somewhere, some bigger town, they got a club in Burlington I think I could work at. I could pay for a room for a week ahead. If I don't use crack or anything, I can make pretty good money in a week. 'Course the hospital's gonna want a shit load, and I don't have time for any of that, anyway. I gotta get outta here now."

"On the phone you said you thought you knew where Debbie sent the material."

"Yeah. The day after Debbie, you know..."

We nodded.

"... a letter came for her. I didn't know what to do with it, but I didn't think I should throw it away. It's from her mother, her name's Barbara Douglass. Debbie'd gotten other ones from her just like it, in a kind of pink color envelope. I thought, you know, there might be some clue there. I read it and thought about calling the police, but shit, you know, they know what goes on at The Doll House, the drugs, prostitution ... shit. They like it like that. They get their cut, they want a little after-hours piece, there it is. Anyway, then I thought about you and found the card you gave me."

I hesitated. She was right, she should have called the police. That's what we should do now. I looked over at Kathy.

"We came out here to find out what was going on, didn't we?" she said.

"Would you mind reading it?" I asked Angi. "I probably shouldn't have my prints on it."

We had all been standing, and we spontaneously took seats as she pulled three salmon-colored pages out of the envelope and began reading.

Dear Debbie, I'm glad you've decided to leave that place. You've done a good job saving up your money. This check is for all that you've been sending me, and I added a little more to it. Let me know when you've settled somewhere. I wish I had some good ideas, but it probably ought to be far away. Maybe California. There's always legitimate work for pretty girls out there. Start taking dance lessons again, and some acting. You can make it, you're still young. But for sure get out of that miserable business.

Angi held up a small, slim piece of paper. "This check is for five fucking thousand dollars. Damn. I thought about getting someone to help me cash it, there are people can do that, hang around the club. But then I'd have to be around those people again. And, well ... anyway."

She sighed before going on.

I've been doing some serious thinking about my businesses, and I've decided to sell them.

"Her mom ran a couple of pageants," Angi added. "You know, like Miss Preteen Georgia, like that." She read on.

It's taken me all this time to realize that what we are encouraging these girls to do is not much different than what you've been doing, except for wearing more clothes. And thank God for that. I made a lot of money selling those get ups. But it's really all the same, strutting for the attention of an audience. I used to think we were helping young women with self-esteem, getting them to feel good about themselves. And we've really done just the opposite, made them feel lousy if they didn't win, if they weren't perfect.

I'm sorry for what I put you through and don't blame you for running off to live with Arnie when you did. You were still really just a kid, and my drinking didn't help things. I didn't think it would be good for you being with him, but even I couldn't imagine how things would turn out.

There was more about what she might do with the proceeds from the businesses and that they might wind up near each other again someday. By the end of the letter, both Kathy and Angi were crying, and I had an ache in my chest. Kathy walked over to Angi and knelt alongside her, putting an arm over her shoulders. Angi laid her head against Kathy.

"So, you think she sent the material, whatever it was, to her mother," I said.

She nodded.

I thought that made sense.

Then I remembered the other part of her call.

"Tell me about Jay," I said.

Kathy got up and went to the kitchen, coming back with damp paper towels and two glasses of water. Angi wiped her face and took a drink.

"He said he worked with you and knew you were worried that the police weren't trying very hard to find out who really killed Debbie and he was helping you. He asked if I knew why Debbie was murdered and why I was beaten up. I told him that I thought it had to do with something they were looking for and whatever it was, Debbie probably had sent it to her mother."

I asked to see the envelope. The return address was in Atlanta.

"I've got to go now," Angi said. "There's a bus leaves for

Greensboro in half an hour."

Kathy and I each lifted a bag. I cringed as pain shot across my shoulder. On the way to the car, I looked around the parking lot. We loaded the bags in the trunk and got in the car, Angi in the back, Kathy driving.

"How did Jay know about you?" I asked.

"He read about it in the paper. He showed me the article."

"When was the last time you saw the green car? Before or after Jay was here?"

"I don't know. I guess before. Yeah. I don't think I've seen it since he was here."

Kathy accompanied Angi into the bus station while she bought her ticket. I kept an eye on the parking lot, looking for shadowy vehicles. The women returned five minutes later. We sat quietly, awkwardly for a couple of minutes before Kathy asked, "How will it be, going back home to your mom?"

"It'll be okay. She's not so bad, really. I mean, you saw how she was at the hospital. It's been like that all our lives. I can live with it some more 'til I figure out what I'm gonna do. And you know, when I was at home before, it was really the men she was with who were more of a problem than her."

Kathy looked over at me, eyes wide, eyebrows raised.

"This last guy she's with seems to be okay, though. At least from what she tells me. And he's all right with me staying there awhile. I just hope he doesn't turn out to be another asshole, excuse me. God! Men!

"She tried, I mean, she had me when she was seventeen. I don't know how she did it. I couldn't do it, man. No way. I couldn't."

Kathy reached an arm between the seats to pat the girl's leg, just a touch, really. Angi was crying.

Almost in a whisper, Angi said, "I had an abortion last year."

"It's okay," Kathy said, matching Angi's quiet voice. "We all do what we have to do."

I heard the sound of a diesel engine down-shifting and saw the big gray coach in the rear- view mirror make the turn into the station lot, disappearing behind the building.

"That's probably mine," Angi said.

The women got the bags out of the trunk and walked into the station while I maintained my vigil. Kathy returned as the bus was pulling back out onto the road.

"Men," she said.

I didn't ask.

48

"Think we should stay until the bus is gone?" Her voice sounded gentler ... or at least less cynical. But maybe that was just wishful thinking.

I shrugged. "I doubt these people would do anything to her if they knew where she was, just be glad she got out of town. But..."

"You never know," she said, finishing my thought. "I know something else you're thinking." She turned to look at me. "You do remember what happened the last time you went down there."

"Yes, I do." I thought of the gun in the glove box, but didn't mention it.

The Greyhound came around the corner of the building, pulled out onto the street, and disappeared into Beaucatcher Tunnel.

She started the Infiniti. "And you're still not supposed to be going out of state, are you?"

"No, I'm not."

"You think the Douglass woman is in danger?"

"I think that's where Jay's gone. Why else would he have been to Angi's except to find out about the material and where it might be?"

"You really think Jay's involved with ... them? Who are they all, again?"

"MTM, The Doll House, Manetti. Senator Simmons. Any or all of the above."

"They're all in this together? A vast conspiracy?"

"I don't know. But I think this. Debbie was killed because of some material she had that she thought would keep her safe. I assume it implicates people in unsavory, probably illegal activities—activities they would not want the authorities or the public to know about."

"Like what we saw with Marilyn Morgan's daughter."

"That's my guess."

"And Jay's involved in that? Jay and his girlfriend?"

"I don't know what to think about him. But he's not talking to me about it, and I don't think that's a good sign. Nor is his quitting the Center."

"Couldn't you call Henderson, tell him what you've found out?"

"I don't think he'd have the same sense of urgency."

"So, you think I should step on it?"

I smiled. "Crack the whip, Watson."

It took three minutes to get to the interstate. Within a few hours we'd be in the suburbs east of Atlanta.

"I hate to be a broken record, Rick," she said as we reached cruising speed.

I knew I wasn't going to like what was coming.

"But you have been a participant in all this."

I thought this could be a very long two-and-a-half hours. "Yes, I've acknowledged that."

"And so have I by putting up with it. I'm out. Done. Finis. I retract what I said before. It's not okay with me if you keep going to The Doll House or places like it. I won't put up with it."

The air in the car felt as if it was gathering static electricity. Somebody saying the wrong thing would set it off.

After a silence that had me wishing there was a safe place I could crawl into, she said, "I wonder if it's possible to explain what was going through your mind when you asked that girl to play tennis."

I thought about it as I had repeatedly for the past week-and-a-half.

"I heard a child once, a young girl, three, four years old, get asked by her mother why she had written on the living room walls with crayon. The girl thought a second and said, 'I guess my brains fell out.' I don't know what else I can say, except my brains fell out. It didn't seem unreasonable at the time."

"And you were sober?"

"I was sober."

I wanted to ask about the guy in Charlotte and how she decided to do that. I knew that conversation couldn't lead anywhere I really wanted to go.

"Do you suppose you would have asked her if you hadn't just seen her naked?"

I remembered flirting with her in the sporting goods store.

"No, I don't think I would."

"So, just like going into bars significantly increases the likelihood you'll drink, going into ... what's the euphemism? Gentlemen's clubs? ... Going into those places increases the chances you'll strike up relationships with strippers."

"I get your point."

It was another Chamber of Commerce postcard day in western North Carolina. Straight ahead, the Blue Ridge Mountains tumbled into the Great Smokies, lining up together against a cloudless blue sky. Against that, it was hard to carry a heavy heart.

I fiddled with the radio for a minute before giving up and looking through the small collection of CDs she kept in the console between the seats. I found Leonard Cohen's Greatest Hits and slipped it in the player. The first song was "Ain't No Cure for

Love." She looked over at me sideways. I leaned over and kissed her lightly on the cheek and started singing along. She smiled and sang with me.

"Okay, let's do this thing," she said, punching the accelerator.

When we hit eighty, I said, "You know, it probably would be a good thing not to be stopped by the cops."

"Oh. Yeah. You are a suspected felon, aren't you? And not supposed to be going where we're going."

We made small talk as we headed into north Georgia, mostly about her work. The conversation petered out as we got on I-85 to make the final approach to Atlanta.

She broke the silence.

"What's the plan?"

"Get the lay of the land. See what needs to be done."

"Doesn't seem like much of a plan."

"All I've got right now."

As traffic began to thicken east of the city, I tapped the address into the GPS. My breathing quickened. My palm was sweaty. We got off the interstate in a suburban community of curving streets, every other one of which was a cul de sac. The GPS called out turns until I saw Jay's old Corolla parked in the driveway three houses ahead, a green Buick behind it.

"There it is. Pull over a couple of houses past it."

I opened the glove box and took out the revolver.

"Oh, shit," she said as she pulled to the curb.

"I don't like it either," I said. "But I have no idea what I'll find in there."

I stuffed the gun in my waistband, pulled my shirt over it and began walking with studied nonchalance toward the Douglass house. I cut across the yard, went up the few steps to a narrow porch, turned the front door handle. It opened. I pulled the gun out, held it to my side and nudged the door with my foot. My stomach dropped when my eyes adjusted to the light in the room. I assumed the same people who tossed Angi's place had been here.

This time it looked like they were really mad. Upholstery was slashed, books torn apart, furniture reduced to kindling. About the only thing that seemed to have escaped their ire was an entertainment console with a big old TV set, an equally old VCR, and an up-to-date DVD player.

There were splotches of blood on the floor, a trail leading out of the room. I began following it toward the kitchen when I heard the sounds coming from what I guessed was the basement. Holding the weapon against my leg, I moved forward, reminding myself to breathe. When I came to the head of a stairway leading down, I went on past, following the line of blood into the kitchen.

I froze when I saw the two bodies on the floor. One was a woman, strands of unnaturally blond hair matted with streaks of crimson. The other was Jay.

"Jay," I mouthed, barely audible.

His head moved slightly in my direction. His face was swollen and covered with blood. His eyes did not open. I stuck the gun back in my pants and, using what I remembered of CPR, assessed that they were both breathing but unconscious. I called 911, gave them my name and the address and told them two people had been shot and or beaten, were breathing but not conscious. When I hung up, footsteps were coming up the stairs. I drew the revolver and held it against my right leg, my left side toward the stairs.

A heavy-set, dark haired man in black pants and shirt appeared at the top of the stairs.

"Who the fuck..." he began as he drew a gun from somewhere I couldn't see.

I fired and hit him in the arm. It spun him around and the gun flew away. Our heads turned in unison toward the front of the house when we heard a siren approaching. He ignored the gun and bolted down the stairs. A door slammed and another pair of footsteps joined his. I ran back into the living room and looked out the front window in time to see the Buick back out of the drive. Less than thirty seconds later, an EMS truck came into view, passing the car speeding away from the house.

49

By the time the ambulances left for the hospital with Jay and Barbara Douglass, two black-and-whites had arrived. I gave as concise a story as I could to explain my presence and what I thought had happened to the victims. When Detective Lieutenant Jeremiah Andrews arrived fifteen minutes later, I had to go through it all again.

"You're the prime suspect in a murder investigation," he reiterated. He was a tall man, well-groomed, short dark hair with the hint of a part. "You believe that some information—some material—was in the possession of Ms. Douglass. And that the people who are actually responsible for the murder of which you are accused were here looking for that information. And Mr. McIntosh—"

"McIntyre," I corrected.

"Mr. McIntyre, a coworker of yours had come before you in search of the same material."

"That's an educated guess. I don't know why else he'd be here. The young woman I'm accused of killing was Debbie Douglass, the daughter of—"

"Yes, I know who she was. And who were the people trying to get this stuff? Girl was a stripper, wasn't she?"

"She was. Used to dance for her stepfather at his place here. Club Elegant."

"Guy named Arnie Camacho," Andrews said.

"Arnie sounds right."

"Yeah. Guy's a real piece of work. Not surprising he'd be involved in a mess like this."

I wanted to hug the guy, to call Ted Henderson and yell, "See! Somebody knows about the Atlanta connection!" Then I had a darker thought. They've known about it all along.

Andrews's eyes slowly took in the room. "If somebody wasn't looking for something here, they sure did a good job of making it look that way. Whose gun is that?" he asked when he saw the one lying on the hallway floor.

I explained shooting the guy and showed him my revolver.

"Got a license for that?"

I started to say 'yes' until I remembered it wasn't my gun.

I grinned like a kid caught with a dirty magazine. "Afraid not."

The crime scene people had arrived. One of them took my gun and wrote out a receipt on a piece of paper.

Andrews told me I'd have to go downtown since all they had right now was my story of what happened. I knew I had to be careful, watch my tone of voice. I had gotten, as Detective Henderson had warned, way out on the skinny ice. I could easily fall through at any minute.

I held my lone arm toward him. "Does it look like I could have beaten the shit out of those two people?"

"Could have had an accomplice."

"Yeah, that would be my wife, the one out there in the Infiniti."

He looked at me and shrugged. "Still. You're gonna have to come downtown. We'll have to do something about the weapon, at least. And I'm guessing you aren't supposed to be out of your home county. That right?"

I shrugged. We were standing in the living room. The crime scene people were busy dusting surfaces, putting things in evidence bags. There was a recliner oriented for TV watching, its stuffing bleeding out into the room. I asked if it was okay if I sat down in it. A crime scene guy came over, pulled some of the stuffing out with tweezers, put it in a bag. Andrews told me I could sit. As soon as my butt touched down, I realized I was exhausted. I leaned over the side of the chair looking for a lever that would make the back go down, couldn't find it and leaned over the other side. I had to look slightly back before I could see the wooden handle. The corner of a brown envelope protruded from under the chair. I reached over and almost grabbed it before I realized what I was about to do.

Interrupting the detective in conversation with a uniform, I pointed to the manila paper. "Lieutenant. That look like a mailing envelope to you?"

"Could be."

"I think that whoever beat up Ms. Douglass and Mr. McIntyre may have been looking for something that was mailed to her."

He came over, leaned down, and retrieved it with a gloved hand. It was the kind of envelope a videotape would be mailed in. It was empty.

"The only thing where the return address should be is 'D. Douglass,'" he said.

The mention of her name brought back images of that rainy morning in the parking lot.

"You all right?" Andrews asked.

"Yeah. Just caught me unprepared."

We both looked at the TV set connected to the tape and disc players. Andrews walked over to it and pushed the eject button on the VCR. A tape slid out

"The label says, 'World Cup Finals, 1999.'"

"I wouldn't count on it," I said. I thought of Shari, Marilyn Morgan's daughter.

He turned the TV on and pushed the tape back in. There was a lot of snow. If it hadn't already been in the player and if I hadn't had a similar experience a few days ago, I might have assumed it had been erased. I suggested he fast forward it. It took another minute until black-and-white images appeared. He slowed it back down. The movie had not been well lit, wasn't something for mainstream commercial use. The angle we were seeing it from suggested the camera might have been hidden from the people on the screen. The point of view didn't change, the "performers" moving in and out of the static frame, people in various stages of undress, some naked.

"That the Douglass girl?" the Lieutenant asked.

I might have figured it out eventually, but the long hair and twenty fewer pounds and poor lighting were sufficient to keep me from recognizing her. It surprised me how quickly Andrews ID'd her until I remembered this was where she had lived, her hometown, and he was a hometown cop. He knew these people. She was still a teenager on that tape, fifteen, sixteen.

It was hard to get a good feel for the room, except that there was a bed with a big cushioned headboard and a table next to it. Debbie, another girl, and an older guy began snorting lines of powder through a rolled-up bill. Another man came into the frame, younger than the other man. In a couple of minutes, no one had any clothes on and a variety of positions were being taken by the players. The older man looked in the direction of the camera, not directly at it, but at the wall beneath it.

"Jeezus," I said.

"What?"

"That's Senator Simmons."

Andrews squinted at the set. "From North Carolina?"

"That's the one."

"You're sure?"

"I just saw him yesterday. He's younger there, of course, but that's him."

Andrews called for someone to bring evidence bags. He popped the tape out of the player and sealed it up. Before doing the same with the envelope, he said, "That's interesting."

"What's that?"

"This thing's postmarked four days ago."

It took a few seconds before I got the significance.

"That means Debbie didn't mail it."

"Not unless she's got zombie powers," he said.

50

Kathy followed in the Infiniti while I rode in a police cruiser to the district station. I dictated a statement, then had to spend two more hours while Andrews called Henderson and Henderson called Bobby Headley, who confirmed that, indeed, he had given me a gun. I was surprised when they gave it back to me. What was found at the Douglass house didn't exonerate me, but it did reinforce the possibility that there were other people who might have had a motive to kill Debbie.

When they were finished with me, I called Nate, who called the DA and got it okayed for me to stay in the Peach State overnight. We weren't allowed into ICU to see Barbara Douglass. Jay was in the adjoining room with serious internal injuries. Nominally conscious, he still wasn't speaking. Maybe we'd get to talk to one or the other or both of them in the morning. I had a lot of questions.

After checking into a motel, Kathy and I walked to a nearby Mexican restaurant.

"Two things I don't understand," Kathy said over a steaming plate of fajitas.

"Only two?"

"Two that come to mind. One, why didn't they think to look

in the tape player?"

"Who knows? You know what I think about the intelligence of your average criminal. You'd think they knew what they were looking for. Maybe nobody told them it would be labeled 'World Cup.' Maybe they did start to watch it, saw a couple of minutes of snow and assumed it had been erased. It took the skills of a highly-trained professional to get the job done."

After a few more bites of my tortilla, I asked, "What's two."

"Who mailed the tape? And when?"

"That's two and three. In answer to number two, it had to have been Angi."

"You think so?"

"Who else? She may be the real stand-up person in all this."

"You mean she had it when they tore up her apartment? Almost killed her?"

"Or, maybe she found it afterward, when she was cleaning up."

"But why? Why not turn it over to the police?"

"Didn't know who she could trust. If a United States senator is corrupt, who isn't? She knows there are cops on the take, knows how The Doll House and places like it get away with what they do."

After flan and decaf, we strolled back to our room. The original Thin Man with William Powell and Myrna Loy was on TCM. We watched as Nick Charles, retired New York City detective, mixed another pitcher of martinis for Nora and himself.

"Oh, yeah," I said, "Those were the good old days."

⨭⨴

We were at the hospital by eight the next morning. Zoey, Jay's girlfriend, had arrived during the night and was in the intensive care waiting room. She said Jay was conscious and trying to talk, but it hurt because of his banged-up ribs. We went to check on Barbara, who'd been moved into the regular hospital population. The police had already been there, and the nurse playing gatekeeper was reluctant to let us in the room. I asked her if she couldn't ask Ms. Douglass if she'd like to speak to us.

"She says she's anxious to talk to you," the nurse said when she returned and grudgingly ushered us into the room. "Please keep it short. You'll see she has very little energy."

"I'm glad to meet you," Barbara said after I introduced Kathy and myself. A smile forced its way out from the swelling in her face. Behind the bruises, I could see where Debbie had gotten her good looks. I wanted to say something about Debbie, but couldn't find words that seemed appropriate. Instead, I asked her when the package had arrived.

"Yesterday ... or I guess it's the day before. There wasn't any kind of letter or anything, just the movie."

Her eyes fluttered and moistened.

"I'm so ashamed of what's on it, ashamed for how I treated her, I don't want anyone else to see it. I don't know if I can trust the police, now that I know who the man on the tape is."

A different nurse came in and told us we'd have to leave. Barbara asked if Kathy and I could stay just a minute longer.

"We'd started to talk again a couple of months ago," Barbara said. "And week before last she told me there was this guy, an older guy who'd asked her to play tennis, a guy with only one arm and the unlikely name of Rick Ryder. She said it made her feel good to think there was a least one man in the world who knew what she did and was interested in something else about her."

I couldn't see Kathy's face, but I could imagine her eyeballs rolling up.

"When I read they arrested you for her murder—it's been in the Atlanta paper because she was from here—I knew that couldn't be true. I just wanted to thank you for being a friend to her." She closed her eyes and seemed to have drifted off to sleep when she added, "And they'll finally be able to get that bastard Arnie Camacho."

The nurse stuck her head back in the room and said, "Now it's really time to go."

"I'd like to stay in touch," I said. She said she'd like that, too.

We got coffee and tea in the cafeteria. Zoey was asleep in a chair when we got back to the waiting room. Within a minute, she opened her eyes, as if she sensed our presence.

"Brought you some coffee," I said.

"Thanks. This isn't the most comfortable bed."

"We've got a room just down the street we're not using. Could probably talk them into a late check-out. You could get a few hours of rest."

"Jay's mother should arrive soon," she said as she dumped sugar into her cup. "I'm just going to wait 'til she gets here."

"How's he doing?"

"I guess he's going to be okay. He's going to have to stay a little while before he can be moved. Might be able to go back home for rehab. I guess it's going to be a long recovery."

"What's that going to do to your movie?"

She looked at me for several seconds without speaking.

"You weren't supposed to know about it."

"I was out there the other night."

"Oh. That was you. Security mentioned they'd chased somebody off."

"A couple of months ago, Jay mentioned you guys were working on a movie, referred to it as your 'project.' He didn't say much about it; I didn't ask. Wasn't any big deal. But then the day the office was trashed, I made some comment about your project, and it was clear he really didn't want to talk about it. Like now it was some big deal. I didn't think a whole lot about it at the time. But then there was the murder, and he started to get weird. Zella and I knew something was up. So I followed him out there one day, before you began shooting, and overheard him say something about how good it was that I wasn't in the office. After that, I figured that you guys were in league with Mountain Timber, and maybe the senator, and C&M Enterprises..."

"You mean that jerk Manetti," she said through a burst of laughter.

"Yeah, well, we didn't know what to think. So, what is going on with it?"

She shifted in the chair, sipped some more coffee.

"The short version," she began. "I've wanted to do a movie about the nexus of environmental destruction and corruption for a long time. Trying to find the right vehicle. Had all kinds of people lined up to be involved, including some pretty good talent. Then Jay goes to work for the Mountain Center and you're involved in this MTM case and, bingo, we've got a narrative. Jay copied stuff from the case file when he could get the chance, when you weren't around and Zella was otherwise occupied. He got Carole to help him—I think she's got a crush on him. When we had enough material, it took a screenwriter friend about three days to turn out a screenplay. Change the names, all that stuff."

"But 'based on actual events.'"

She nodded. "And then, of course, Jay had to quit."

"Conflict of interest," I said.

She nodded.

"How did you ever decide to go see Manetti?"

"Somebody said—I don't even remember who it was—they heard about this outfit just came to town, were in the business of making movies. I'll talk to anybody about making movies. That's how you get a buzz going. Get everybody who has anything to do with them excited about what you're doing. So it was just a shot. We didn't realize he was making porn. And he's a real asshole. Suggested that I might want to be in one of his projects. God, it still makes my skin crawl."

"I still don't understand why Jay couldn't tell us what was happening."

"We didn't want people to think the Center was in any way involved, especially not while the lawsuit was going on. From what Jay was saying, it looked like MTM would probably settle this thing pretty soon, before the movie gets distributed. Assuming it ever does."

"Zella actually wanted to get an injunction against you guys," I said, "stop the thing, thinking you were doing a propaganda flick for the other side."

"You don't really know Jay very well, do you?"

"Well, that's the thing. I couldn't imagine him doing it, but couldn't figure out what else you were up to, what with all the secrecy and spooky behavior."

"We knew we were taking a chance and just wanted to get it in the can before the wrong people found out about it."

"The wrong people being me and Zella."

"And MTM and all that crowd."

"Did you know he was coming down here?" I asked.

"Yeah, he called. He said he thought the murdered girl's mother might be in danger, that something had been sent to her that other people might want to get their hands on."

"And why couldn't he tell me that?"

"He figured you'd just tell him not to do it."

"Well, he got that right."

A nurse came into the room. Maybe Kathy's injunction was working: I almost didn't notice how cute she was in her whites.

"Ms. Magnuson?"

"Yes?" Zoey answered.

"Mr. McIntyre would like to see you."

"Can we just stick our heads in and say 'Hi'?" I asked.

He looked terrible, much worse than Barbara Douglass. Zoey stepped up to him and held his hand as she kissed him on the forehead.

After letting the moment linger a few seconds, I said, "You probably saved that woman's life. Who knows what might have happened if you hadn't shown up to take the heat."

A small smile crept out over his lips.

"I guess I've gotta go back to work since you've quit." I wanted to get out of the room before the tears that were welling up began to spill out. "So we're going back up the mountain. Rest easy." Before I could do anything about it, my chest was heaving. I walked over and held his hand. "See you in a while," I whispered.

We were on the road by ten, Kathy behind the wheel. The weather was acutely Georgia summer, hot, humid, cloudless blue sky. We cruised in air-conditioned comfort. Out of recent habit, I kept an eye behind us through the passenger-side rear-view mirror.

A half-hour out of Atlanta, I said, "I think we're being followed."

"Damn," she said. "I thought we'd be done with that. What do they want now?"

"Just letting us know they're still around. I don't know. But I'm damned tired of it. Speed up a little and if they stay with you, slow down and see what happens."

The car stayed with us, fast or slow. I pulled the map out from under the gun in the glove box and looked to see where we were.

"Get off at the next exit," I said.

She looked over at me.

"Just indulge me here."

"Don't do anything stupid," she said.

"Who? Me?"

As she glided to the stop sign at the bottom of the ramp, I said, "Take a right and, if they're still behind us, stop about fifty yards or so down the road."

It was a two-lane road with little traffic. The Buick came behind us, stopping about twenty yards back.

"Back up slowly," I said, "until you're about ten feet or so from him."

I turned around to watch as we approached. There was only the driver in the car. When Kathy came to a stop, I reached in the glove box and retrieved the revolver.

"Rick! What the hell are you doing?" she yelled.

Before she'd finished the sentence, I was out the door. As soon as I'd cleared the back of the Infiniti, I shot out the Buick's passenger-side front tire, then ran the several steps back to our car, hopped in and said, "Just go straight."

I leaned back in the seat and breathed.

"God, that felt good."

"You are a cowboy, aren't you?"

"Just call me 'Red,'" I said.

51

The cats were vocal about our having gone off without feeding them.

"Sorry, guys. Stuff came up," I said as I scooped food into their bowls.

As soon as they had eaten, they went outside and ignored us. We had dinner on the deck, comforted by the gurgle of the creek.

Just after eight the next morning, my phone rang.

"Dominic," he announced. "I'm here at Triple A Security. Mr. Chatham and Lieutenant Henderson are gonna be here about nine. Wanna come down?"

I said I'd be delighted.

The company was housed in a small strip mall on the near east side of town. Nate and I pulled into the parking lot almost simultaneously. Henderson was already there.

Herbert Ackerman was the technician who played the recordings for us. The first one showed a pickup truck pulling into the sports bar's parking lot. It caught the vehicle head-on until the truck turned to the right. It was hard to see clearly, but a man, apparently having gotten out of the passenger side, came around the front of the truck. The time on the bottom of the tape read 01:43. If we all had left the club at one-thirty, Jimmy would have had to drive directly to the parking lot to be there in thirteen minutes.

The next tape was shot from the right rear of the lot. In this one, we could see clearly two people—a man and a woman—getting out of the truck. They looked vaguely like me and Debbie. It appeared that the woman leaned over and gave the man a peck on the cheek, then got back in the truck. The man walked over to another vehicle. It looked like my old Honda. The time signature was the same as on the first tape.

We were all quiet for a minute until Henderson said, "Looks like you getting out of what looks like Jimmy Crawford's truck."

"Looks like it to me," I said. "And Debbie was alive at the time. Are we all guessing the same thing?"

We let Henderson say it.

"After he drops you off, he drives to your office. Probably wants the girl to get out before shooting her, but she resists, so he has to do it with her still in the car. He unloads the body, drives up to Sandy Creek, disposes of the truck."

"And," I said, "calls Tom Longo to come get him."

❧❧

The clock radio read 7:15 when the buzzing started. I hit the button twice and stared at it for a few seconds before I realized it was my phone.

"Kemosabe. I wake you up, bro?"

"Matter of fact, you did, Nate."

"Ah, gonna miss the worm, my man. Seen the paper yet?"

"I just woke up."

"Ah, yeah. Seems to me I heard that. Must be nice to be retired, homie."

The bathroom door opened, and Kathy stepped into the room wearing nothing but a towel—wrapped around her head. I was tempted to tell Nate I'd call him back. She mouthed, "Who is it?"

"It's Nate, my lovely, taking me to task for still being in bed."

"Why, I think it's the perfect place for you."

"Hear that?" I said.

"Sounds like you ought to get arrested more often. Which is what, actually, I'm calling about. This is worth being said out loud, so I'll narrate."

The gist of it was that Senator Simmons had resigned "for personal reasons."

"And, that's not all. On page three, it reads, 'The U.S. Department of Agriculture announced yesterday that it had settled out of court a lawsuit that had been brought by a consortium of environmental groups in North Carolina.' Blah blah blah. 'The Department acknowledged no wrong-doing in the case, claiming problems arose from differing interpretations of federal regulations.'"

"So," he said, "all's well that ends well?"

"The really good ending would have been better if Simmons, that paragon of virtue, God-fearing upholder of family values, had been nailed for his role in the whole thing, instead of getting off with simply resigning from the Senate."

"Whatever happened to that tape anyway?" he asked.

"Way I heard it, they gave it back to the Douglass woman. Part of the deal. Saves her the embarrassment of people seeing her daughter like that, saves the senator's ass."

"Ah, yes, the wheels of justice," he said.

"Yeah, I know. They don't always take us where we'd like to go."

"A very unsatisfactory ending, Nate."

"What is it you're always telling me about life, Rick?"

"You mean, life's not fair?"

"Yeah. That."

52

The weather was, as they say in these parts, fixin' to change. When my phantom arm behaved like this, it was not a mere apparition.

Daylight savings time had ended two nights before. At six-thirty in the morning, the sky above the ridgeline was white and foreboding, confirming what my arm told me. Kathy and I had settled back more or less into a routine, which included me taking a cup of tea and the newspaper to her after I'd had my first cup of coffee and a quick scan of the paper. I'd gone over the sports page and turned to the front section. A headline on Page 3 caught my eye.

"Wife of former Senator Malcolm Simmons files for divorce."

It was like someone had fired a gun. My heart raced. My first thought was, I hope she takes him to the cleaners. Followed by, Maybe there's some way to help her stick it to him. I almost tripped over the cats in my hurry into the kitchen, where I turned the tea kettle on, anxious to share this with Kathy. In four minutes I was on my way up stairs.

"Look at this," I said, as I laid the tray holding the tea and the paper in her lap.

She took a moment to read the article.

"So?"

"I was thinking we might be able to help her out."

She gave me that have-you-lost-your-mind look, the squinched-up eyes, the nod of the head.

"And how would we do that?"

"I don't know. It's just set me off, thinking how the SOB got off easy and this might be an opportunity to—"

"I thought your spiritual program involved letting go, forgiveness, all that."

"Yeah, well. This guy was behind at least one murder and perpetrated a number of—"

"I get that. I don't get how we could be of any help to Mrs. Simmons, however."

"I need to think this out."

"Good idea."

I donned a windbreaker, grabbed a bottle of water, and headed out to the road. The sign warning that the pavement gave out ahead deterred most people from continuing down this way. If they decided to be adventuresome or missed the sign, they usually turned around when they reached our property, the last before the gravel road began, leaving the lane to the likes of me and a few four-wheelers. The road followed a serpentine route up and over the ridge, an ideal setting for introspection.

Simmons's going scot-free annoyed me. More than annoyed. Irritated me, like a piece of sand in an oyster, but what was growing in me was not a pearl. It was something darker. I knew it would be healthy to let go of my desire for revenge. But that morning I decided that I was not thinking of revenge, but rather a balancing of the scales.

Forty-five minutes later, I had no better idea of what I wanted to do, but my heart was lighter.

Kathy was up and dressed and seated at the kitchen table when I returned.

"How about something like this," she said as soon I'd gotten a cup of coffee and taken a seat across from her. She laid out a plan. It seemed like a good one.

It began with a trip to town. We bought a new long-sleeved shirt for me, all the others I owned having had their left arms amputated to match my body, followed by stops at craft and party-supply stores, then a pancake place for late breakfast. That night we invited Jay and Zoey over for dinner.

Jay had mostly healed, at least on the outside. The only visible clues that something bad had happened to him were a couple of wondrous scars on his face and his right arm in a cast. It was iffy if he'd have full use of the limb. Nevertheless, I thought wryly, not-quite-full use would be better than no arm at all.

A bottle of wine anchored the center of the deck table, although Jay, still taking pain meds, joined me in sticking to club soda. Very quickly we discovered that none of us had managed to the take the spiritual high road: we were all hoping to find a way to serve up the senator's just desserts.

"He's an addict," I said. "Like a junkie who needs to score. He's not going to go all over the place looking for his fix. He's going to go to the same people and places he's gone to before."

"Meaning he's going to return to Club Elegant."

"And no doubt already has."

"You need someone on the inside," Zoey said, after we laid out our scheme.

"That would be nice, of course," Kathy said. "But—"

Zoey cut her off. "I bet I could get inside."

If we hadn't been paying close attention before, we were now.

"I've got creds," she said. "I've done that kind of work before, you know. I'll bet I could pass an audition for them."

"What?!" Jay exploded. "You're kidding. You'd dance for them? I mean, take off your clothes for them? And God knows what all else you'd be expected to do if you worked for them. No. No way."

"Hey. When did you become the boss of me, buddy?"

"Wait a minute here," I said. "They kill people, you know. Dancers who have become a problem for them. If you went in there undercover and they found out…"

"I understand that. But if I was only there a few days—I'm sure you can work up whatever I.D. I might need for an alias. I doubt they do much in the way of background checks."

After a moment to let that settle, I asked, "And what would you do on the inside?"

"What!" Jay blurted. "You're not actually thinking this is a good idea, are you? To repeat what you just said, Rick, 'They kill dancers.' That's why we're here today."

"Yes," Zoey said, "and today we get to put the hammer down on a very corrupt politician."

"Former politician," Jay said.

"He may not hold office today," I suggested, "but that doesn't mean he's not actively involved in what goes on behind the scenes."

"Aren't there other corrupt politicians we could go after that wouldn't require nude dancing in front of large rooms full of sleazy people?"

"Jay," Zoey said, in a parental-lecture voice, "you do not tell me how I can use my body."

He glared at her. She glared back.

I played elder statesmen. "I can't say I'm thrilled about the idea either. To repeat what Jay said, 'These are not nice people and we know what they're capable of doing to people who've crossed them.'"

Zoey turned her glare on me. "I can take care of myself, Rick. It's not like I'd be going in there with blinders on. Kathy, what do you think?"

"It's risky. But the whole project is risky. That hasn't stopped us before. If you're comfortable with it..." Her voice trailed off.

Jay's glare turned sullen.

Zoey called the club and was told to stop in between eleven a.m. and two p.m., Monday through Saturday. Ask for Mr. Camacho. Be ready to dance.

Kathy reserved two rooms at a nearby hotel. It had been a Thursday at four o'clock when I saw the senator at the club. If, as I predicted, he was being guided by habit, he would be there the day after next. We picked up Zoey and Jay at seven the next morning.

Zoey left for the club at ten-thirty wearing a short black leather skirt, a gauzy button-up blouse with a dark bra underneath, and patterned hose inside over-the-calf leather boots. The consensus was that, if we were running a strip club, we'd hire her on the spot. We went on to a nearby café to while away the time until we could check into our rooms. Zoey called at twelve-fifteen.

"They want me to start today, like, now," Zoey said. "Some girl called in sick. Happens a lot in this business. I said I could. He also agreed that I only have to do floor and bar dances. I tried to get out of the latter. But since I'd already said I wouldn't do lap dances or private dances it was a kind of a deal-breaker. I go on at two. They will, of course, be glad to sell me any outfits I need."

"Be careful, Zoey. When will your shift be done?"

"The girl I'm filling in for was supposed to start at twelve, go 'til eight. One of the second-tier girls. Working later gets you the big tips."

We'd thought it would take a day before she'd start so we had a day to kill before we expected the senator to arrive. Visits to The Underground and the Georgia Aquarium plus a couple of meals filled most of the time. We were back at the hotel at eight-fifteen when Zoey returned.

"Gawd! My feet are killing me," she said as she came into our room. "I forgot how much physical work this shit is."

"You don't have to do this," Kathy said.

"Yes. I do. And, it's okay. The floor dancing isn't so bad, much as I remembered it. But the bar dancing? I'd forgotten that. There will be different guys at the tables tomorrow, but those guys at the bar? It will be like they never left. It's sad, but they're also very creepy."

She had more to tell but she wanted to take a bath and get into some other clothes. It was hard to think of the freshly scrubbed young woman who returned wearing print cotton pajamas as a strip-tease dancer.

"Arnie 'interviewed' me. Boy, there is one sleazy character. You could keep a lamp going with the oil that comes off of him. Anyway, I didn't want to go in there asking too many questions the first day. But, I was also being intentionally naïve. I asked about the V.I.P. Room. I learned that it takes a special membership and it's not just money that decides who will be admitted. According to one girl, Vera I think her name is, there are very special services there. She wouldn't go into detail but said if I stuck around long enough I'd probably find out. We can't tell any of the regular customers anything about it. They have to talk to Arnie, personally. I guess it's pretty serious money for those who get admitted."

"I wonder how long is 'long enough,'" I said.

"Me, too," Zoey said.

"Maybe talk to someone else. Tell them you understand you can't tell the patrons about it, but your curiosity is up."

"Yeah," Zoey said. "And we all know what happened to the cat with that."

Through all of this, Jay was silent. From his expression, he was judging the rest of us—and it looked like we weren't coming out well.

⊷⊶

We met for a late breakfast in the hotel restaurant before Zoey was due at the club. Jay's spirits were improved, a lot. My guess was that Zoey had used some of her charm on him overnight. He returned to his room while Kathy and I window-shopped, before we, too, went to our room, resting up in anticipation of what might happen later that afternoon.

At two-thirty, I put on the new shirt, its empty left sleeve stuffed with cotton. The sling went around my neck and the new "prosthesis" lay limply inside, a false hand adhesive-taped to the end, the hand itself also wrapped with tape. I walked around the room. Kathy thought it worked. With new fake eye-glasses, Kathy doubted that I'd be recognized by any of the people who'd seen me there before. Jay declined to join us, believing that he would get literally sick seeing Zoey perform.

Kathy and I split up before arriving at the block on which Club Elegant was located. I headed directly for the main door. She went around the block before arriving at the entrance to the V.I.P. Room. I wished I could watch her, but we both knew hanging around on the street wasn't a good idea.

She was going to knock on the door or ring the bell or whatever one had to do to get the attention of someone inside. And then, in her most innocent manner, ask what this place was and attempt to engage whoever opened the door until the senator arrived. A mini-camera, of the type we P.I.s use, was affixed inconspicuously to her handbag, inside of which a voice recorder was hidden.

Neither the door guard who had met me before, nor Yuri,

or the guy who had thrown me out was in sight. I took a seat at a table a couple of rows back from one of the three big stages and waited while I accustomed myself to rap music and strobe lights from three directions. I had no idea what time Zoey would go on. A woman who, from the look of it, had been doing this for a long time, finished her routine. She received a smattering of perfunctory applause.

I couldn't see Zoey on either of the other stages or on any of the bars. A young woman took the stage in front of me. Probably eighteen, but little more than that. I imagined they would be scrupulous about age out here in the "public" area. The girl was pretty. Had a nice smile that seemed real—though I was pretty sure it would be replaced by a plastic one in the near future. Her routine was not particularly imaginative, but the mostly male audience appreciated her physical attributes and gave her a warm, and lucrative, send-off.

I walked to the men's room, taking the opportunity to look around. It was much as I remembered. Back at my seat, I ordered another Coke and was rewarded for my patience with the announcement, "And now, a new treat. All the way from merry old England, give it up for ... Cassie!" From England? Were English women supposed to be particularly sexy? Moderate applause greeted her. She looked great, even if she lacked the figure of her predecessor. Her dancing was inspired, giving off an "I'm having a great time here" vibe. Jay would no doubt have been incensed. By the time she had her clothes off, the crowd was hootin' and hollerin'. I was about to join the spontaneous outburst when shame washed over me. I was appalled with myself. What was I doing watching this spectacle? I felt sick to my stomach. This is not what I'd come in here for.

The next time a dancer-waitress came over, I asked, "What goes on in the V.I.P. Room?"

"You'll have to speak to the owner about that, hon," she said with a big smile and a lot of boob in my face. I wondered about the hierarchy, the waitresses and the dancers, the table dancers and the stage dancers, and how it was that Zoey got to dance on one of the main stages from the start.

"Can I speak to the owner?" I said, returning the smile. We were yelling at each other to make ourselves heard.

"He's not here."

"When will he be here?"

"Here's the deal, sugar. You need a referral to talk to him. You know, somebody you know knows somebody. That kind of thing."

"That's the only way to get in there?"

"Only way I know of." Her gaze slid down to the sling. "What happened to your arm?"

"Bar fight," I deadpanned. "Somebody wouldn't tell me something I wanted to know."

Her eyes widened. Then she grinned. "Come on. Really."

"Car accident," which was, of course, the truth. "So, if I've been referred, how do I talk to the owner?"

She shrugged. "I guess whoever refers you tells you that. Then I think you have to have an interview. It's a B-F-D man. I know that."

The noise level was affecting my equilibrium. I accepted that this had been a failed, let's-just-go-in-and-see-what-happens reconnaissance, and that I wasn't going to get any further with her. I checked my phone for the time. I needed to be outside in five minutes. Scanning the room again, I noticed my waitress talking with the guy who had bounced me on my previous visit. He looked over at me, started to walk my way. I guessed they were interested in people interested in getting into the V.I.P. Room. I threw a few bills on the table and got up, affecting nonchalance. Looking back from the doorway, I saw the big guy watching me. He hadn't moved in my direction.

Outside, a limo was pulling up. Kathy was talking to Yuri. I crossed the street to get the entire scene in frame and started taking pictures. The senator getting out of the limo. The senator under the canopy. Kathy talking to the senator with the canopy and the main entrance to the Club Elegant in the frame. I kept clicking. Yuri looked up. Saw me. I moved on down the sidewalk, back to the hotel.

⊰⊱

"Mission accomplished," Kathy announce as she entered the room.

"You sound like Bush," I said.

"'Cept I'm not on an aircraft carrier and I'm not wearing a borrowed Marine jumpsuit."

I'd already fixed a tonic and lime for myself and handed her a glass of dry Zinfandel.

"Tell me."

"The timing was immaculate. You are a genius … sometimes."

I rolled my eyes.

"Really." She grinned. "Well, very smart, anyway. So, I walk up to the door. There's a button. Big guy comes out. Says, in this, very deep, Slavic voice, 'Yes?'"

"Yuri."

"I guess. I asked, 'Can I come in?' He says, 'Who are you?' Whoops, I think. Hadn't prepared for that. Pretty silly. I came up with 'Annie Hall.'"

"You're kidding."

"I couldn't imagine he'd get the reference. Anyway, he says, 'who sent you?' Really. Like some old speakeasy."

"Yeah. I understand you need a referral."

"I said, 'No one. I just wanted to know what goes on here.

Can I come in?' Of course, I was working on my most fetching look. I also had my arm on his bicep. He didn't seem to mind it."

"Imagine that."

"I was out of material at that point when who should show up?"

"The recently retired senior senator from North Carolina."

"The same. You are so smart. Yes. When the limo—how's he still get a limo?—pulled up, I stepped aside so I could see who was getting out. And there he was. I started taking pictures, bursts, you know. I said, 'Senator,' with a big grin. Talk about being caught off guard. Yuri tried to get in between us, but I moved to him like I wanted his autograph or something, calling out so the tape recorder in my purse could hear, 'Imagine meeting you here outside of the Club Elegant V.I.P. Room in Atlanta.' His eyes. I mean. If they'd gotten any bigger they'd have popped out of his head. Really. He didn't know what to do."

"Whether to shit or go blind, as the saying goes."

"That's it! Poor guy."

"'Poor guy'?!"

"Well. I had my hand out and leaned in around Yuri who put his hand on my shoulder like he was going to pull me away. I pushed it off and turned and said, 'Hey. What do you think you're doing? Keep your hands off me, buddy.' I think that was a new one for him, too."

"Sounds like you were having way too much fun."

"Until I saw him look across the street at you. So, I reached in my bag and got the pad and a pen I had them ready for the opportunity, whipped them toward Simmons and asked for his autograph. His look turned into, like, 'Lady, are you out of your mind?' Finally, Yuri was able to put himself between us and get the senator in the door. I walked away. I'm dying to see the pictures."

We called Jay in for the reveal. We had a visual record of the senator approaching the V.I.P. Room of the Club Elegant in Atlanta, date- and time-stamped, synched to the audio recording of same. We thought the estranged Mrs. Simmons might find it interesting as, perhaps would her lawyers and, perhaps, some media outlets.

Tempering our feelings of success were worries about Zoey. Added to the possibility that whatever information-gathering she was doing would raise suspicions among the staff was a concern that Yuri or others there might associate our presence with this new dancer who appeared out of nowhere. Jay wanted to call her and tell her to get out of there. That would be difficult: the club checked all employees' bags on the way in and on the way out, and cell phones were not permitted.

By eight-thirty, silence had descended over us, broken by Jay grumbling, "God, I wish I could have a drink." At eight-forty-five, he said he was going to the club. I was about to object when there was a knock on the door. I opened it to see Zoey with a conspiratorial expression on her face. She leaned into the room after looking up and down the halls.

"Wanna snort some coke?" she said in a stage whisper.

"You didn't!" Jay said.

"Snort any? Hell no. I gave them the 'I-need-it-for-later' routine. And, I also gave some to one of the other dancers. An older girl. We're all girls, you know. Like a sorority. Anyway, she complained after her first set that she was worn out, didn't know how she was going to make it through her shift. It may have been a con, you know, to get sympathy from the new kid, who would then do just what I did. However, it turned out to be a good investment. She knows all about the V.I.P. Room and wasn't reluctant to share after she'd done a couple of lines."

The "girl," now twenty-three, had started working at the place when she was sixteen, dancing in the V.I.P. Room. "That's the deal there," Zoey said. "Underage girls. That's why they don't let just anybody in. You gotta be checked out and a current member has to, you know, say you're cool. I told her I understood there were videos of what went on in there. She didn't bat an eye, either about how I might know that or about telling me about them. She had worked in the office for a while at one point. They have a mailing list they send those things out to. She said it's hugely expensive."

Kathy looked like Zoey was telling her that she'd seen God. Intense. "Why was she telling you this? Couldn't she get in a whole lot of trouble?"

"She said she had known Debbie and had heard about what happened to her. She wanted to get out but didn't know how. With me coming there, she felt like I was someone she could talk to."

"You don't think it was a set up?" Jay asked.

"No, I don't. She said she had most of her things packed. They'd been packed for a month, just waiting for the right time. She'd decided tonight was the night. As soon as she got home she was calling a cab. There was a three a.m. bus going in the direction she wanted to go. She wouldn't tell me where so I could honestly say I didn't know where she went. She gave me keys she'd kept to the office and the storage closet where the videos are kept."

Zoey reached in her pocket and pulled out two keys. "Voila! Then she told me not to say another word about the V.I.P. Room to anybody."

The room got quiet. Jay said, "No. You're not going back in there to get a video. That's crazy. Insane. They will kill you and then they will find her and kill her. I won't let you do it." His face was red, his fists were clenched, tears welled in the corner of his eyes. Zoey went to him, embraced him. Their tears flowed into each others'. The crying turned to laughter. "I just love you so much," Jay said.

"Maybe it's time for you two to say goodnight," Kathy said.

After a group breakfast, Kathy and I dragged Jay around town, sightseeing, shopping, eating, distracting him, as well as ourselves, from thinking about Zoey and letting our imaginations run wild.

Lazy cocktails and late dinner kept us out of our rooms until eight-fifteen. Jay joined us. It was if we were waiting to hear from the governor about a reprieve from execution. The earliest she would get back to the hotel if she worked the full shift was eight-thirty—under ordinary circumstances, which these were not. Her plan was to go into the office after her shift. No one would find it unusual that she wasn't in the dressing room. According to Zoey, getting the girls ready to go on stage was like herding cats. It was Arnie's pet peeve. Any down-time on a stage drove him nuts. He would ordinarily be hovering around, haranguing dancers, threatening firing for slow appearances. But this was the night of the week he went trolling the town for talent, checking out the competition. She would slip off, let herself into the office, then into the video cabinet. She knew the date she was looking for. Then remove the DVD from its cover, stick it in her pants, put the jewel case back and skedaddle.

Jay paced. I scrolled through the stations on the TV repeatedly until Kathy said, "Stop doing that. Please. Light on something, would you?"

"There's nothing I want to light on."

"Then turn it off, for crying out loud. This is nerve-racking enough."

Nine o'clock came and went. At nine-fifteen, Jay said, as he had the night before, "Okay, I'm going over there."

Unlike the night before, there was no knock on the door as he said it.

"I'll come with you," I said.

"No. You won't. You're the one responsible for this. I might have to kill you if something has happened to her."

Oh, God, I thought. What if something has happened and he shows up and makes a scene? With Yuri and the other bouncer there, who knew who would land in jail? Neither Kathy nor I had anything to say at that point, nor after he left. We sat in our thoughts.

The knock came at nine-thirty on the dot, weeping and laughing after we opened the door.

"So, it was going fine," she said, after we'd all settled down and had gotten ourselves something to sip on. "I found the videos, had them in my hands, when I heard a key in the lock. In the movies, they always hide behind the door at this point. So, I did. Rolled myself into a little ball and scrunched up in the corner. Someone, I think it was Yuri, opened and closed drawers in a desk. I remembered that I hadn't closed the cabinet door. He walked over to it. I thought, Oh, shit. He closed it—apparently it was no big deal—and came back to the door, went out, closed the door."

She held a thumb and forefinger up a quarter of an inch apart. "I came this close to peeing my pants," she said. She then reached into her bag and produced DVDs. "Voila! There are three here. Since I knew he came every week, I just went seven days forward and back in the drawer. I do want you to know, it is very awkward walking around with these things in your underwear."

53

Tom Henderson agreed to meet with the four of us and Nate. We quickly learned that we did not have the slam dunk that, in our excitement, we had allowed ourselves to believe. The material, Nate and Tom agreed, could be useful for Mrs. Simmons in her upcoming divorce negotiations. Nate would contact her lawyer to pursue the best avenue for making this disclosure.

We all understood that there was collusion between some of the city's powers-that-be and Club Elegant in order for the latter to operate as it had been doing. Since much of the club's operations were within legal bounds, albeit at the margins, city officials could claim ignorance of the illegal activities there. A problem with the material we had was that there was no way to prove that they were filmed at that V.I.P. Room at that club. Yes, the senator was clearly implicated. Yes, we documented that he went to that place. No, we couldn't prove that what was on the DVDs took place there. Would the dancer who had given the keys to Zoey and had worked there—according to her statements to Zoey—testify to that fact? Probably not. Zoey could, theoretically, testify about where she got the videos, but we knew to what extremes "they" could go to exact revenge. The DVD evidence revealed that Senator Simmons cavorted with females who appeared to be underage for such activity. The senator could claim that he did not know they were underage. In fact, we only had hearsay evidence that this was so.

"And the evidence of our own eyes," I said.

"Oh," Nate said, "they just look young. That's what they're going to say. My guess is there is nothing prosecutable here but I do think it will have the effect of shutting the operation down. At least at that location. They have the girls. They're gonna use them somewhere."

"What about a raid on the place? There's got to be somebody in or around City Hall who would be outraged at this, some good church-going type."

Tom said, "I know the chief down there, although we're not what you would call buddies. I'm not sure how much latitude he has, politically. I also know the folks in the neighboring county, where you wound up in the hospital, Jay. I imagine they know more than I do about the machinations in the big city."

❧❧

Our excitement turned sour, moving towards cynicism. Both Nate and Tom Henderson urged patience, accept that the wheels of justice turn slowly. Kathy and I invited Jay and Zoey to come over and talk about the possibilities of taking more direct action on our own. The next day, before the young couple arrived, Nate called.

"You're gonna want to be watchin' the evening news."

"Oh? And why is that?"

"Just watch, okay? Talk to you later."

He hung up.

It was a rare, late fall day, warm enough in mid-afternoon to sit on the deck. The menagerie seemed to like the company, the cats occupying the borders of the space. The creek murmured down the mountain. As the sun disappeared behind the western ridges, we moved inside.

Just before six, Kathy clicked on the TV, and as the theme music faded down and the camera zoomed in on the news desk, the anchor announced, "Malcolm Simmons, the former senior senator from North Carolina, was arrested today on multiple counts of indecent liberties with a minor." The visual showed Simmons getting out of car at the courthouse, covering his face with a newspaper, as if this would keep us from knowing who he was. All four of us sat bug-eyed for a few seconds, before cheering. The anchor handed the story off to a reporter who said, "Yes, Belva. The charges are related to the senator's alleged participation in the activities of Club Elegant, a self-styled gentlemen's club in Atlanta. This follows a raid on the club last night by federal, state, and local officials, after accusations that the club was involved in producing child pornography." Here, the video of the senator outside the club appeared. "The senator, through his lawyer, had no comment other than that the senator denies all charges. Back to you, Belva."

We danced around the living room as if we'd won a million-dollar lottery, until the landline phone rang.

"Yo, homie. You see that?"

"Yes, Nate. Did you know this was coming?"

"Knew it was coming. Didn't know when. Thought you'd like the surprise."

54

The crash came as always after an adrenaline rush. The smug satisfaction at having gotten the bad guys, tempered by the knowledge that there were still many others doing the same thing that snared the senator, that the industry was huge, and that what we'd done made not so much as a dent in it.

Kathy ruminated. "Was that the point? Just to even the scales in one instance? Is that all we can do, all we can hope for? Justice, one case at a time? Find someone doing bad stuff and bring 'em to light?" She sighed, then said, "Put your coat on. Let's go for a walk."

From the hill behind the house we could see forever between the leafless trees, the winter view the realtors all talk about. It was beautiful, branches reaching like fingers into the azure sky. The antithesis of evil.

Also available from Pisgah Press:

Mombie; The Zombie Mom
$16.95
Barry A. Burgess
illustrated by Jake LaGory

Letting Go: Collected Poems 1983-2003
$14.95
Donna Lisle Burton

MacTiernan's Bottle
$14.95
Michael Hopping

rhythms on a flaming drum
$16.95
Michael Hopping

Musical Morphine: Transforming Pain One Note at a Time
$17.95
Robin R. Gaiser

Guide to the Edible and Medicinal Plants of the Finger Lakes Trail
$22.00
Heather Housekeeper

I Like It Here! Adventures in the Wild & Wonderful World of Theatre
$30.00
C. Robert Jones

Lanky Tales, Vol. I: The Bird Man & other stories
$9.00
C. Robert Jones
illustrated by Jennie Jones Branham

Lanky Tales, Vol. II: Billy Red Wing & other stories
$9.00
C. Robert Jones
illustrated by Jane Snyder

Lanky Tales, Vol. III: A Good and Faithful Friend & other stories
$9.00
C. Robert Jones
illustrated by Jane Snyder

Red-state, White-guy Blues
$15.95
Jeff Douglas Messer

A Green One for Woody
$15.95
Patrick O'Sullivan

Reed's Homophones: a comprehensive book of sound-alike words
$10.00
A.D. Reed

Swords in their Hands: George Washington and the Newburgh Conspiracy
$24.95
David Richards

Trang Sen: A Novel of Viet Nam
$19.50
Sarah-Ann Smith

Killer Weed: A Rick Ryder Mystery
$14.95
RF Wilson

To order:

Pisgah Press ~ PO Box 1427, Candler, NC 28715
www.pisgahpress.com